Wynthrop
Serpents Pass
Thalonia
Thalondor
Vindoria
Serendell

THALONDOR SHADOWS OF DESTINY

Shane Lege

* * *

Thank you to all my family and friends who support me
through these efforts.

Table of Contents

Chapter 1 He's Alive

"Valaric!" Aria's voice sliced through the thick fog of my unconsciousness, her words laced with a desperate urgency. Her gentle shaking transformed into frantic jostling as if she were trying to awaken me from a nightmare I couldn't remember. My eyelids fluttered open, and the world came rushing back in a whirlwind of disorientation.

Lucas said wryly, "If he weren't already gone, Aria's yelling would surely finish the job." His words carried a hint of amusement, easing the seriousness of the situation.

Ethan chimed in, relief lacing his voice, "Well, he's still breathing. That's a good sign." The weight of worry lifted, replaced by a glimmer of hope.

Always calm and composed, Arabella urged the others, "Let's give him some space. It seems he might regain consciousness." Her soothing words conveyed assurance and empathy, offering reassurance to everyone present.

As I opened my eyes, the world snapped into focus. The surrounding voices became familiar, and the faces of my companions became recognizable. My breathing steadied, aligning with the rhythm of the moment.

I took a moment to gather my thoughts, piecing together fragments of memory and sensation. The fog in my mind cleared, and clarity returned. My surroundings and the concern on my friends' faces became more apparent.

With a gentle sigh, I felt my weak voice emerge, acknowledging my return to consciousness. The relief mirrored in my companions' eyes matched my own, a shared triumph over the looming uncertainty.

"Are you injured?" Aria's voice was concerned as she examined me for signs of injury.

Feeling the lingering effects of my daring action, I said, "No, I think I'm alright. Just a few bumps and bruises." Wincing, I realized the toll my impulsive choice took on my body.

Aria's frustration overflowed as she delivered a sharp smack across my cheek. "How dare you take such a reckless gamble! We thought you might have been dead!" Her words were a mix of relief, worry, and a touch of anger.

Rubbing my stinging cheek, I protested, "Ouch! What did you hit me for?"

Aria responded, "That's payback for tricking us into believing you may be dead."

Now more composed, I turned my attention to the rest of my companions. "Is everyone else alright?" I said.

Lucas, always composed, reassured me, "Yes, we're all here. A bit shaken, but otherwise unharmed." His words brought a collective sense of relief to the group, knowing we all survived the ordeal.

"What happened? Where did all the creatures go?" I asked.

With a puzzled expression, Ethan responded, "That's an excellent question, and we hope you may have some answers. When you jumped through the rings of fire, something extraordinary occurred. The influx of creatures stopped as if something entirely focused them on you. We feared the worst and thought you met your demise."

Lucas said, "We were just about to escape, thinking there may be no hope left. Then a blinding flash of light and violent shaking shook the ground."

Nodding in agreement, Ethan continued, "Once the effects subsided, we found ourselves in a bewildering sight. All the creatures that plagued us disappeared as if they vanished. And there you were, lying unconscious."

As I absorbed their words, the puzzle pieces came together. The rings of fire, my daring leap, and the subsequent events unfolded. My actions triggered a cataclysmic event that expelled the creatures and transformed our surroundings.

"We were terrified for you, Valaric. We thought you sacrificed yourself to protect us. But your bravery brought about a miraculous change," Aria stated.

"Can you provide more details about what happened? Can you explain why you took such a daring leap?" Lucas asked.

After gathering my thoughts, I wanted to explain the events that led me to make that risky decision. I understood the importance of my companions understanding my motivations and the purpose behind my actions.

"Well, what happened was..." I said, gathering my words. "I stumbled upon a set of intricate symbols in one of the ancient manuscripts we discovered in Serpents Pass. Through careful study and deciphering, I realized these symbols were key to restoring the Kingdom of Thalondor to its former glory."

"How did you think that would help our situation?" Arabella asked.

I sighed, realizing the audacity of my decision. "To be honest, that part is unclear to me. It was a leap of faith, a desperate attempt to grasp any chance for us to survive. I took a risk."

"So, you decided to 'pull a Boudreaux' and go for it without a simple plan," she remarked, implying that this was a familiar occurrence.

I nodded. "Yes, I suppose you could say that. Sometimes, when faced with overwhelming challenges, all we can do is trust our instincts and seize the opportunity. It may not always be the safest or most predictable course of action, but it can lead us to unforeseen breakthroughs."

Aria interjected, "So, what exactly happened?"

Taking a deep breath, I prepared to recount the events that unfolded. "Well, I reached into my bag and retrieved an ornate dagger that I had gained earlier," I began, focusing on the group before me. "I made my way towards the source from which the creatures emerged. The dagger was in my hand."

Aria's eyebrows furrowed in anticipation as she listened.

"As I approached the location, it appeared the creatures sensed my presence and launched a desperate assault to stop me. They lunged and swarmed, their feral instincts driving them to protect whatever lay behind the entrance."

My words hung in the air, and my companions exchanged glances, their expressions a mix of astonishment and admiration for my bravery. I pressed on, recounting my struggle against the overwhelming odds. "I needed to think, dodge their attacks, and outmaneuver their relentless pursuit. It was a harrowing dance, navigating through the chaos, as I fought my way closer to the heart of their stronghold."

I paused momentarily, memories of the fierce battle playing in my mind. "After overcoming countless obstacles, I reached the entrance, where the creatures were emerging. The air crackled with energy, and a sense of foreboding hung heavy in the atmosphere. I knew that what lay beyond held the answers we sought, the key to our survival."

My words hung in the air, a palpable tension filling the space. The group remained silent, their eyes fixed on me, awaiting the story's resolution. My gaze met each of theirs, my expression a mix of determination and satisfaction.

"I then took the ornate dagger and plunged it into the narrow crack," I explained. "As I did so, I spoke the ancient magic I discovered within the texts we found in Serpent's Pass. It was a solemn invocation, resonating with the power of forgotten days."

My companions leaned in, their anticipation growing. I continued, my voice carrying the weight of the moment. "The words echoed through the air as I recited, 'From the ashes of forgotten days, let the light of rebirth illuminate our ways. Rise, O city of Thalondor, once lost in time, now embrace your destiny divine.'"

A hushed silence fell upon the group as they absorbed my words. It felt like they infused our quest into the magic. I continued, a flicker of awe in my eyes. "And then, just as I finished uttering those ancient words, a blinding flash of light erupted from the crack. A brilliant radiance bathed the surroundings, illuminating everything in its path."

"There was something even stranger," I said. "Moments before you checked on me, I witnessed the battle that devastated this place and led to the creation of the Eldoria Forest."

My companions gathered closer, their eyes wide with anticipation. My voice took on a mesmerizing quality as I recounted the scene I witnessed. "It was unlike any battle I ever saw or imagined. The clash of swords, the thunderous galloping of horses, and the rain of arrows filled the air. Warriors fought with unparalleled courage and determination, their cries echoing across the desolate land. The ground shook under the weight of their struggle, and the sky seemed to hold its breath in awe."

My words vividly depicted the chaos and grandeur that unfolded during that ancient conflict. My voice was reverent as I continued, "Amidst the fury of battle, I witnessed acts of heroism and sacrifice, moments of both triumph and tragedy."

"Oh my," Aria exclaimed. "We better understand the events that unfolded over a thousand years ago. But what transpired when you placed that dagger in the hole?" she inquired, eager to uncover the mysteries before us.

Lucas chimed in, his voice filled with urgency. "What about the creatures lurking down here? What happened to them? Where else in the land could they emerge from if they emerged from this location?"

Arabella, ever practical and thoughtful, nodded in agreement. "These questions are of great importance. We should gather all our information and bring it back to Father. However, before we do that, we must ensure everyone is ready to return to Vindoria."

A collective affirmation resounded through the group as we acknowledged our readiness to return to the Kingdom. Arabella took charge, her voice commanding yet filled with warmth. "Very well. Let's head back to Vindoria. The road ahead will have challenges, but we stand united, and together, we shall uncover the truths within Thalondor."

"Alright then, let's retrace our steps and ascend how we came down. Our destination is Vindoria," Arabella declared, her voice resonating with determination. The crew gathered their belongings, stood up, and walked towards the staircase that led back to the surface.

Chapter 2 The Rise of a Kingdom

As our team ascended the stairway, our footsteps echoed in the chamber, and we reached the next level with curiosity and anticipation. However, what we encountered left us in awe-struck disbelief. The once grim and dilapidated surroundings had undergone a remarkable transformation. We felt like a veil had lifted, revealing a realm untouched by the passing of time.

The walls, once covered in layers of dust and decay, now showcased vibrant tapestries depicting scenes of courage and grandeur. Active Colors shone resplendently as if someone had woven them just moments ago. It vividly brought the once-hidden intricacies of the tapestries to life. Each thread seemed to tell a story, whispering the forgotten legends of Thalondor.

Once cracked and discolored, the portraits in the corridor appeared newly painted. Faces of the long-departed rulers and heroes of Thalondor were now rendered with striking realism. Their eyes held wisdom and determination, urging the present generation to continue their legacy.

As we ventured further, the flickering torches along the walls burned with a radiant flame, casting a warm and inviting glow. The once stale air was now fragrant with blooming flowers as if an unseen garden had sprung to life within these hallowed halls.

Our footsteps echoed softly on the marble floors, gleaming with a polished luster. The elaborate designs on the stone, concealed for years, are now evidence of the talent of ancient artisans. Each step seemed to echo the whispers of the past as if the essence of Thalondor's history was beckoning us forward.

We stood in awe, our eyes filled with wonder, as we beheld this unexpected transformation. It was a surreal experience as if we had stepped into a portal that transported us back to the glory of Thalondor's past. Time seemed to lose its grip, and we found ourselves immersed in a living tapestry of forgotten splendor.

"What an incredible transformation!" said Aria, scanning the magnificent surroundings. How is it even possible?"

Ethan pondered for a moment before responding. "Remember the ancient parchments we discovered in Serpents Pass? They spoke of a prophecy, suggesting that the Kingdom of Thalondor would regain its former glory to ward off the forces of evil. Perhaps, by inserting the dagger into the portal, Valaric triggered a powerful enchantment that reversed the effects of time."

Lucas nodded in agreement. "Valaric's actions restored the castle to its grandeur and revealed its hidden beauty. This is a sight to behold."

I said, "It's as if the castle has awakened, embracing its destiny to stand against the darkness. Thalondor is regaining its rightful place in history because of the magic released from these walls."

Arabella's gaze swept across the resplendent hallways. "This does not limit the transformation to the physical appearance. It feels as though the very essence of Thalondor came to life. It charged the air with renewed purpose as if the castle was preparing for future battles."

Filled with astonishment and anticipation, we resumed our ascent, guided by the radiant light illuminating our path. Each step brought us closer to the grand hall, where we hoped to uncover more of the castle's secrets.

As we walked, we marveled at the intricate details of the architecture. Elaborate murals adorned the walls, depicting heroic tales and triumphs of the Kingdom's past. The chandeliers overhead gleamed with an unmatched brilliance, casting a warm glow that bathed the corridors in a soft, inviting light.

Reaching the grand hall, we saw a breathtaking scene. The once-dilapidated space now stood as a majestic chamber fit for royalty. The grand hall had marble pillars and colorful stained glass windows.

"This is beyond anything I could have imagined," whispered Aria.

With determination, our team explored the castle, impressed by the renovations. Once filled with debris and decay, halls now exuded an air of majesty and grace. Ornate tapestries lined the walls, vibrant and alive with scenes of Thalondor's rich history. Elaborate statues stood tall, depicting legendary heroes frozen in time.

As we traversed the corridors, we couldn't help but be captivated by the intricate details restored to their former glory. Elaborate stained glass windows fill the castle with colorful patterns of light. Polished suits of armor stood sentinel, a testament to the courage of Thalondor's warriors.

Our astonishment deepened when we stepped out of the castle and into the open. The transformation we saw in the castle affected the entire kingdom. A scene of pristine beauty replaced the overgrown, tangled landscape.

Gone were the twisted vines and encroaching vegetation that had marred the Kingdom's exterior. Instead of them, there were lush green plants, beautiful gardens, and newly built buildings.

The team stood in awe, taking in the breathtaking sight before us. Rays of sunlight filtered through the leaves, glowing gently upon the rejuvenated land. It was as if nature had responded to the restoration within the castle, mirroring its resurgence with its reawakening.

Aria's voice broke the silence. "It's incredible! The outside of the Kingdom has transformed just like the inside. This is a sight to behold."

I nodded in agreement. "We have witnessed an extraordinary phenomenon. This Kingdom, once lost in time, was new and refreshing. We must seek answers and understand the forces at play."

Our eyes scanned the surroundings as we walked through the revitalized streets of the Kingdom of Thalondor. We took in the astonishing transformation that had occurred so quickly. The ruins we had witnessed earlier had now blossomed into a thriving kingdom, brimming with life and grandeur. It was difficult to fathom the magnitude of the change that had transpired.

As we approached the outskirts of the Kingdom, a sense of bewilderment overtook us. The once dense forest that had enveloped the area was nowhere to be seen, and in its place stood open fields and a vast expanse of unfamiliar terrain.

Lucas voiced the perplexity that echoed in everyone's minds. "What... what happened to the forest? This is unexpected."

My voice quivered with concern as I shared my apprehension. "I had a fear that this might happen," I admitted.

Arabella's eyes widened, reflecting her growing unease. "What are you talking about?" she inquired.

I took a deep breath before continuing. "Considering the transformations in the kingdom, I couldn't help but wonder if the forest would also be affected," I explained. "Eldoria Forest emerged once the enchantment was complete. It engulfed the once desolate wasteland and turned Thalondor into ruins."

Arabella's brows furrowed. "So, you're suggesting that now that the enchantment has been reversed, the forest might have receded?" she asked.

I nodded solemnly. "It's a possibility," I confirmed. "If the enchantment that birthed the forest has changed, the forest itself may have retreated or changed."

Arabella's panic became apparent as she urgently exclaimed, "We must make haste to Vindoria!" Her voice quivered with urgency and fear. The team's collective worry deepened as we contemplated the extent of the changes on the land.

We pressed on, our steps growing more determined as we ventured further away from the transformed Kingdom of Thalondor. The once-familiar landmarks had vanished, leaving us to rely on our instincts and memory to find our way. After what felt like an eternity, we stumbled upon the entrance to the Glimmering Caverns, a glimmer of hope flickering within our hearts.

"There it is," Lucas exclaimed. I nodded in agreement, my gaze fixed on the cavern entrance. "Let's go in and see if the passage still leads us to our desired destination," I suggested.

With cautious anticipation, we stepped into the caverns, our eyes scanning the surroundings for any signs of change. To our relief, the caverns remained untouched, maintaining their mystical allure. The familiar glimmers danced across the walls, illuminating our path as we remembered.

A collective sigh of relief escaped our lips as we realized that, at least for now, the caverns remained unaffected by the recent upheavals. It offered us a semblance of stability in a world that seemed to shift and transform at an alarming pace.

"Looks like the caverns have stayed true," Arabella remarked.

We exchanged nods of agreement, our spirits lifted by this small but significant victory.

We anxiously retraced our steps through the winding passages of the Glimmering Caverns. The weight of uncertainty pressed upon us, and our hearts pulsated with anticipation and trepidation.

Our footsteps quickened as we approached the cavern's exit, propelled by hope and fear. What awaited us on the other side? Would we find ourselves in the familiar embrace of the Kingdom of Vindoria, or would our fears come to life as a changed and unrecognizable land?

The threshold of the cavern drew near, and our hearts pounded in unison. We stepped out into the open air, our eyes scanning the surroundings, desperately seeking familiarity amidst the unknown.

And then, a moment of sheer joy washed over us like a warm embrace. The Kingdom of Vindoria stood before us, unchanged by the recent upheavals. The once-thriving forest remained vibrant and verdant, its ancient trees whispering tales of resilience and endurance.

Relief flooded our beings, and joy painted our faces. The fear that had gripped our hearts moments ago was replaced with triumph and gratitude. We had returned to a sanctuary, a place that had weathered the test of time and emerged unscathed.

Eyes met with glistening tears of joy, and a collective sigh of relief escaped our lips. The team embraced one another, our spirits lifted by the sight before us. The familiar sights and sounds of Vindoria reassured us that some things remained constant amidst the chaos of our journey.

With renewed determination, we set forth into the heart of the Kingdom of Vindoria, ready to seek counsel from the elders and share the incredible tale of our adventures. We were no longer burdened by the weight of the unknown but fueled by the knowledge that we had emerged victorious from a world in flux.

"Looks like everything here is still the same," remarked Aria, relieved by the familiar sight of the Kingdom.

"Let's hope so," agreed Ethan. We pressed on, our steps quickening as we approached the Kingdom's entrance. However, our arrival met an unexpected challenge.

"Halt!" commanded the guards, their spears raised. "State your business in this area," one of them demanded, their tone stern and cautious.

Arabella, taken aback by the guards' response, stepped forward. "It is I, Princess Arabella," she announced with a touch of authority.

The guards stared at her in disbelief, their eyes widening. "We thought you were dead," one of them yelled out, struggling to regain composure.

Arabella's brows furrowed in confusion. "Dead? We've only been gone for a day. Why on earth would you think that?" she asked.

The guard stammered, trying to find the right words. "Princess, you've been missing for over a year," he said. "The King sent search parties to look for you and the others. We feared the worst."

Shock and disbelief washed over us as we exchanged bewildered glances. "What do you mean, over a year?" Aria questioned, her voice filled with disbelief.

The guard continued his recollection, recounting how the King had dispatched the army to the ruins of Thalondor after receiving word from a lone returning guard. They had discovered that the ruins had vanished from their long-standing location.

We stood stunned, grappling with the realization that time had played tricks on us, distorting our perception of the world outside. The passage through the enchanted castle had unknowingly transported us not only through space but also through time.

Arabella's mind raced, trying to make sense of the situation. "We must inform the King," she declared, her voice tinged with urgency. "Lead us to him."

Chapter 3 Thalondor Army

With heavy hearts and minds clouded by uncertainty, we proceeded toward where we would find the King—the weight of the news we had received hung heavily upon us.

"Dead," echoed Aria.

"Gone for a year," added Ethan.

Lucas, ever curious, sought answers. "What exactly transpired during our time away?" he wondered aloud.

Deep in thought, I shook my head. "I have no answers yet, but hopefully, we will unravel this mystery soon," I said. "Undoubtedly, the people here are just as perplexed as we are."

Arabella, the beacon of composure amidst the chaos, spoke with a measured tone. "I cannot claim to comprehend the events that have unfolded fully, but it is evident that recent circumstances have caused significant changes. We must take the time to piece everything together."

As we walked through the bustling streets, we observed the faces of the Kingdom's inhabitants, sensing a shared confusion and bewilderment. The once-familiar sights and sounds of Vindoria now carried an air of uncertainty. It was a landscape altered by time, where we had become mere strangers in a world that had moved on.

As we arrived at the King's location, a cloud of mystery and uncertainty hung over our minds. The sound of approaching footsteps caught the king's attention, causing him to turn around. When his eyes fell upon Arabella, his face lit up with relief and overwhelming joy.

"Arabella!" he exclaimed, moving towards her with outstretched arms. "I thought we had lost you forever," the King expressed, his voice brimming with emotion. His heart swelled with happiness at the sight of his daughter's return.

However, his joy was short-lived as his gaze shifted to me. A sudden change in the King's expression revealed a storm of suspicion and anger brewing within him.

"Cease him!" the King bellowed, his voice filled with authority. "Throw the outsider into the dungeon for kidnapping the princess!"

"Wait, what?" I questioned, disbelief evident in my tone. "I didn't kidnap the princess!" I exclaimed, desperately trying to defend myself against the sudden events.

Without hesitation, the guards swiftly surrounded me, their weapons drawn and ready to seize me. Amidst the mounting tension, Arabella rushed to intervene, her voice filled with urgency and desperation.

"Father, please! He is innocent," she pleaded, her words laced with sincerity. "Valaric didn't kidnap me. Shadowfang and I willingly joined them without your knowledge or permission."

Despite Arabella's heartfelt plea and attempt to clarify the situation, the King remained unyielding. He stubbornly refused to entertain any alternative perspective or listen to the truth. "Bring him to the dungeons immediately!" the King commanded, his voice unwavering in its resolve, as he watched the guards seize me and lead me away.

The team's pleas were ignored as the King adamantly refused to listen to anyone at that moment. "Guards, escort the princess to her quarters!" the King commanded, his voice resonating with authority. However, before the guards could even step toward Arabella, a guard came running into the area, breathless and filled with urgency.

"Your Highness, we are surrounded!" the guard exclaimed, his words eliciting alarm.

The King's eyes widened in disbelief as he processed the gravity of the situation. "Surrounded? What do you mean we are surrounded?" he demanded, a hint of fear creeping into his voice.

Anxiety washed over the guard's face as he struggled to find the right words. "An army has encircled the Kingdom," he explained, his voice trembling unease.

The news struck the King like a thunderbolt, leaving him

momentarily stunned. "An army? How is this possible? Our Kingdom is shielded from view," the King questioned, his voice laced with concern.

The guard could only shake his head in response. "I don't know, Your Highness. The enemy forces have managed to breach our defenses somehow," he admitted, his voice tinged with confusion and fear.

"Well, what do they want?" the King inquired, a hint of desperation creeping into his tone.

"We don't know yet, Your Highness. The head guard is attempting to establish communication with them," he relayed.

The gravity of the situation hung heavy in the air as the Kingdom found itself thrust into a state of emergency. The arrival of an unknown army had disrupted the delicate balance of power, and the kingdom's fate now teetered on a knife's edge.

In a flurry of urgency, the head guard rushed into the area, where a sense of anticipation and anxiety hung thick in the air. Gasping for breath, he addressed the King with urgency and trepidation. "Your Highness," the head guard exclaimed, his voice strained, "they wish to speak with you."

"Me? Why do they want to speak with me?" he questioned, a mix of curiosity and concern in his voice.

"I don't know, Your Highness. They stated their desire to speak directly to the King," the head guard replied.

The King's mind raced with possibilities and conjectures, trying to make sense of the enigmatic situation before him.

"Did they make any other demands or express any intentions?" the King inquired.

"No, Your Highness. They did not reveal any other details. They requested an audience with the King," he answered.

Perplexed, the King surveyed the room, seeking guidance or insight from those present. Silence filled the space as the weight of the moment settled upon them. After a moment of contemplation, the King made a decisive choice. "Summon the elders," he commanded, his voice steady yet filled with concern.

Recognizing the gravity of the situation, messengers were dispatched to gather the esteemed elders of the Kingdom. With their wisdom and experience, the elders would play a vital role in navigating this unforeseen challenge. As the Kingdom braced for the meeting with the mysterious army, the realm's fate hung in the balance, and the King's every decision carried immense weight.

With a sense of urgency hanging in the air, the elders entered the room, commanding respect and authority. The King took a brief moment to compose himself before explaining the situation, his voice steady yet laced with concern. The elders listened attentively, their faces reflecting a mix of contemplation and wisdom.

Silence enveloped the room after the King had finished recounting the events and the mysterious army's request. The elders exchanged meaningful glances, their collective wisdom converging into a unified perspective. Finally, one of the elders stepped forward, his voice carrying a tone of gravity and reason.

"You must go and meet with this army, Your Highness," the elder advised, his words carrying a weight of responsibility. "By addressing their concerns directly, you have the opportunity to prevent any potential escalation and safeguard the well-being of your people," he continued, his tone measured and resolute.

To prevent a potential conflict, the King resolved to engage in dialogue with the army that had encircled the Kingdom of Vindoria. As the King walked through the bustling streets, a notable contingent of his loyal subjects accompanied him, creating an aura of strength and unity. The guards, stationed both ahead and behind, maintained a vigilant presence, ensuring the safety of the King. Arabella, Aria, Lucas, and Ethan were walking closely alongside him—eager to support their monarch and discover the encroaching army's intentions.

As the procession advanced, the streets hummed with anticipation, with curious onlookers gathering to witness this historic moment. The atmosphere was a blend of trepidation and hope as the fate of the Kingdom hung in the balance. Every step carried significance, and the King felt the weight of responsibility upon his shoulders.

As the King arrived at the designated area, his eyes scanned the surroundings before settling on the head guard. Determined to assert his position of authority, he raised his voice in a commanding bellow, seeking to demonstrate his role as the true leader.

"Which one was making the request?" he demanded.

The head guard pointed towards a particular soldier among the ranks. "That one right over there, Your Highness," he replied, acknowledging the King's inquiry.

The King's gaze turned piercingly towards the soldier, his face a mask of stern determination.

"You there," the King called out, his voice carrying a weight of authority. "What is the meaning of this? Why have you surrounded my kingdom, putting my people at risk?" Each word was enunciated with purpose, conveying his expectation of a swift and respectful response.

In an audacious display, the soldier who had made the request looked back at the head guard, a dismissive smirk on his lips. Disregarding the King's presence, he posed a condescending question, "Where is the King?"

Before the head guard could respond, the king's anger ignited. His voice thundered through the air, reverberating with an intensity that demanded attention.

"I am the King, and you will address me when I am speaking to you!" he roared, asserting his rightful place as the ruler of the Kingdom.

As the tension escalated, the soldier's words reverberated through the air, causing a momentary pause in the unfolding confrontation. The King, still brimming with authority, glanced around at his guards and companions, their eyes reflecting a mix of confusion and curiosity.

Undeterred by the King's denial, the soldier in front maintained a composed demeanor.

With a firm voice, he continued, "Your Highness, we understand your disbelief, but our mission is clear. We have come in search of the one true heir to the legendary King Eldramir, the rightful ruler of Thalondor."

The King's expression shifted from defiance to intrigue, a flicker of uncertainty crossing his face. He pondered the soldier's words, trying to reconcile the tales of an ancient King with the reality of his reign.

"We have long awaited the return of the descendant of King Eldramir, the one destined to unite our fractured land and restore balance," the soldier elaborated, his tone conveying a deep reverence for the legendary figure.

The King's words dripped with sarcasm and skepticism as he

responded to the soldier's claim. "I'm afraid you're mistaken. Thalondor, the ancient ruins realm, has been desolate for centuries. Moreover, it has vanished from the very location it occupied for all that time."

The soldier remained resolute, his voice unwavering in the face of the King's doubt. "I assure you, your Majesty, that Thalondor has risen from the ashes and returned to its former glory."

Arabella stepped forward, her voice filled with urgency, hoping to finally be heard by her father. "Father, we've been trying to tell you this all along. Thalondor has been restored, and it's not a mere fabrication. It's the truth."

The King's confusion mingled with a glimmer of curiosity. He leaned forward, his eyes fixed on Arabella. "What are you trying to say, Arabella? Speak plainly."

Arabella took a deep breath and recounted the group's perilous journey to the King. She painted a vivid picture with her words, describing the treacherous path they braved through Serpents Pass. She spoke of the hidden chambers they discovered, where an army of stone statues stood guard, frozen in time and awaiting release.

With each word, Arabella's voice carried the weight of their encounters, the fear and awe they experienced as they ventured deeper into the dungeon of the castle ruins. She vividly described the haunting creatures that lurked in the shadows, their eyes gleaming with malice and their presence filling the air with an unsettling energy.

But amidst the darkness, there was a glimmer of light. Arabella's voice swelled with admiration as she recounted Valaric's selfless act of heroism. She depicted the pivotal moment when he, with unwavering courage, sacrificed himself to seal the portal to the dark world, saving all their lives. His bravery became an indelible mark in their shared journey, a testament to the power of loyalty and friendship.

The most astonishing revelation of all was Thalondor's transformation. Arabella's words conveyed the miraculous resurrection of the once-ruined Kingdom, now vibrant and restored to its former glory. She described the grandeur and majesty that now adorned its streets and architecture, evoking a sense of awe and wonder in all who listened.

However, one aspect remained a mystery—the inexplicable time difference. Arabella explained that while their adventure had spanned only a day, a year had passed within Thalondor. The implications of this temporal anomaly lingered, leaving them with unanswered questions and a sense of intrigue.

Silence filled the area as Arabella concluded her tale. The listeners absorbed the weight of their shared experiences, their imaginations ignited by the wonders and dangers they had encountered. The King's gaze reflected a mix of astonishment, pride, and a deepened understanding of the extraordinary world beyond their borders.

Upon hearing the tale, the soldier spoke up. "Only he who is a direct descendant of King Eldramir has the power to wield the ornate dagger and the ability to restore the Kingdom of Thalondor," said the soldier.

The soldier's words hung in the air, stirring a mix of astonishment and intrigue among the gathered group. The revelation that only a direct descendant of King Eldramir possessed the power to wield the ornate dagger and restore the Kingdom of Thalondor sparked a flurry of questions and uncertainties. The area buzzed with anticipation as everyone exchanged bewildered glances, searching for confirmation and answers.

"Valaric?" The name rippled through the area as if carried by a gust of wind, each person sharing the same thought and seeking reassurance from one another. The weight of the Kingdom's fate now seemed to rest upon Valaric's shoulders, a destiny intertwined with the bloodline of a long-lost King.

Sensing the urgency and significance of the moment, the King wasted no time. With a swift gesture, he summoned his guards to fetch Valaric.

Aria's voice trembled with excitement and disbelief as she questioned, "Valaric, a King?"

Arabella, still grappling with the magnitude of the revelation, replied honestly, "I don't know. We can only hope that once he arrives, the truth will become clear."

A pause settled over the area as they awaited Valaric's arrival. Each person's thoughts swirled with anticipation, their hearts fluttering with curiosity and trepidation. The air crackled with electric energy, charged by the potential discovery of a hidden legacy and the prospect of Thalondor's restoration.

As the guards escorted Valaric to the gathering, a remarkable sight unfolded before them. The soldiers who had encircled the Kingdom, their swords held high and faces masked with determination, suddenly dropped to one knee. It was a gesture of profound reverence and loyalty, a spontaneous display of allegiance to the new found King.

The air grew heavy with the moment's weight as the soldiers, their voices harmonizing as if guided by a single purpose, spoke in unison. "My King," their words resonated, carrying the echoes of centuries past and a deep-seated respect for the authority bestowed upon Valaric.

Chapter 4 The Rise of a King

I took a moment to survey the scene with a mix of confusion and disbelief, still bound in shackles. The soldiers' proclamations and their kneeling gestures seemed surreal to me. Searching for answers, I turned to those who stood beside me.

"What's happening? Who are they referring to?" My voice echoed uncertainly, my eyes darting between Arabella, Lucas, and the rest. The weight of their words began to sink in, but I struggled to accept the sudden realization.

"They are speaking to you, Valaric," Arabella replied, her voice steady yet tinged with excitement. "You, my friend, are the chosen one, the rightful King of Thalondor."

"Me? A King?" I questioned, my disbelief seeping through my words. The concept seemed inconceivable, as if plucked from a realm of fantasy.

As my gaze darted from person to person, my skepticism remained palpable. Sensing my need for clarification, Arabella stepped forward to offer some context, particularly regarding the tale of the ornate dagger.

"Valaric, let me explain," Arabella began, her voice infused with conviction. She recounted the ancient legend of the dagger, its connection to the rightful ruler of Thalondor, and its significance in restoring the Kingdom. However, my disbelief lingered, casting doubt on the unfolding events.

"This all sounds incredibly far-fetched. After all, I am not even from Thalondor; I hail from Aurelia," I proclaimed.

The soldier, patiently waiting, seized the moment to offer his contribution. Stepping forward with a parchment, he sought permission to address the situation. "Your Highness, with your permission, may I present this parchment to you?" he requested respectfully.

I regarded the soldier. However, intrigued by the soldier's request, I granted permission with a nod, inviting him to proceed. "Yes, please go ahead," I responded.

"Is there any chance we can remove these shackles from my King?" the soldier respectfully inquired, addressing the guards. Sensing the moment's significance, the King swiftly motioned for the shackles to be removed, allowing me to embrace my newfound role fully.

With the weight of the shackles lifted, I took hold of the parchment and began deciphering the ancient symbols inscribed. My eyes scanned the lines, and awe and revelation flickered across my face. The silence grew thick with anticipation as everyone waited for me to share the parchment's contents.

"Well, what does it say?" asked Aria

Ethan said, echoing her sentiment, "Don't keep us in suspense any longer. Share the truth with us."

"According to this ancient document," I began, "the King, in a desperate bid to safeguard the royal lineage, decided to send the prince, his wife, and their newborn son away before the final battle. It was done in preparation for invoking a powerful enchantment."

The assembled group listened intently, their eyes fixed upon me as I continued to unravel the secrets of Thalondor's past. "Furthermore," I said, my voice carrying a weight of destiny, "the King entrusted them with the ornate dagger, a symbol of their rightful claim to the throne. It was a beacon of hope, destined to guide the true heir back to Thalondor, to resurrect the fallen Kingdom."

My mind was filled with skepticism and confusion as I processed the weight of the revelation. "This can't be possible," I declared, my voice tinged with disbelief. "None of this adds up. I've never heard of Thalondor, the dagger, or this story."

Arabella, undeterred by my doubt, posed a thought-provoking question. "But have you considered how you arrived here in the first place?" she asked, her eyes searching my face for a flicker of realization.

I paused, contemplating her words. "I haven't quite figured out the circumstances of my arrival," I admitted, "but that doesn't prove anything."

Arabella pressed on, her voice laced with curiosity and concern. "Doesn't it strike you as peculiar that you stumbled upon the ornate dagger in a trunk that washed up on the shore?" she inquired.

My expression shifted, a flicker of recognition appearing in my eyes. "Well, when you put it that way..." I trailed off, my voice laden with newfound uncertainty.

The pieces of the puzzle started to align in my mind. The inexplicable arrival, the fortuitous discovery of the dagger—it was as if the hand of destiny had guided me towards Thalondor. A sense of awe and apprehension washed over me as I realized the significance of the trunk and its contents. Could it be that my path was intricately intertwined with the fate of the Kingdom?

My skepticism began to waver, replaced by a growing realization that a grander design was at play. The synchronicity of my arrival and the appearance of the ornate dagger held a deeper meaning, one that I could no longer dismiss as mere coincidence. The doubts that had clouded my mind were slowly replaced by a newfound sense of purpose and the acceptance of my role in Thalondor's restoration.

As Arabella and I delved deeper into our conversation, I became increasingly aware of the multitude of eyes fixed upon us. The previously kneeling army stood tall, their gazes unwavering. I couldn't help but feel a surge of curiosity as I observed the sheer number of individuals surrounding us.

Breaking the silence, I addressed the assembled soldiers, my voice carrying a mix of awe and bewilderment. "Please, rise," I implored, watching as the vast army gracefully elevated themselves to their feet. As the soldiers stood, their unwavering presence resonated with a sense of purpose and loyalty.

Seeking answers, my gaze swept across the assembly, my eyes alighting upon the soldier who had spoken earlier. "If Thalondor had been reduced to ruins, where did all of you come from?" I inquired, a mix of wonder and confusion in my voice. With a solemn expression, the soldier stepped forward to explain.

"As part of the ancient enchantment that safeguarded Thalondor's future, we were positioned in Serpents Pass, transformed into stone until the prophesied heir would come to restore Thalondor to its former glory," the soldier revealed. My mind whirled with astonishment, struggling to comprehend the intricacies of the enchantment that had kept the army hidden for so long.

"How many of you were positioned in Serpents Pass?" I inquired.

"Approximately a hundred thousand of us stood sentinel within those ancient grounds," the soldier stated.

My eyes widened in astonishment at the magnitude of the number. Realizing that such a formidable force had been waiting in the shadows filled me with awe and renewed hope. "A hundred thousand," I exclaimed. "With numbers like that, we could have turned the tide of the impending battle I witnessed in my vision."

The soldier's expression turned solemn as he spoke, acknowledging the potential within their hidden ranks. "Indeed, the possibility exists that our presence could have altered the course of that fateful battle," the soldier admitted. "However, the enemy we faced at the time was a formidable force. We had already engaged in a grueling, decades-long conflict, and with each passing year, our strength waned. In his wisdom, the King conceived a plan to pause the battle and wait for a thousand years, allowing the land to repopulate and our forces to grow even stronger before conquering the unknown."

I took a moment to absorb the soldier's words, contemplating the immense sacrifice and strategic foresight behind the King's decision. The realization that our ancestors had intentionally chosen to bide their time, banking on a future heir to lead us to victory, stirred my heart's deep sense of responsibility. I understood the weight of the legacy entrusted to me and the potential impact our united forces could have in shaping the destiny of Thalondor.

"But we only have thirty thousand guards here in the Kingdom of Vindoria," the King projected, his voice tinged with concern. "Compared to the hundred thousand forces you possess, it seems insufficient to effect significant change," he continued.

The soldier met the King's gaze, understanding the weight of his words. "The scope of the situation extends far beyond the borders of Vindoria," the soldier replied. "Numerous kingdoms and regions surround Thalondor, each with their armies and warriors ready to join our cause. Together, we will amass a formidable force to confront the dormant evil that has haunted us for centuries."

The soldier's words resonated deeply with us, offering a glimmer of hope in the face of adversity.

"What about the creatures of the forest?" Arabella asked.

"Indeed, the forest holds powerful allies," the soldier explained. "Over the years, the creatures of Eldoria Forest have grown and evolved, becoming aware of the looming threat that shadows our land. They understand the stakes better than most, and I believe they will willingly join forces with us to combat the greater evil."

"How do we unite everyone and rally them for this cause?" Arabella questioned. "Even as one of the central figures in this tale, I find it challenging to grasp and believe everything fully."

The soldier regarded us with empathy, understanding the weight of our doubts. "We have time to gather our forces and establish alliances," the soldier reassured us. "As the truth of your lineage spreads, and as the threat becomes more apparent, others will understand the urgency and importance of our mission."

"With the army's emergence from Serpents Pass, what became of the artifacts stored within?" I inquired. The pass housed the army and advisors, elders, workers, and various others. What happened to them, and where are they now?"

The soldier nodded, understanding the importance of my questions. "Indeed, it was not solely the army that resided within Serpents Pass. A significant number of individuals, including advisors, elders, and workers, were also present," the soldier explained. "At this very moment, those people, along with half of the army, are diligently transporting all the artifacts and belongings from Serpents Pass back to the Kingdom of Thalondor."

I listened intently, envisioning the logistics and efforts required to relocate such a significant cache of artifacts. My thoughts then turned to the location of the Kingdom itself. "Where precisely is the Kingdom of Thalondor located?" I queried, seeking a clear understanding of our destination.

"The Kingdom of Thalondor lies west of our current location, approximately four days' walk from here," the soldier revealed.

My mind raced, realizing the urgency of our mission and the need for comprehensive knowledge to persuade others to join our cause. "We must gather as much information as possible about Thalondor, its history, and its people. This knowledge will be crucial in convincing others to rally to our cause swiftly," I stated with determination.

"What are your suggestions?" I inquired, turning to the King, seeking his guidance.

The King pondered for a moment, considering our next steps. "I propose that we gather as much information as possible to prepare ourselves adequately. We can send some of our elders to Thalondor to exchange knowledge and insights, allowing them to understand our history better. At the same time, we educate them on the events of the past few hundred years," the King suggested.

I nodded, impressed by the King's proposal. "That sounds like an excellent plan. Let us proceed with it and make preparations to set out as soon as possible," I agreed, my tone filled with determination.

"Father, I wish to travel with Valaric, or rather, King Valaric, back to Thalondor," Arabella declared.

"For now, it's just Valaric," I responded firmly.

"Arabella, you've been missing for a whole year, and now you've returned!" the King exclaimed.

"To you, it may have been a year, but for us, it has only been a single day," Arabella explained while emphasizing the importance of having someone to aid our cause. "Furthermore, one of us needs to join the effort, and I believe I can provide valuable assistance. Besides, you would be better suited to command the army here," Arabella reasoned.

The King paused, contemplating Arabella's words. "I suppose you are right," the King conceded, acknowledging the logic behind her argument.

Seizing the opportunity, Lucas, Aria, and Ethan all spoke up in unison, expressing their desire to accompany me on the journey. The King, taken aback by their request, exclaimed, "You too?"

"Yes, Your Highness," Lucas replied confidently. "We believe we can contribute to the effort. We have been traveling together, completing missions as a team. We work well together."

The King considered their words, recognizing the bond formed between the group and their potential to be of assistance. "Very well," he conceded, acknowledging our capabilities.

"We must organize everything swiftly as we still have a four-day journey ahead. Time is of the essence," the soldier urged.

I wore a sly grin as I interjected, sensing an opportunity. "We might have a solution for the main party," I teased, evoking a chuckle from those privy to the plan.

"Go ahead and send the army toward the Kingdom, but you stay back," I declared determinedly. I locked eyes with the King, seeking his approval. He returned my gaze, offering a subtle nod of agreement.

"Very well," the King acknowledged.

"Gather everything and everyone we need swiftly. We must reach the Kingdom of Thalondor before daylight fades," I proclaimed, emphasizing the urgency of our mission.

"Let's reconvene here in one hour to depart," I directed, setting a timeline for our preparations. With those words, the group dispersed, each member venturing in different directions to gather the necessary supplies and equipment for our upcoming journey.

Arabella paused outside the doors of the King's quarters, taking a deep breath before entering. She knew she had to address the situation and mend their rift.

"Father, I understand that my actions in the past were deceiving, and I apologize for that," Arabella began with a heartfelt tone. "I wanted to explore the past and see its secrets firsthand, but I never anticipated it would lead us to this momentous journey we find ourselves on now."

The King listened intently, his concern etched across his face. "You put yourself before the Kingdom, and that worries me, Arabella," he admitted, his voice filled with disappointment and apprehension.

Arabella nodded, acknowledging her father's concerns. "You're right, Father. I was selfish, and I'm sorry for that. But please understand, this time it's different. Our mission isn't about personal curiosity anymore; it's about the restoration of Thalondor and the well-being of all of us."

The King sighed, the weight of his worry still visible in his eyes. "Yes, I understand that, but it doesn't mean I have to like it," he confessed, his love for his daughter mixed with his parental concerns.

With genuine affection, Arabella wrapped her arms around her father in a warm embrace. "I know, Father, and I appreciate your love and concern. I promise to do everything I can to protect and serve our Kingdom. We're in this together, and I won't disappoint you."

The King returned the embrace, a mixture of emotions swirling within him. As they pulled away, a glimmer of pride appeared in his eyes. "Be safe, my dear Arabella," he whispered. "Now, catch up with the group so you can get going."

As we gathered together, making our final preparations before embarking on the journey toward the Kingdom of Thalondor, the soldier, our guide, pointed in a particular direction, indicating our intended path.

"Wait a moment," I interjected, a mischievous glint in my eyes. "I know a shortcut that might save us some time."

Curiosity piqued, and the group turned their attention to me, intrigued by my proposal. With a confident grin, I, the newly acknowledged King, guided them away from the familiar surroundings of the Kingdom of Vindoria and deeper into the lush expanse of Eldoria Forest.

Chapter 5 Creatures in the Cavern

With Whisperwind and Scorch nestled safely in my bag, I led the group through the depths of Eldoria Forest. We ventured deeper into the ancient woodland, following a path known only to me. The forest hummed with life, its vibrant foliage whispering secrets of ages past.

As we neared the entrance to the Glimmering Caverns, a sense of anticipation filled the air. I took the lead, and my steps were confident and purposeful. Apart from the elders and soldiers, the rest of the group had previously experienced the awe-inspiring beauty of the Glimmering Caverns. It was a familiar sight to them—a place of wonder and enchantment. However, this was a moment of sheer excitement for the elders, who had only read about the caverns in ancient tomes and heard tales of its ethereal glow.

The elders' eyes sparkled with curiosity as they took in the otherworldly glow emanating from the cavern entrance. The soft, iridescent light danced upon their weathered faces, reflecting their newfound enthusiasm. This was a chance for them to witness firsthand the storied wonders that had captured their imaginations for so long.

With reverence, the group stepped into the Glimmering Caverns, its ethereal beauty captivating their senses. The air grew cool and filled with a subtle luminescence, casting an otherworldly glow upon the walls adorned with shimmering crystals. The echoes of our footsteps reverberated, creating an enchanting melody that filled the cavernous space.

As we ventured deeper into the caverns, I turned to the soldier by my side and inquired, "By the way, I don't believe I caught your name earlier amidst all the excitement. I apologize for not asking sooner." He met my gaze with a steady and respectful expression. "Roderick, Your Highness," he replied, his voice carrying a sense of unwavering loyalty.

"Nice to meet you, Roderick," I responded, a playful smile tugging at the corners of my lips. "I'm guessing you're about a thousand and twenty-five years old."

Roderick couldn't help but chuckle, a hint of amusement in his eyes. "Well, when you piece together all that has transpired, I suppose I would be about a thousand and twenty-six years old," he replied, his voice tinged with irony.

My gaze lingered on Roderick, taking in the soldier's commanding presence. He stood tall, his sturdy frame exuding strength and resilience. His neatly trimmed beard framed a strong jawline, accentuating the determination in his expression. I couldn't help but notice Roderick's piercing emerald green eyes, which seemed to hold a depth of experience and wisdom.

A closer look revealed Roderick's disciplined demeanor, reflected in his well-maintained appearance. His short, dark brown hair was neatly styled, hinting meticulous attention to detail. The muscles in his arms hinted at years of wielding a sword, a testament to his skill and dedication as a warrior. Adorning his form was a suit of armor, meticulously crafted and decorated with intricate engravings. Each symbol told a story, representing the Kingdom's rich heritage and the courage that defined its warriors.

I couldn't help but feel a sense of respect and admiration for Roderick, recognizing the soldier's dedication to his duty and the embodiment of honor that he represented. As we continued our journey through the caverns, I found comfort in knowing that I had Roderick by my side, a steadfast ally in the face of unknown challenges.

I listened attentively as Roderick shared his origins and his hardships. His hometown, a small village west of Thalondor, sparked my curiosity. I couldn't help but ponder Roderick's challenges, stepping back into a time frame where his family and friends had long passed.

"I can only imagine how difficult it must be for you, having to confront these memories and face the absence of loved ones," I empathized. "Were they affected by the evil we are preparing to defeat now?"

Roderick nodded solemnly. "Indeed, they were. By the time the King decided to enact the enchantment, the evil had already ravaged our lands, claiming the lives of many innocent people. I was but a young child when I lost my family. It was this tragedy that fueled my resolve to join the fight against the darkness, hoping to bring an end to its reign of terror."

My expression softened as I realized the weight of Roderick's burden. "I am sorry for your losses. Your firsthand experiences and knowledge will be invaluable to our cause. I trust that your fellow soldiers, who have also faced this evil, will provide crucial insights and strategies."

Roderick nodded, a glimmer of determination shining in his eyes. "We have seen the horrors of this enemy and stood strong against it. We shall draw upon our collective experiences and forge a path towards victory."

As we reached the location where I had defeated the Gem Golem, a sense of awe filled the air. I gestured towards the area, addressing the elders, "This is where the Gem Golem met its demise." The elders, still marveling at the sight of the Glimmering Caverns after centuries, took a moment to absorb the significance of their surroundings.

Curiosity brimming, Roderick couldn't help but inquire about the Gem Golem's downfall. "How did you defeat the Gem Golem?" he asked. I chuckled lightly before responding, "It was a stroke of luck. A fortunate strike while I was defending myself." Roderick's eyes widened, his gaze shifting towards the ornate dagger I carried. "Was it with the same dagger you used to awaken us?" he queried.

I nodded, confirming Roderick's assumption. "Indeed, it was with this very dagger. Its power proved instrumental not only in awakening you all but also in defeating the Gem Golem." Roderick's interest was piqued, finding the connection intriguing. "Fascinating," he murmured.

Roderick's thoughts then turned to the nature of the Glimmering Caverns. "I recall that the entrance of the caverns tended to move around randomly in the past," he said.

As Roderick shared his memories of the Glimmering Caverns, I nodded in acknowledgment. "Yes, the entrance tended to shift its location unpredictably," I confirmed, recalling the strange phenomenon that had occurred during my previous encounters in the caverns.

Steering the group towards the exit, I glanced at the cavern wall. The inscription that had been present when I defeated the Gem Golem remained: "Victor of Glimmering Caverns possesses mystical abilities within the caverns." However, to my surprise, new words had materialized beside the original inscription, sending a shiver down my spine: "Protect the caverns, for evil lurks within the shadows."

Whispering to myself, I attempted to decipher the hidden meaning behind the cryptic message.

Seeing my contemplation, Arabella turned to me and asked, "What was that?"

I quickly regained my composure and replied, "Oh, nothing. Just musing to myself." Yet, my unease persisted, and I couldn't shake the feeling that there was more to the Glimmering Caverns than met the eye.

With a determined stride, I led the group towards the exit of the Glimmering Caverns, my mind still occupied with the enigmatic warning inscribed on the cavern wall. The mention of lurking evil heightened my curiosity and sense of responsibility to protect what lay within.

As we moved forward, the dim glow of the caverns gradually gave way to a brighter light, indicating our approach to the exit. My companions – Arabella, Aria, Ethan, and Lucas – were well acquainted with the caverns' magical properties and anticipated what lay ahead. However, the elders and Roderick, uninitiated to the caverns' enchantments, were about to be met with a surprise.

Knowing the nature of our emergence, we shared knowing glances, opting to keep the revelation to ourselves for the moment. The elders and Roderick, still unaware of what awaited them, followed closely, their anticipation growing with each step. It wouldn't be long before they, too, witnessed the wonders the Glimmering Caverns had in store.

A soft and enchanting hum filled the air as we approached the entrance, captivating our attention. Before I could inquire about the mysterious sound, Lucas suddenly winced in pain, a small, dragon-like creature with shimmering scales darting away. Alerted to potential danger, I swiftly called for everyone to take cover, preparing ourselves for whatever lay ahead.

We scanned our surroundings with weapons ready, trying to locate the elusive creature. But it seemed to vanish and reappear unpredictably, making it difficult to pinpoint its exact location. It moved with uncanny speed and agility, flitting in and out of view like a fleeting dream.

During a moment of respite, when the creature briefly emerged, Ethan drew his bow and launched an arrow. However, the beast evaded with a graceful shift, leaving the arrow to miss its mark and instead strike Ethan in the chest, momentarily taking him out of the fight. It became apparent that we needed a different approach to capture this agile foe.

Aria, ever resourceful, stepped forward with determination in her eyes. She unleashed a lightning bolt to catch the creature in its electrifying grasp. Her hands crackled with energy as she focused her power. Still, even with her precision and intent, the creature deftly evaded the electrical discharge, continuing its elusive dance through the caverns. We were left to regroup, reassess, and find a way to outmaneuver this enigmatic and agile creature.

"It's like trying to catch a flickering flame," I exclaimed, my frustration evident. "We need to devise a plan to anticipate its next move and strike before it can evade us."

Before anyone else could respond, Scorch, the tiny dragon hatchling, burst out of my bag and zoomed after the elusive creature with unwavering determination.

"Scorch, no! You're still too small to chase after it!" I shouted, but my words fell on deaf ears as Scorch darted through the caverns in pursuit.

Frantic, the group strained their eyes, searching for any sign of Scorch or the creature.

"Did anyone see where they went?" I asked, concern creeping into my voice.

"I didn't," Arabella replied.

"When did Scorch learn to fly?" Aria wondered aloud.

"I had no idea he could fly so soon after hatching," I admitted, surprised by Scorch's newfound skill.

As we listened intently, wings flapping echoed through the cavern, a mix of the creature's and Scorch's. However, our eyes failed to catch a glimpse of the ongoing chase. The beast emerged from the darkness, hurtling towards the group. Urgently, I called out, "Hold your fire! We can't risk hitting Scorch!"

We braced ourselves as the creature quickly dived, only to veer away at the last moment, narrowly avoiding a collision. Scorch continued his pursuit, swooping and diving with remarkable agility, keeping the creature on its toes. The tiny dragon proved surprisingly adept at keeping pace, displaying an uncanny understanding of the chase.

As the creature sped past our group, with Scorch in hot pursuit, we strained to keep our eyes locked on the two figures. Suddenly, we were all blinded by a radiant, fiery orange light emanating from Scorch's maw. The intensity of the brightness overwhelmed us, and we instinctively shielded our eyes. As we did so, a wave of heat washed over us, accompanied by the sight of flames engulfing the elusive creature. It tumbled towards the cavern floor, its once elusive nature now subdued by the relentless pursuit of the tiny but courageous dragon hatchling.

"Since when could he breathe fire?" Lucas asked, his curiosity evident.

I chuckled, still in awe of Scorch's unexpected display of power. "That's a great question and one I can't quite answer," I replied with a bemused smile.

As Scorch fluttered back to me, I gently stroked the dragon hatchling's head. "Well, it seems you're growing up faster than anticipated, my fiery friend," I said, my voice filled with astonishment and pride. "You certainly have more surprises hidden within that tiny body of yours. What else are you capable of, I wonder?" I mused, my eyes gleaming with anticipation.

With the diminished threat, I carefully stowed the torch back into my bag. "Let's get out of here before we encounter more of those," I said, my mind still grappling with the words and the mysterious creature we had just faced. It was the first creature we had encountered in the Glimmering Caverns since our victorious battle against the Gem Golem. Taking a moment to ponder the writing on the wall, I wonder if that was precisely what the enigmatic message was trying to tell me.

Chapter 6 The Castle

As we emerged from the depths of the Glimmering Caverns, the sight before us confirmed our expectations, but for the elders, it was a moment of overwhelming awe. The Kingdom of Thalondor, once ravaged by time and ruin, now stood before us in all its restored glory. The once crumbling walls now boast magnificent architecture, and vibrant banners fluttered in the gentle breeze. It was a testament to the power of our mission and the hope that had guided us thus far.

Roderick, still absorbing the scene's grandeur, couldn't help but comment on the newfound ease of our travel.

"That seems to be a much easier mode of travel," he stated, his tone filled with admiration. Curiosity shining in his eyes, he turned towards me and asked, "But how does it work? How can it reach the desired destination by merely thinking of it?"

I smiled, recalling our previous conversation. "Remember when I mentioned that the entrance to the Glimmering Caverns has a unique quality of shifting and moving?" I began. Roderick nodded, his attention entirely focused on my words. "Well, that's exactly how it works. By envisioning where we wish to go, the entrance responds and transports us there. It's as if the caverns have become attuned to my thoughts and intentions. It is one of the mystical abilities granted upon defeating the Gem Golem."

Roderick couldn't hide his amazement. "So, all you need to do is imagine our destination, and the caverns will carry us there?" he asked.

"Exactly. It's a remarkable gift bestowed upon us, a testament to our connection with the ancient forces within these caverns. It allows us to traverse great distances instantly, sparing us days of arduous travel."

As the group approached the grand gates of the Kingdom of Thalondor, we couldn't help but notice the bustling activity that filled the once-desolate surroundings. People were coming and going, engaging in lively conversations and going about their daily tasks. It starkly contrasted the emptiness we had left behind only a few hours ago.

I couldn't hide my surprise as I took in the vibrant scene. "This looks quite different from when we left, and it feels like only a short while ago," I remarked, my voice filled with astonishment.

Pondering over the mysterious passage of time, Arabella added, "It's perplexing how we seemingly lost an entire year during our journey. The whole situation is quite strange."

Lucas chimed in. "Indeed, it's hard to comprehend. The Kingdom was empty when we departed, and we were the only ones present. And now, it's teeming with life."

"It makes you wonder what else has changed in the surrounding areas during that lost year," Aria said, nodding in agreement.

Ethan's voice carried a sense of curiosity as he voiced his thoughts. It may have something to do with the enchantment cast upon the Kingdom. It might have altered not just the physical state of Thalondor but also the passage of time."

I nodded in agreement. "That's a possibility we should consider. The enchantment might have had far-reaching effects beyond our understanding."

As the group approached the gate, the guards there halted our progress. One of the guards, engrossed in paperwork, absentmindedly addressed us without even looking up. His lack of attention irked Roderick, who could not tolerate negligence.

"Are you truly paying attention to the individuals entering and exiting this gate, or are you merely going through the motions without even looking at them?" Roderick spoke up, his voice firm and commanding.

Startled, the guard finally lifted his gaze from the paperwork. Realizing his mistake, he hastily tried to rectify the situation. "Apologies, General. I was caught up in reviewing this roster," he stammered. "I assure you, I will be more attentive in the future."

Roderick's stern expression softened slightly, but his tone remained firm. "It is imperative that you perform your duties with utmost diligence. Now show proper respect to your King."

The guard's eyes widened as he recognized me. "Your Highness!" he exclaimed. "I offer my sincerest apologies. I did not realize it was you."

I chuckled, finding amusement in the situation. "I suppose I will never quite get used to the 'Your Highness' treatment," I mused. "But indeed, something does feel peculiar about all of this."

As we made our way through the lively streets, surrounded by the bustling activity of the Kingdom, we couldn't help but be captivated by the vibrant atmosphere. The sounds of chatter, laughter, and the clamor of market stalls filled the air, creating a sense of liveliness that seemed out of place for a Kingdom that had recently emerged from ruins.

"This is truly remarkable," Aria exclaimed.

Lucas nodded in agreement, scanning the market square. "It's as if Thalondor has seamlessly returned to its former glory, as if it had been thriving for years."

We marveled at the sight, struggling to reconcile the reality before us with our memories of a dilapidated Kingdom. The transformation was nothing short of extraordinary.

"This feels like a strange dream, doesn't it?" I mused.

Arabella said, "It may feel surreal, but we are all experiencing it together. It must be real, and there must be an explanation."

I nodded, accepting her reasoning. "You're right. We need to find answers. Let's go to the castle and see if we can uncover the truth behind all this."

As we arrived at the majestic castle, the elders paused to take in the grandeur of its imposing structure. They remained silent, their eyes tracing the intricate details of the castle's architecture, filled with reverence for its history and significance.

I led the group up the grand staircase and into the expansive hallway. My mind was filled with thoughts and plans, and I turned to address the group.

"Let's ensure everyone is settled in their respective rooms first, and then we can discuss our next course of action," I said.

"Roderick, you mentioned there are elders here. Could you arrange for someone to escort the Vindoria Elders to a suitable meeting place where they can begin collaborating?"

Roderick swiftly motioned to a servant, instructing them to guide the elders to their designated location.

I then turned my attention to the group. "Please make yourselves comfortable and take some time to settle in. We will reconvene shortly to discuss our plans."

Following my instructions, the servants led the guests to their rooms, ensuring their comfort and privacy within the castle's walls.

"Roderick, could you show me around the castle, taking the longer route? I would appreciate familiarizing myself with the surroundings."

Roderick nodded respectfully. "Of course, Your Highness. It would be my pleasure."

As Roderick and I strolled through the grand hall, our footsteps echoed against the stone floor, a reminder of the weight of history within these walls. Roderick gestured towards the banners adorning the walls, their vibrant red hues catching the flickering light.

"These banners represent the legacy of Thalondor," Roderick explained, his voice filled with reverence. "The crossing swords symbolize the valor and strength of our Kingdom, while the shield displays the intricate designs that signify our noble heritage."

My gaze lingered on the banners, my mind drifting back to the vision I had experienced after the bright light in the dungeon. The images flashed vividly in my memory—the chaos, determination, and the sight of those banners fluttering amid the conflict.

"I witnessed those banners flying high during the final battle," I shared a hint of awe in my voice. "Although, it was more of a vision that came to me when I plunged the dagger into the opening in the dungeon."

Roderick listened intently, intrigued by my connection to the past. "A vision from the depths of history," he mused. "It seems your destiny has long been intertwined with the fate of Thalondor."

He continued, his voice carrying the weight of ancient stories. "Before the enchantment was cast, your noble ancestors ruled over Thalondor for over a century. They guided the Kingdom, ensuring peace reigned throughout the land."

He paused, his gaze meeting mine. "Your family played a pivotal role in seizing and building up this Kingdom. Their determination and foresight forged the path to the Thalondor we see before us today."

As Roderick and I made our way through the castle, he gestured towards different areas, offering me insight into each location's significance. I listened attentively, my curiosity growing with each new revelation.

As we approached a familiar staircase, Roderick pointed towards it with a knowing smile. "Ah, the dungeon area," Roderick remarked. "A place that held great challenges and mysteries, but now lies transformed after your encounter with the creatures and the use of the dagger."

I nodded, memories of our intense battle flooding back. "Yes, I remember. The creatures seemed impossible initially, but when I wielded the dagger, they vanished as if defeated by its power."

Moving onward, we ascended a flight of stairs, and Roderick directed my attention to a grand room. "Here we have the library," Roderick explained. "It houses a vast collection of ancient parchments and texts retrieved from Serpents Pass. These documents hold invaluable knowledge about our history, the land's secrets, and perhaps even clues to aid us in our quest."

My eyes widened with anticipation, knowing those hallowed halls lay answers that could help guide us on our journey. Delving into the ancient wisdom of the parchments ignited a spark of determination within me.

As we continued our tour, Roderick gestured towards a set of imposing doors. "And over there, Your Highness, lies the meeting chamber of the High Council," Roderick stated. "It is a gathering place where the important matters of the Kingdom are discussed, and decisions are made."

"The High Council," I repeated. "Who comprises the council?"

Roderick smiled, understanding the weight of my question. "As the rightful ruler, it will be your prerogative to select individuals whom you deem wise, capable, and loyal to sit on the High Council," he replied. "Their counsel will prove invaluable as we navigate the challenges ahead and make critical decisions for the welfare of Thalondor."

I took a moment to absorb the information, realizing the

importance of assembling a council of trusted advisors. It would be an opportunity to unite individuals with diverse skills and perspectives, united by their dedication to the Kingdom's prosperity.

Roderick guided me through the castle, pointing out various locations and their purposes. As we walked along, he gestured in a particular direction.

"Over there, Your Highness, you will find the chambers where the esteemed elders convene, discussing matters of great importance to the Kingdom," he explained. "And adjacent to that area is the assembly point for the heads of our formidable army."

I nodded, taking note of the designated areas. The presence of a dedicated space for both the wise elders and the military leaders emphasized the Kingdom's commitment to collaboration and strategic decision-making.

Continuing our journey, we ascended another staircase, and Roderick indicated a series of rooms along the hallway. "Here are the guest quarters, where dignitaries and visitors can find rest and respite during their stay in the Kingdom," Roderick said.

I surveyed the elegant rooms, imagining the conversations and alliances forged within those walls. Welcoming esteemed guests and fostering diplomatic relations would be essential for Thalondor's growth and security.

As we strolled further down the hallways, my attention was captured by a series of captivating paintings adorning the walls. Each painting tells a story, portraying scenes from the Kingdom's rich history. I paused momentarily, my gaze shifting from one artwork to another.

"These paintings chronicle the tales of times past," I remarked. It's as if they hold the essence of our heritage within their brush strokes."

Roderick smiled, acknowledging my fascination. "Indeed, Your Highness," he replied. "These masterpieces have been carefully crafted to immortalize the pivotal moments, legendary figures, and cherished traditions that have shaped Thalondor throughout the ages. They serve as a reminder of our glorious past and a source of inspiration for the challenges ahead."

I nodded, appreciating the depth of symbolism woven into each stroke of the artist's brush. The paintings ignited a sense of pride and responsibility, knowing I now held the key to continuing Thalondor's legacy and protecting its future.

As we ventured further along the hallway, we ascended a grand staircase leading to the castle's uppermost level. Roderick gestured towards the vast expanse before us. "This entire upper area is dedicated to you, Your Highness," he explained. "There are two sets of stairs that provide access, the one we just climbed and another set located over there." Roderick pointed towards the second staircase, emphasizing the security measures in place. "Guards are stationed at the bottom and top of both staircases, ensuring your safety and outside your chambers."

With anticipation, Roderick pushed open the doors to the King's chambers. I stepped inside and marveled at the spaciousness of the room. The chamber was designed to resemble three interconnected rooms, each serving a distinct purpose. A designated sleeping area was adorned with a lavish bed and fine linens, offering respite and comfort. Adjacent to it was a cozy sitting area with plush chairs and a small table, perfect for discussions or moments of relaxation. The third area was a well-equipped space for strategizing and developing plans, featuring a large desk, maps, and shelves filled with books and scrolls.

I took a moment to absorb the grandeur of my new quarters. The ample space provided a sense of freedom and the opportunity for introspection. It was a place to rest, gather my thoughts, and make crucial decisions for the Kingdom's future.

"I am truly grateful for this space," I said, my voice filled with appreciation. "It is more than I could have ever imagined."

Roderick smiled, pleased with my response. "It is befitting of a King, Your Highness," he replied. "May it serve as a sanctuary where you can find solace and inspiration as you navigate the challenges that lie ahead."

I nodded, my mind already brimming with plans and ideas for the Kingdom's resurgence. This chamber would become my haven, where I would strategize, contemplate, and lead with conviction.

"Alright, Your Highness, I will take my leave now to allow you to settle in," Roderick said respectfully.

"Thank you for the tour. How can I reach you if I need anything?" I inquired.

"Simply inform the guards, and they will promptly notify me," Roderick replied.

"Good to know," I acknowledged.

"Goodbye for now," Roderick said as he exited the chambers.

I took a moment to soak in the atmosphere of my new surroundings, sinking into one of the plush chairs in the sitting area. I was grateful for the chance to unwind after a long day finally. As I reflected on the events that had led me to this point, uncertainty still lingered in my mind about my role as a King. Yet, I couldn't deny the thrill and excitement of the adventure that had brought me here.

Chapter 7 Waterfalls and Mystery

As I took a moment to unwind, I lifted Whisperwind and Scorch from my bag, allowing them to stretch their wings and settle into the room. Whisperwind nestled into one chair, observing his surroundings, while Scorch hopped onto my shoulder, emitting small bursts of warmth from his fiery breath.

I chuckled at Scorch's newfound abilities. "You've been keeping some surprises up your sleeve, haven't you, my little friend?" I remarked, scratching Scorch's scaly head. "Flying and breathing fire, quite impressive indeed. Just remember, no setting anything ablaze in here."

Curious, I rose from the chair and walked towards the window, beckoning Scorch to join me. I opened the window, allowing a gentle breeze to sweep into the room. "It's time for you to stretch your wings and explore the open skies," I said to Scorch. "Fly around, build up your strength, and survey the area. Once you grow larger, we'll have to find a suitable place for you."

Scorch responded with a joyful chirp as if understanding my words. With a flutter of his wings, he soared out the window, his scales glinting in the sunlight. I watched him disappear into the horizon, feeling a sense of excitement and pride in my newfound companion.

As I gazed out of the window from my chambers, my eyes scanned the transformed kingdom below. The once desolate ruins had blossomed into a vibrant community. People moved about purposefully, engaged in their daily activities, unaware of the mysteriously disappearing time.

I attempted to make sense of the dissonance between my experience and the reality of the world around me. How could a year have passed for the Kingdom while I and my companions felt like only a day had passed? The perplexing nature of our time displacement nagged at my thoughts, stirring curiosity and unease.

Lost in contemplation, I pondered the enigma that had unfolded. What unseen forces had played a hand in our journey, altering the flow of time? Questions swirled in my mind, seeking answers that remained elusive.

With a deep sigh, I resolved to uncover the truth behind our temporal displacement. I knew that the key to understanding our peculiar predicament lay hidden within the secrets of Thalondor's past. I was determined to solve this puzzle for my companions and the Kingdom.

As my gaze extended beyond the boundaries of the Kingdom, I was drawn to the expanse of Eldoria Forest. The lush green canopy stretched as far as the eye could see, inviting me to reminisce about past adventures and tales of exploration.

In my mind's eye, I could almost hear the booming voice of Captain Stormrider, the fearless leader of the Silver Serpent crew. Memories flooded back, recalling the exhilarating moments when we sailed through the open waters, seeking new horizons and untold treasures. Captain Stormrider's words echoed in my ears as if carried by the wind itself.

Captain Stormrider stood tall at the helm, his eyes fixed on the distant horizon. His voice carried across the deck, blending authority with enthusiasm. "Maintain course and heading!" he called out, his words resonating with unwavering determination.

The disciplined and skilled crew sprang into action, ensuring the ship stayed true to its intended path.

My mind wandered back to that momentous day when the anchor plunged into the depths of the sea, signifying their arrival on an uncharted land. With a swift and coordinated effort, the crew lowered the boats into the water and paddled purposefully toward the mysterious shoreline. As the ships neared the unknown land, my heart quickened with excitement and trepidation.

As the boats approached the shore, we worked in unison to

navigate the shallow waters and reach the beach. I joined my comrades in pulling the vessels ashore, our muscles straining under the weight. The rhythmic sound of their efforts harmonized with the crashing waves that greeted the sandy shore.

Soon, Captain Stormrider emerged from the boat, his presence exuding leadership amidst the untamed wilderness. His keen eyes surveyed the surroundings, ever watchful for signs of life or adventure. The crew, their senses heightened, followed his lead, their gazes scanning the vast expanse before them, eager to embrace the unknown that awaited.

Ahead of us lay not an empty beach but a sprawling forest stretching. Towering trees reached for the skies, their lush canopies weaving a tapestry of green that spoke of enigmas and concealed wonders. The forest stood in quiet invitation, enticing them to delve into its depths and uncover its mysteries.

The whispers of the leaves seemed to caress my ears, a gentle rustling that promised untold stories and undiscovered creatures. We exchanged glances, our curiosity and excitement mirrored in each other's eyes. While we had braved the unknown, this untouched wilderness held a unique allure, an air of uncharted possibilities that ignited our adventurous spirits.

"Shall we step into the unknown, my loyal crew, or will you linger here on this sandy shore, basking in the sun?" Captain Stormrider's voice rang out with a mix of excitement and playfulness.

The crew, a band of fearless souls from different walks of life, responded with a resounding "Arrr!" Our hearts yearned for the thrill of exploration, eager to embrace the mysteries that awaited them.

Captain Stormrider took the lead without hesitation, planting his feet firmly on the forest floor. We followed closely behind, our footsteps in sync as they delved deeper into the dense foliage. The ancient trees embraced us, their branches forming a natural canopy that filtered sunlight and created a mystical ambiance.

With each step we took into the dense forest, the weight of the unknown pressed against my senses. The crew forged our path through the thick undergrowth, guided by our shared spirit of adventure and Captain Stormrider's unwavering determination.

As we ventured deeper into the wilderness, the forest enveloped us, its canopy casting dappled shadows upon our path. The air was alive with the scents of earth and foliage, and the symphony of nature echoed around us. We were explorers, pioneers in a land untouched by human hands, driven by a thirst for discovery and the thrill of the unknown.

"This bloody forest is one of the thickest ones we've encountered yet," grumbled Finnegan, his voice laced with frustration.

Undeterred by the challenging terrain, Captain Stormrider forged ahead, his determination etched on his weathered face. He navigated through the dense undergrowth, pushing aside tangled branches and foliage with every step.

Struggling to keep up, I voiced my curiosity. "Are most places you venture into as difficult to traverse as this forest?" I asked.

Captain Stormrider paused, his gaze scanning the towering trees surrounding us. His eyes reflected the wisdom earned from a lifetime of exploration. "When a forest may grow undisturbed, it becomes a labyrinth of intertwined foliage," he conveyed reverence. "Such thick forests bear witness to the passage of time, often revealing untrodden paths that no one has traversed in ages, if ever."

With every step, Captain Stormrider continued to lead the way, sharing his knowledge of the natural world with his eager companions.

"In contrast, forests humans have frequented leave a unique mark," he explained. "Trails become more defined, and signs of civilization are scattered throughout. While these places may offer easier passage, they often hold fewer hidden treasures and untold secrets."

As we pushed deeper into the forest's heart, we could sense the wilderness whispering ancient tales, its thick vegetation embracing our every movement. The air grew heavier, carrying the scent of damp earth and the symphony of unseen creatures. Each step brought us closer to the unknown, an exhilarating dance between man and nature.

Captain Stormrider's weathered features softened as he turned to me, offering a reassuring smile. "Fear not, my friend," he said. "Though this forest tests our mettle, it also promises unparalleled discoveries. The challenges we face are but a small price to pay for the wonders we may uncover within these hallowed grounds."

As we pressed onward, our ears caught the distant melody of rushing water, reminiscent of a majestic waterfall cascading down rocks. Captain Stormrider's keen senses perked up, attuned to the possibilities ahead.

"Listen," Captain Stormrider called out. "Do you hear that? The symphony of freshwater beckoning us towards new opportunities."

We, the crew, followed the sound with eager curiosity. With each step, the thunderous rush of water grew louder, harmonizing with the rhythm of our excited hearts. The air became charged with anticipation, buzzing with the energy of our impending discovery.

We emerged from the dense foliage into a breathtaking clearing. Before us lay a scene of unparalleled beauty. The once-overgrown wilderness had given way to an idyllic paradise—a serene oasis with vibrant flowers, bountiful fruit-laden trees, and a waterfall that tumbled down a rocky cliff. Sunlight pierced through the mist, painting a radiant rainbow across the sky.

We stood in awe, our eyes wide with wonder. Captain Stormrider's weathered face broke into a smile as he surveyed the scene. "What a sight!" he exclaimed. "A place untouched by time, where nature's splendor unfolds before our eyes."

We took a moment to absorb the magnificence of the scene, immersing ourselves in the moment's serenity. The air was infused with the sweet scent of blooming flowers, and the soothing sound of cascading water filled our ears. It was a sanctuary, a respite from the trials of our journey, offering a glimpse into the world's untamed beauty.

The crew, overcome with delight and uncontainable enthusiasm, wasted no time plunging into the crystal-clear pool at the waterfall's base. Laughter and joyful splashes filled the air as they frolicked in the refreshing water, forgetting our surroundings.

Captain Stormrider watched the playful scene unfold with his eyes twinkling with amusement. "Well, if anyone or anything nearby wasn't aware of our presence before, they know now," he remarked with a chuckle.

I joined in the lighthearted banter, adding, "Indeed, Captain. At least some crew can wash away the grime and odors accumulated during our journey. It's about time, as some were emitting quite an aroma."

The atmosphere shifted from joyous celebration to urgency and concern as something pulled several crew members beneath the pool's surface, disappearing. A stubborn determination replaced the shock and alarm on Captain Stormrider's face.

With unwavering determination, Captain Stormrider dove into the water, his powerful strokes propelling him toward where his men had vanished. His eyes scanned the depths, searching for any signs of his crew. As he resurfaced, gasping for breath, he wasted no time rallying his remaining crew.

"They're being drawn towards the waterfall! Sound the alarm, men!" Captain Stormrider's urgent voice echoed as he called for immediate action. With a unified sense of purpose, the crew members leaped into the pool, their bodies slicing through the water with determined strokes.

Feeling concerned for my fellow crew members and a sense of duty, I followed suit, plunging into the pool alongside my comrades. The water enveloped me, its cool embrace urging me onward. I swam with determination, my eyes fixed on the distant waterfall where my crew members were being pulled.

As we approached the waterfall, the force of the current grew more robust, tugging at our bodies relentlessly. The rushing water drowned out our desperate calls and cries, adding an eerie backdrop to our treacherous journey. We fought against the powerful current, our strokes growing more vigorous as we neared the waterfall's edge.

My heart raced with a mixture of fear and determination as I reached the precipice of the waterfall. I propelled myself forward without hesitation, bracing myself for what lay beyond. The sight that greeted me was both awe-inspiring and terrifying.

A hidden cavern revealed itself behind the waterfall, its mysterious depths beckoning us forward. I could hear the faint echoes of my crew members' voices, showing they were still alive. Determined to rescue my comrades, I steeled myself for the unknown ahead.

Navigating through the hidden cavern, we pressed onward with determination, our senses heightened as we moved deeper into the unknown. The air grew heavy with anticipation, and every twist and turn of the labyrinth brought us closer to our goal. We relied on our instincts and the faint sounds echoing through the cavern to guide our path.

Footsteps echoed against the rocky walls, our hushed whispers mingling with the distant water drip. We exchanged glances, communicating as we continued our search. We moved cautiously, aware that any wrong turn could lead us astray or into danger.

As we ventured more profoundly, a faint flicker of light illuminated the way, drawing us closer to our missing mates. We quickened our pace, eager to find them...Knock Knock.

Startled by the unexpected knocking, my attention snapped back to my chambers. The sound reverberated through the room, breaking the silence that had enveloped me. I turned from the window and approached the door.

With anticipation and caution, I reached out to grasp the door handle. I dragged it, the creak of the door adding an air of mystery to the moment. As the door swung open, I found myself face to face with an unexpected visitor.

Standing before me was a messenger clad in the Kingdom's regal attire. The messenger's eyes sparkled with urgency as they delivered a scroll into my outstretched hand. The messenger bowed and left without uttering a word, allowing me to read the scroll. Secrets and revelations filled the message, sparking events that would mold Thalondor's future.

Chapter 8 The Messenger

As I held the scroll in my hands, my gaze fixed on the impressive wax seal adorned it. Crafted from high-quality wax with a deep royal blue hue, the seal immediately caught my attention. The intricate design etched into the wax depicted a mighty lion standing proudly on its hind legs with its forelegs raised, emanating strength and courage. Above the lion, a regal crown adorned with precious gems symbolized the wealth and prosperity of the kingdom.

I couldn't help but marvel at the attention to detail and the regal elegance of the seal. It was evident that whoever had sent this scroll wanted to make a statement. The lion's fierce posture and the crown atop its head conveyed a sense of authority and nobility, befitting a message from a person of significant importance.

Curiosity gnawed at me as I pondered the identity of the sender. Who in the realm possessed such a striking and distinctive seal? The answer to this mystery lay within the scroll's contents, and I couldn't wait to unravel its secrets. With a sense of anticipation, I carefully unrolled the parchment, eager to discover the message that lay within.

I gingerly unrolled the scroll and began to read the message inscribed within.

"To Whom It May Concern."

"To Whom It May Concern," I echoed. "Are they seriously playing coy with me? They sent it to a castle, for heaven's sake!"

"Behold, your golden ticket to bask in the glory of my majestic presence; I, the illustrious Queen of Serendell, summon you!"

I couldn't help but roll my eyes. "Majestic presence, huh? Someone's got an overinflated sense of grandeur."

"Listen up, my devoted messenger will lurk around, eagerly waiting to see if you possess the brains to grace the Kingdom of Serendell with your esteemed company. Or, of course, you can choose the path of ignorance and pass up this once-in-a-lifetime chance."

"Oh, the audacity!" I scoffed. "This Queen sure knows how to stroke her ego."

"Should you embark on this extraordinary journey, my envoy will be your trusty guide to the dazzling Kingdom of Serendell." "Yours imperiously, Queen Amelia."

"Queen Amelia," I mused, chuckling softly. "Well, we've got ourselves quite the character here." After reading the note, I knew it was time to gather everyone in the castle. Oh, the tales we'd have to tell!

I briskly made my way to the door and swung it open.

The guard stationed outside greeted me, "Yes, your Highness."

"Could you please inform Roderick to gather all those who traveled with us today and assemble them in the High Council Chambers?" I requested.

"Certainly, your Highness," the guard acknowledged, and he set off to find Roderick.

Once the door shut, I retrieved my bag from the room. Whisperwind lifted his head, curious about the commotion.

"Don't worry, my little friend. Everything's alright. You rest up; we might need all the energy we can get in the coming days." I gently patted Whisperwind's head, assuring him, before leaving the room to head towards the High Council Chambers.

Descending the stairs on my way to the High Council Chamber, I couldn't help but be captivated by the walls and tapestries that adorned the castle. The kingdom's transformation was astounding, and I remained in awe of the changes that had taken place. Once a place of dilapidation and ruin, the castle now gleamed as if everything had been renewed. The sight was unbelievable, a testament to the power of restoration and the potential for growth and change within Thalondor.

Upon entering the High Council Chambers, I was surprised to find

Roderick, Arabella, Aria, Ethan, and Lucas already present. I couldn't help but wonder if I had lingered longer than I realized when I asked the guard to gather them.

"Hello, everyone. I hope you had a moment to relax or get things in order," I greeted them.

"We did, but we also took the opportunity to discuss some ideas," Arabella replied.

"Ideas? About what?" I inquired.

"Just brainstorming, throwing ideas around to see what might work," Ethan explained.

"And you didn't include me in the discussion?" I raised an eyebrow.

"We didn't have anything concrete to share yet, just preliminary thoughts," Lucas replied. "There was no need to involve you until we had something more substantial."

"I understand. So, did anyone come up with anything promising?"

"We're still waiting for information from the elders, but we agree that we'll need assistance from other kingdoms and cities. Our army alone isn't enough to defeat this threat," Roderick explained.

"Which we all agreed upon, but it's frustrating that we don't know anything about the other kingdoms out there," Aria said passionately.

"And that's precisely why I called this meeting; now I have information about at least one kingdom," I responded enthusiastically.

"Although I must admit, it's quite extraordinary."

Passing around the scroll, I watched as their eyes widened with surprise.

"Oh my," Arabella exclaimed. "That's one way to exude confidence!"

"That's putting it mildly," I chuckled.

"So, any ideas on what our next move should be?" Lucas spoke resolutely,

"Frankly, I don't think we have much of a choice. We need strength in numbers, and we have no clue how formidable her army may be." Roderick agreed, "He's right. We can't ignore the possibility that her forces might be considerable."

"It's worth noting that her messenger is still here somewhere in our kingdom, awaiting a response from 'To Whom It May Concern,'" I revealed. "I think we should find him and gather any information we can."

"I'll have the guards track him down and bring him here immediately," Roderick declared, determination etched across his face.

"However, I also think it's crucial to start sending scouting parties out across the land to see who else is out there," I suggested assertively.

"Agreed," Lucas chimed in.

"Arabella and I can go and meet Queen Amelia. We can probably get there and back in a day if we use Glimmering Caverns," I proposed.

"Oh, you can't just use Glimmering Caverns for this important encounter," Ethan interjected.

"Why not?" I inquired.

"Because you need to show up with force, letting her know you are not to be underestimated," Ethan explained. "You must present yourself as a mighty King with a formidable army, setting the story straight from the start."

"Okay, I'm listening," I replied, intrigued by Ethan's idea.

"Yeah, I can't wait to see how this unfolds," Lucas chimed.

"You need to ride out there as a King, not as Valaric," Ethan continued. "Show her that you are a powerful ruler with a massive army. This will make her see that you both stand on equal ground and are not inferior to her. By doing so, you'll be better positioned to ask for her assistance in the upcoming battles."

"I must admit, that wasn't exactly what I expected him to suggest," Lucas remarked, amused.

"Agreed, Lucas, but he does make a valid point," I acknowledged.

"So what's the plan, then?" Aria inquired.

"Valaric and Arabella head to Serendell with at least twenty thousand men," Ethan relayed. "The idea is not to send a hostile message but rather to travel with a significant force to ensure your protection."

"Are you sure traveling with so many soldiers won't be considered a threat?" I questioned.

"It's a calculated risk. But I presume she has more soldiers at her disposal, though probably not as many as we currently do," Ethan explained. "So it shouldn't be seen as a threat, and it demonstrates that you can casually roam around with twenty thousand men."

"Alright, so that's the plan for Arabella and Valaric. What about the rest of us?" Lucas inquired.

"Roderick and I can head in one direction, and you and Aria can go in another," Ethan proposed.

"I must say, Ethan, that sounds like a feasible plan," I stated, holding the scroll in my hands. "Roderick, do we have a seal and wax in my chambers? I need to write up some mandates for them to carry."

"Yes, they are available at your desk in your chambers," Roderick replied.

"Now that we have everything figured out, let's bring in the messenger to give him an answer," I suggested.

"I will fetch him from the hallway," Roderick said promptly.

As the messenger entered the room, I began, "Welcome to the Kingdom of Thalondor. I am King Valaric. According to this scroll, you are awaiting an answer regarding whether or not I will grace your Queen with my presence."

"Yes, your Highness. Those were my orders," the messenger confirmed.

"Could you please tell me the exact location of the Kingdom of Serendell?" I inquired.

"It's near the coast, about three days from here, in a southwesterly direction," the messenger replied.

"If we give you a map, could you mark the approximate location of Serendell?"

"Yes, Your Highness," the messenger responded.

"Excellent. Someone, fetch a map so the messenger can mark the approximate location," I instructed. "Say I am willing to bet you have delivered similar messages to the other surrounding kingdoms or villages. Would you please mark those as well?"

Once the messenger marked the location of Serendell and the neighboring areas, I called over one of the guards to prepare to escort him.

"It's rather late to start heading back tonight," I said. "Why not stay the night in one of our accommodations, and I will prepare a note for you to bring to your Queen in the morning."

"That sounds like a good deal, Your Highness," the messenger replied.

I motioned for the guard to lead the messenger out of the room and take him to his quarters for the night.

"Well, I suppose the rest of us should get some shut-eye before tomorrow as we all start traveling," I suggested. "I need to write some edicts for you and a memo for Queen Amelia."

"Yes, it has already been a long day," Arabella said.

"I would say so, considering it seemed like just this morning, this place was in ruins," Ethan added, prompting a chuckle from all of us.

"I'm going to head back to my quarters to get those items written," I informed everyone. "See you all in the morning."

Each of them bid me goodnight as I left the High Council Chambers. Climbing the stairs, I reached my floor and entered my room, finding Whisperwind undisturbed during my absence. On the other hand, Scorch had settled on my bed after his flight around the kingdom.

"I'm guessing flying around is hard work," I said with a chuckle.

Taking a moment, I wrote up several mandates for the others to carry, showing they were under the protection of our kingdom and stating the purpose of their visit to request assistance. Without existing relationships, this endeavor was going to prove quite challenging.

As I prepared to write the scroll for Queen Amelia, I pondered the right words to use. Her earlier message had been rather bold and self-assured, so a cordial and respectful tone would be appropriate. With that in mind, I set to work, carefully crafting each sentence with diplomacy and courtesy.

"This missive is to the esteemed Queen Amelia of Serendell," I began, hoping that such a formal introduction would set the right tone. "I, Valaric, King of Thalondor, extend my greetings and salutations to you and your noble kingdom."

I continued, expressing our intention of seeking an audience with her and the desire for an alliance between our realms. I emphasized the mutual benefits that could be achieved through cooperation and assistance in these difficult times.

Though I couldn't shake the lingering uncertainty of how she might react to our proposal, I remained optimistic. After all, forging new alliances required taking risks, and it was the only way we could hope to face the looming threats together.

With the scroll now complete, I placed it with the mandates for the others to carry, ensuring they would be delivered safely. As I settled into the soft embrace of my bed, I contemplated the potential outcomes of our upcoming journey. It was a risky venture that could lead to a warm embrace or a hostile reception. But in times of uncertainty, boldness was necessary, and the potential rewards far outweighed the risks.

Excited and apprehensive stirred within me as I closed my eyes, eager to see how our fate would unfold. Tomorrow marked the beginning of a brand new day filled with hope and anticipation. There was much ground to cover in the coming days, and as the sun dipped below the horizon, I welcomed the embrace of slumber, knowing that the journey ahead would be one of challenges and triumphs.

Chapter 9 The Great Alliance

The following morning, anticipation coursed through my veins as I prepared for the adventure ahead. Queen Amelia's message had ignited a spark within me, and I knew this encounter would be etched into my memory forever. Despite my expectations, the meeting was inevitable—our kingdom's fate hinged on forming alliances, and we couldn't afford to falter. Who knew, it might even turn out to be an intriguing affair.

As I gathered my belongings and carefully packed my essentials, my mind couldn't help but drift between the extraordinary events of the past and the uncertainties ahead. It seemed like only yesterday that the kingdom stood in ruins, a relic of a bygone era, but now, it shone with newfound life and vibrancy.

Amidst my preparations, questions swirled in my mind like a storm. How long had those sinister monsters been seeping out of the crack in the dungeon's depths? And beyond our kingdom's borders, where else were these creatures emerging from, threatening the peace we desperately sought to uphold? Would we be able to endure the fierce battles that loomed ahead, and would they stretch on for years, reminiscent of the epic struggle a millennium ago?

Yet, amidst the contemplation of these daunting challenges, my thoughts inevitably turned to the surreal nature of it all. I awoke on an unfamiliar beach not long ago, devoid of memory and identity. Now, I stand as a king—a leader of a thriving kingdom responsible for safeguarding its people. The weight of the crown upon my shoulders was a testament to the gravity of the situation. Fate had intertwined our destinies, and it was now my duty to ensure the safety and well-being of everyone under my care.

As the king, I was embarking on an adventure far grander than I could have imagined. Each step, each decision, would influence the course of history, shaping our kingdom's future and its inhabitants' lives. Realizing the extent of my role in this unfolding tale was both exhilarating and overwhelming.

Turning my attention back to the present, I lovingly scooped up my two faithful companions, Whisperwind and Scorch, and gently placed them in my bag. As I secured them in their cozy spot, I couldn't help but marvel at Scorch's growth.

"My fiery friend," I told him affectionately, "you're increasing. Soon, you might not fit in this little bag anymore."

Scorch responded with a playful nudge as if understanding every word I said.

I had grown incredibly fond of Scorch's company. There was something special about having a dragon as a companion—a magnificent and rare creature. With every passing day, I wondered how much bigger he would become, but at the same time, a part of me secretly wished he could stay this size forever. Having such a loyal and endearing friend was heartwarming, and I cherished the moments we spent together.

As I looked at Whisperwind and Scorch nestled in my bag, I couldn't help but smile. They were more than just loyal companions; they were like family to me. The thought of sharing countless more adventures with them filled me with excitement. Together, we would face the challenges ahead, drawing strength and comfort from each other's presence.

With everything in order, I went downstairs to meet the others, but only after stopping in to see the Elders.

"Your Highness, what can we do for you," asked one of the Elders.

"I just stopped in to see if we have uncovered anything interesting," I said.

"Right now, we do not have anything that would help us defeat the monsters, but we are continually pouring through the manuscripts to search for clues," the elder said.

"Understand as it has been but a day, and there is much to uncover," I followed up. "By chance, do we have anything on the

Kingdom of Serendell? Maybe something that tells of an alliance from a thousand years ago or something."

"Hmm, let me look at the manuscripts to see what I can find," said the elder, searching the shelves. "Ah, here they are, the manuscripts on Serendell."

"Thank you," I said as I started to look through the manuscripts.

As I looked through the ancient symbols within the manuscript, I deciphered that the Kingdom of Serendell is a land of enchantment and mystery, nestled near the coast and shrouded in legends. With its majestic landscapes and lush greenery, Serendell exudes an otherworldly charm that captivates all who venture into its domain. The kingdom's natural beauty is said to be unparalleled, with cascading waterfalls, meandering rivers, and dense forests that stretch as far as the eye can see.

I took a second to imagine what that would look like and whether it would be the same today as it was written in this thousand-year-old manuscript.

I continued to decipher some more symbols to learn that the people of Serendell are known for their warm hospitality and deep connection with nature. They have a rich cultural heritage, marked by storytelling, music, and art passed down through generations. Festivals and celebrations are common in Serendell, offering a glimpse into the kingdom's vibrant and colorful spirit.

As I delved further into the ancient manuscripts, I stumbled upon a section that recounted the history of Serendell's allegiance to Thalondor in the previous great war a thousand years ago. The tale spoke of a time when the forces of darkness threatened to consume the entire realm, and the Kingdom of Serendell found itself on the brink of destruction.

Amid chaos and uncertainty, the wise rulers of Serendell sought aid and unity to combat the encroaching darkness. Recognizing the need for a powerful ally, they reached out to the Kingdom of Thalondor, a land renowned for its strength and courage in the face of adversity. Queen Amelia's ancestors, who ruled over Serendell during that time, sent forth a delegation of emissaries to meet with the ruling monarch of Thalondor.

The emissaries embarked on a long and arduous journey to Thalondor, conveying peace, friendship, and the desire to forge an unbreakable alliance. Upon their arrival, the reigning king of Thalondor welcomed them with open arms, and after days of discussions and negotiations, the two kingdoms sealed their pact of loyalty.

The treaty solidified their bond, pledging mutual aid and support in need. It was agreed that the Kingdom of Serendell would stand as a steadfast ally of Thalondor, and in return, Thalondor promised to protect and defend Serendell from any threats that might arise. The two kingdoms swore to stand side by side in the face of adversity, united in their quest for peace and prosperity.

"I've found what I was seeking," I declared with satisfaction. "This should be enough to convince them of their pledge to Thalondor."

"Perhaps," the elder replied thoughtfully.

"Can we have this written into a scroll promptly?" I inquired.

"Yes, your Highness," the elder assured me.

As I waited for the information to be transcribed, I observed the intriguing exchange between the elders of Thalondor and Vindoria. It was a mix of humor and frustration as the Thalondor elders tried to recount the history of their kingdom from a thousand years ago. In contrast, the Vindoria elders attempted to bring them up to speed on the past millennium. It was a comical sight, and I couldn't help but imagine that a barrel of wine might have eased the conversation or made it more coherent.

"Here you go, your Highness," the diligent elder presented the finished scroll to me.

"Thank you," I said, quickly taking the scroll and excusing myself from the room.

As I stepped outside, the group was assembled and eager to embark on the day's adventure.

"Look who decided to grace us with his presence," Lucas teased.

"I guess royalty demands a bit of extra sleep," Ethan jested, causing everyone to laugh.

"Well, I couldn't let everyone have all the fun without me," I replied, playfully defending my tardiness.

Aria chimed in with a playful remark, and Arabella joined the lighthearted banter, further lightening the mood. In the company of my friends, even the prospect of a daunting journey seemed less formidable.

As we readied ourselves, Roderick announced the messenger's arrival.

"Here, my good man, take this scroll with utmost haste to Queen Amelia of Serendell," I instructed, handing over the carefully crafted message.

"Yes, Your Highness," he replied dutifully, mounting his horse and set off on his mission.

"Before I forget, here are the edicts for you both," I announced, handing the scrolls to Lucas and Ethan.

"Thank you," they both replied, tucking the edicts into their bags.

"Use them to initiate conversations," I advised. "The mandates should explain everything they need to know. If they choose not to come to Thalondor, please request a scroll to bring back so we can better understand the terms they may want to meet."

"Will do," said Lucas.

"We will do our best," added Ethan.

"I hope we can all meet back here in a week or so with new allies to help the cause. Make sure everyone stays safe on their journeys."

Before we set off on our separate paths, we exchanged hugs and handshakes, wishing each other well in our endeavors. We watched as Lucas, Aria, and about a thousand soldiers headed to their destination. Next, Ethan, Roderick, and another thousand soldiers departed in another direction.

"Well, are you ready to head out?" I asked Arabella as I turned towards her.

"Yes, we might as well get this adventure started," she replied.

"Good deal," I said with a smile as we started our journey.

As we began our trek, my mind was filled with anticipation about the unknowns ahead. I wondered what sights we would behold and what challenges we might encounter. Hopefully, nothing that we couldn't handle, but I knew we were about to find out very soon. The fate of Thalondor and the success of our quest now rested on our shoulders, and I was determined to face whatever came our way with courage and conviction.

Chapter 10 The Gromlins

As Arabella and I embarked on our journey on horseback towards
Serendell, accompanied by an impressive twenty thousand soldiers, I
couldn't help but ponder how the meeting with the Queen would turn
out. Here I was, a regular guy one day, and the next, I was suddenly
dubbed a King. It was all surreal, and honestly, I wasn't entirely
convinced that the whole lineage thing was a hundred percent real.

As our journey continued, I opted to give Scorch a chance to stretch
his wings. It was an excellent opportunity for him to exercise and take
in the scenery. With a release of my command, he soared into the open
skies. Watching him ascend, I was relieved to see him still within
sight. I hoped that he'd stay close by, exploring the expanse above.

"What you are thinking about over there, King Valaric?" asked
Arabella, breaking me out of my contemplation.

"Now, don't you start," I replied with a smirk. "Let's just stick with
Valaric for now. I mean, I see why you didn't want to be called
Princess. You've been one your whole life, and I've only been a King for
a day or so."

Arabella nodded, understanding my predicament. "True, but your
lineage supposedly dates back over a thousand years," she pointed
out.

I shrugged, still skeptical. "Yeah, supposedly. But it's hard to believe
when there's a story in some old manuscripts. It feels like there's a
thin line between truth and fantasy."

"Sure, it may seem that way," Arabella agreed. "But think about it.
There are so many coincidences that point to the story being true.

Maybe you should consider looking at it from a different perspective."

Curious, I asked, "What perspective would that be?"

She flashed a mischievous grin. "Well, you have a whole Kingdom, a grand castle, and a massive army of a hundred thousand soldiers supporting you. If that doesn't scream King, I don't know what does! Who cares what others believe when you've got all that?"

I chuckled, realizing she had a point. "You've got a knack for finding the silver lining, Princess."

She playfully rolled her eyes. "It's Arabella to you, Your Majesty."

We both laughed, finding humor in our newfound roles.

"I wish we were using the Glimmering Caverns route to Serendell. We'd probably be there by now," I remarked.

Arabella nodded, understanding my sentiment. "I get what you're saying, but let's look at it differently. This journey allows us to spend time together and explore what else is out there."

"You're right," I admitted. "I sometimes forget that all of this is just as new to you as it is to me."

She smiled, her eyes sparkling with excitement. "Absolutely. Eldoria Forest was all I knew before this, and I never even imagined there was a world beyond the trees. Everything we're seeing now is like an adventure waiting to unfold."

"I understand that," I agreed. "For me, this is like another adventure in a new land. Only this time, it's not just about the thrill of discovery – it's about preserving what we find."

Arabella's expression turned playful. "Once all of this is settled, you should take me on one of those grand adventures you're used to."

A grin spread across my face. "I'd be more than happy to. I'm taking you on one right now."

She raised an eyebrow, intrigued. "Oh? I can't wait to see what surprises are in store. Ancient artifacts, epic battles, maybe even something a thousand years old?"

"Who knows," I chuckled. "And speaking of things a thousand years old, I'll just have to bring you back to Thalondor. That place is practically a treasure trove of ancient stuff."

Amid our shared laughter, a screech pierced the air from above, immediately snapping my attention skyward to check on Scorch's safety. Yet, the expansive heavens revealed no imminent danger surrounding him. Could he have detected something from his vantage point high above?

Coincidentally, at that very moment, our organized formation abruptly stopped. Arabella and I exchanged swift glances, scanning our surroundings for any signs of disturbance, but to no avail. Scorch continued his aerial circling, reassuring me with his unharmed presence. Nonetheless, the puzzling cessation of our progress left me questioning its reason.

One of the soldiers approached us from the front of the formation, his expression serious. "Your Highness, there are roughly a thousand Gromlins ahead," he informed us.

"A thousand what?" I inquired, unfamiliar with the term.

"Gromlins, Your Highness," the soldier reiterated.

"And what precisely are these Gromlins?" I inquired further.

"Gromlins are humanoid creatures with rough, mottled skin that comes in shades of green, brown, or gray. They possess distinctive jutting jaws, sharp tusks, and evil, beady eyes," the soldier detailed.

"Their description doesn't suggest they're native to this land. Then again, my understanding of this realm is still evolving," I mused aloud.

"No, Your Highness, they were adversaries we faced over a thousand years ago before the enchantment was cast," the soldier elaborated.

"So they're unaware of our presence for now?" I probed.

"That is correct, Your Highness," he confirmed.

"Excellent. How can we effectively counter them? Would we require some form of magic?" I queried.

"No, Your Highness. Gromlins are vulnerable to conventional means such as arrows, swords, staffs, etc. However, their raw physical strength makes direct one-on-one confrontation challenging at close quarters," the soldier explained.

"Got it. So, what's our strategy for the attack?" I inquired.

"With your approval, we have devised a plan that will enable us to catch the enemy off guard, giving us the advantage to handle the remaining threat," the soldier explained.

I quickly exchanged a glance with Arabella, and she nodded in agreement.

"You have my permission," I affirmed.

With that, the soldier dashed to the front of our formation. Arabella and I watched in anticipation as the arrangement shifted from encircling us to stretching out ahead in a formation ready for battle.

The foremost line of soldiers held their shields at approximately chest height, creating a protective barrier. The following two rows brandished long spears, poised towards the sky. Rows four through seven were composed of sword and shield wielders, while the rear ranks were made up of skilled archers.

"That was truly impressive," I remarked to Arabella.

"Absolutely. Their coordination and proficiency are remarkable," she concurred.

A signal was given to the archers, indicating it was time to prepare their bows.

"Nock," the commanding officer's voice rang out as arrows were positioned on bowstrings.

"Draw," the officer commanded, prompting the archers to pull back their bowstrings.

"Loose," the order echoed, and the archers released their arrows towards the target.

Once more, the officer's voice carried across the field, commanding, "Nock! Draw! Loose," the archers obediently repeated the sequence.

Before the Gromlins could even comprehend the situation, a deluge of four thousand arrows was already hurtling toward them, leaving them no time to react. The barrage of arrows brutally wounded most of the Gromlins, but a little over a hundred survived the onslaught, still capable of fighting.

Reacting swiftly, the Gromlins pivoted toward the source of the arrows and charged with an unsettling ferocity.

However, the officer's seasoned voice resounded, issuing the familiar commands, "Nock! Draw! Loose."

The archers responded impeccably, further decimating the charging Gromlins and sending a significant portion of them to the ground. The surviving enemy force continued its advance, yet they found themselves met with a formidable defense this time. Soldiers armed with long spears lowered their weapons between the shields in front of them, thrusting the spears several feet ahead. The charging

Gromlins inadvertently impaled themselves on these awaiting spears, allowing the second row of spearmen to deliver swift, finishing blows that inflicted critical damage.

With the immediate threat neutralized, the formation opened up, granting space for the sword and shield-bearing ranks to sweep through the remaining battleground. As I observed the scene unfold, it appeared to be a choreographed masterpiece. A meticulously trained and coordinated army stood before us, their efficiency and precision awe-inspiring.

While the soldiers meticulously ensured that no remnants of the enemy lingered, the same soldier who had shared the initial information returned to us.

"Your Highness, the threat has been quelled, and our troops are currently securing the area to prevent surprises," the soldier reported.

"That was genuinely remarkable, if I may say so," I praised the soldier.

"The men are well-trained, but the strategic advantage played a significant role—both in terms of numbers and the element of surprise," the soldier explained. "Had either of those factors been different, the outcome might have been far more challenging."

"I comprehend that," I acknowledged.

Arabella inquired, "Do we have any information about their origin?"

"We're actively investigating that now," the soldier responded.

"As soon as you find something out, please let us know so we can investigate the location," she said. "We don't want to deal with another batch of these things on the way back."

"Understood, Princess," the soldier answered and then ran off to check on the other soldiers' progress.

"So, what precisely is going through your mind?" I inquired.

"Well, before the battle began," she began, "the soldier mentioned that these creatures were the same ones they faced over a thousand years ago. Considering that, it's plausible that they're accessing our realm through some portal or opening, much like the one we discovered in the castle's dungeon."

"I had a feeling you might bring up something along those lines," I admitted.

"Imagine if we had the opportunity to seal it off," she proposed. "I'm not in disagreement with your logic," I replied, "but we also need to consider this: while they're currently trickling out, sealing up one might lead to a reaction among the rest. There's a real risk of an overwhelming surge due to the sheer number of enemies trying to break through."

"You're raising a valid concern—one we don't have an answer to now," Arabella conceded.

The soldier from earlier reappeared, announcing, "We've pinpointed the source of the Gromlins."

"Where?" Arabella inquired.

"Over yonder, in an underground cavern," the soldier responded.

"I had a feeling that would be the answer," I sighed.

"Alright then, lead us to the cavern. We'll see what can be done about it."

We set off toward the cave's location with the soldier as our guide. Arabella and I followed him closely, eager to get a firsthand look.

"The troops have established positions on both sides of the cavern," the soldier explained. "They're prepared to intercept any creatures emerging from it. Right now, a creature emerges approximately every few minutes."

"At least this time, we won't find ourselves surrounded," I remarked optimistically.

"Let's head down there and end this so we can proceed with our journey," Arabella suggested.

"There's no 'we' in this scenario," I replied firmly. "I'll venture down there, and you should stay up here in case anything goes awry."

"Fine, I'll stay up here then," Arabella conceded.

I descended into the underground cavern, finding the path surprisingly manageable. The soldiers were strategically positioned along both walls, forming an unassailable line of defense. The torchlight they held cast a subdued glow that proved adequate for navigation as my eyes adapted to the surroundings.

Drawing nearer to the opening, the soldiers motioned for me to pause before the hole in the ground. Almost on cue, another Gromlin emerged from the hole. The soldiers responded swiftly, incapacitating the Gromlin before it could retaliate. The signal to advance was given, and I was directed toward the hole.

"We've got a brief respite now, so make it quick," a soldier urged.

"Got it," I acknowledged.

I swiftly retrieved the ornate dagger from my bag and approached the hole where the creatures were emerging. As I poised to insert the dagger, a Gromlin sprang from the hole without warning. This time, the Gromlin was armed and managed to stab me in the shoulder. The soldiers acted promptly, neutralizing the threat, but the damage was done.

Without delay, I drove the ornate dagger into the hole, mirroring my actions in the dungeon. A brilliant flash of light erupted from the opening as it began to seal shut. The intense illumination and force momentarily disoriented the soldiers lining the walls.

As the hole closed, I experienced another vision from bygone years.

Chapter 11 The Missing Gold

"Ethan, how long have you been journeying and adventuring with the King?" Roderick inquired.

"I haven't had any previous experiences with the King, as he usually remains within the confines of the Kingdom of Vindoria," I explained.

"Not the King of Vindoria, King Valaric," Roderick clarified.

"Oh, my apologies. I'm still adjusting to the fact that Valaric now reigns as King over Thalondor," I admitted. "I haven't known King Valaric for a considerable amount of time. We've completed a couple of adventures together. What prompts this question?"

"I was simply curious because you readily volunteered to support this mission alongside him," Roderick explained.

I took a moment to reflect as we journeyed toward this unknown kingdom. It was true: I had spontaneously joined this quest alongside someone I had known for only a few days. Perhaps it was my desire to aid King Valaric or the intrigue sparked by the dungeon mission that motivated me. Regardless, there was no turning back now. I was riding alongside the King's General and five thousand soldiers, heading toward a pivotal chapter in my life.

"Yes, you're right about that. But I think my motivation was more about understanding Thalondor, a realm that had been in ruins my entire existence and now stands as a thriving Kingdom," I explained. "I couldn't bear idly watching as malevolent creatures overran the land."

"I comprehend both those sentiments," Roderick acknowledged.

"That's how I initially became involved with the Army of Thalondor. I couldn't stand by and do nothing while innocent lives continued to be lost."

"So, what's the path to becoming a General in the Army?" I inquired.

"To earn the rank of General, one must prove themselves as a capable battle commander," Roderick explained. "Leading troops into battle successfully and consistently rising through the ranks based on those successes is the key. Keep in mind, I'm the sole General of this Army."

"What do you mean by that?" I asked, seeking clarification.

"The Army of Thalondor used to be vast, with several Generals. Each General led their troops, but they also had to collaborate to ensure the success of the Kingdom of Thalondor," Roderick elaborated.

"I'm following your explanation so far," I assured him.

"Well, after establishing my capabilities, King Eldramir appointed me as a General and entrusted me with my army to command. However, there was a condition attached to this promotion," Roderick continued.

"What was that condition?" I inquired.

"The condition was that the Army and I would be frozen in time as part of an enchantment meant to eradicate the evil forces. Unfortunately, it would eradicate everyone else within the vicinity," Roderick revealed.

"That must have been a tough decision to make. I can hardly imagine how I would handle such a situation," I remarked.

"It did take me some time to come to terms with it," Roderick admitted. "The King was honest about the situation. He knew there was a possibility that we wouldn't survive the impending battles, and he was determined to safeguard humanity. He couldn't guarantee its success, but he was willing to try anything to prevent the creatures from seizing control of the land."

"I can only imagine how challenging that decision must have been for a King," I commented. "And it couldn't have been easy for all of you soldiers either."

"As a soldier, most of us, given the choice, would opt to die in battle with honor while defending our land," Roderick began. "However, the prospect of being dormant indefinitely was undeniably unsettling."

"It's difficult to fathom what everyone must have been going through mentally during that time," I responded. "I can't even predict what decision I would have made in such a situation."

"The battles leading up to that point were brutal and harrowing," Roderick stated. "We were triumphing over the enemy, but the cost was high, with thousands of our soldiers falling in each engagement while the creatures kept pouring out of the portals. Ultimately, it became evident that we were running out of the workforce, while the creatures seemed endless."

"So, the ultimate decision boiled down to hope, and that hope is what we're experiencing now," I replied.

"Exactly," Roderick agreed. "Thus, we gathered those with fewer remaining family ties and asked them to make a choice, and this is the path we ended up taking."

"That sounds incredibly tense and was a difficult choice," I acknowledged.

"In addition to not knowing whether the day would ever come for us to walk the lands again, the notion of not being by the side of my fellow soldiers in battle was even more difficult to bear," Roderick explained. "Nonetheless, the King was very explicit that this choice was not about a few individuals among us, but rather about the future of an entire kingdom and the fate of humanity."

"Wow, that sounds incredibly intense," I commented. "I'm still unsure which decision I would have made. I'd like to believe I would have arrived at the same conclusion, but I can genuinely admit that it's an exceedingly tough choice to confront."

"Indeed, but enough about my tale and the stone men," Roderick said with a chuckle. "I'm curious about your story now. Where do you hail from? How did you become an Archer? And how did you begin your adventures with King Valaric?"

"I'm not entirely certain I can match a tale like that," I responded a hint of self-deprecation in my voice. "Anything I have to share might pale in comparison."

"I'm not trying to compare war stories," Roderick clarified. "I'm simply hoping to get to know you better. I'm sure there's more to your story than being known as Ethan the Archer."

"Well, I hail from the Kingdom of Vindoria, nestled within the Eldoria Forest," I began. "Although, as I understand it, this forest didn't quite exist during your time."

"That's indeed true," Roderick acknowledged. "There was no forest in that location back then. Discovering a forest there when we passed through Serpents Pass was quite a surprise to us."

"According to King Valaric, Eldoria Forest seems to be intertwined with the same enchantment that froze all of you in time," I explained. "When he inserted the dagger into the first portal, he recounted seeing a vision of a magnificent forest spreading across the land, encompassing Thalondor."

"That's an intriguing tidbit I hadn't been aware of," Roderick noted. "I suspect we'll uncover more about the connections between the two time periods as the elders continue their discussions. But I didn't mean to steer you off track. You were telling me about your upbringing in Vindoria."

"Indeed," I continued. "I grew up in Vindoria under the guidance of my parents. My father was an accomplished archer, following in the footsteps of his father and forefathers. He began teaching me the art of archery from a very tender age. He set up various targets throughout the forest for me to practice. He managed to make the process engaging and captivating."

"That certainly sounds more engaging than simply swinging a sword around in the air, which is often how sword training goes," Roderick commented.

"Absolutely," I replied. "My father had a knack for injecting fun into our training, ensuring we stayed interested. Shooting at various targets scattered around the forest was far more appealing than just aiming at a solitary target in front of me. The latter approach might have discouraged me from pursuing archery altogether."

"That approach sounds quite interesting," Roderick remarked. "So, how did you find your way into the service of the King of Vindoria?"

"It all traces back to Arabella," I explained. "Arabella tends to become engrossed in whatever task she's undertaking, often neglecting her safety. One day, she was researching in the woods, and a group of Earthbound Gorgons stumbled upon her. Just as they were about to attack her, I unleashed a barrage of arrows, startling them. That momentary distraction allowed her to regain focus and join the fight against the Gorgons. After the threat was neutralized, we started a conversation and got to know each other."

"That does sound intriguing, rescuing the Princess," Roderick commented.

"Well, at the outset, I wasn't even aware she was the Princess. All I saw was a woman in peril," I explained. "I was merely aiming to help someone in distress. Of course, she later brought me to the castle, where she revealed my actions to her father, the King. He then requested my assistance with a couple of missions the Kingdom required to aid with."

"I can understand that. But how did you end up embarking on adventures with King Valaric?" Roderick inquired.

"Through Princess Arabella," I responded.

"So the Princess knew King Valaric?" Roderick inquired.

"Not exactly. I explained that she found herself in yet another difficult situation involving Forest Trolls if my memory serves me right," I explained. "Coincidentally, King Valaric was in the vicinity when he saw her running frantically with two trolls hot on her trail. He intervened, neutralizing the threat and preventing any harm. Princess Arabella then escorted him back to the kingdom, where his reception was not as warm as I had experienced. His status as an outsider seemed to overshadow his heroic act."

"But how does being an outsider overshadow saving the life of the Princess?" Roderick asked. "You would expect the King to be overjoyed that someone saved his daughter."

"It's not as straightforward as it may seem," I clarified. "While one would logically assume that the King would be grateful for his daughter's savior, the history of the Kingdom played a significant role. The Kingdom of Vindoria had a history of being wary of outsiders due to past betrayals and threats. So, despite his courageous act, King Valaric's outsider status sparked concerns about his intentions, clouding his reception at the time."

"What led to this skepticism towards outsiders?" inquired Roderick.

"The tale goes that the King's father, on a certain occasion, extended his hospitality to outsiders," I recounted. "Regrettably, these outsiders exploited the King's generosity and used it as an opportunity to serve their agenda. It is rumored that they not only took liberties with the courtesies offered to them but also helped themselves to some undeserved privileges. The most unfortunate part of the story is that they allegedly made off with a significant amount of gold. In their bold exit, they left behind a trail of bloodshed by ending the lives of several guards stationed within the Kingdom."

"The audacity of such actions is truly astonishing," Roderick commented. "It must have left a significant impact on the Kingdom."

"It certainly did," I continued. "The incident became a lesson learned for the King's father, and it ripple effect on how the Kingdom dealt with outsiders and visitors ever since. The consequences of that event shaped their approach to security and trust.

"Well, were the culprits behind this crime ever apprehended?" inquired Roderick.

"According to the accounts I've heard, they did manage to track down the outsiders, in a way," I explained. "The outsiders were discovered in the woods, but they were already deceased."

"And what about the stolen gold?" Roderick pressed.

"That remains a larger enigma. The gold was never located or returned," I responded. "Up to this day, no one has come forward claiming to have stumbled upon the missing gold."

"Interesting. It makes you wonder if there was some other force at play, intercepting those outsiders," Roderick mused.

"That's the intriguing aspect of Eldoria Forest—it seemingly looks out for its own," I mentioned.

"Exactly, and this is precisely why I wanted to know more about you," Roderick stated. "Our conversation has not only shed light on your experiences but also offered insights into the Kingdom of Valaria, the King, Princess, and yourself. Plus, it's made this journey much more engaging."

"I'm glad I could provide some clarity," I remarked. "Now we only have around nine centuries left to cover," I added jokingly.

Roderick chuckled. "Let's hope the elders can fill those gaps and offer guidance for our upcoming mission."

"Absolutely. We'll need all the assistance we can gather to save this land successfully," I agreed.

Chapter 12 The Village

"Valaric, what in the world happened to you?" Arabella's voice carried a mix of concern and shock as the soldiers assisted me out of the cavern.

"It's nothing. You should see the other guy," I replied with a faint chuckle, attempting to maintain some fun despite the situation.

"I can tell your sense of humor is still intact, so you must not be too badly hurt," Arabella remarked, her voice a blend of relief and amusement.

"Yeah, it's not too serious. Just a lucky strike from the Gromlin," I explained, retrieving Whisperwind from my bag to begin healing. "But this does emphasize why I was against you coming into the cavern with me."

"I got your point the first time, don't worry," Arabella assured me. "But seriously, what happened in there? Especially when soldiers surrounded you."

As I started recounting the incident to Arabella, Scorch chose that moment to land on a nearby rock as if to check on the situation. I gave him a quick, reassuring head scratch, letting him know everything was under control.

"The soldiers weren't to blame for this," I clarified. "We had the timing down pretty well for when the Gromlins emerged from the portal. But this one seemed to have its schedule."

"Timing? What do you mean?" Arabella inquired.

"The Gromlins were coming through every few minutes," I explained. "When I first attempted to approach the portal, the soldiers stopped me because they knew another one was about to appear. They swiftly resolved that issue."

"Alright, but get to what happened," she urged, her impatience apparent.

"Once they had dealt with the previous one, the soldiers signaled for me to step forward," I continued. "Yet, this one caught me off guard. It emerged just a couple of seconds after the last, and unlike the others, it was fully armed and ready for a fight."

"So, because of the unexpected timing, it managed to catch you off guard," she summarized.

"That about sums it up," I admitted. "Though to their credit, the soldiers swiftly dispatched the Gromlin, so it wasn't as dire as it might sound."

"Well, at least the wound doesn't appear life-threatening," Arabella noted. "People might even call this a mere scratch in some places."

"A scratch? Well, this is one sizable scratch then," I retorted with a hint of sarcasm.

With that said, the soldiers swiftly applied bandages to my injuries to stem the bleeding. Although the wound wasn't severe, it was essential to prevent it from worsening, given our journey through the exposed terrain. I felt confident that I would barely feel it in a few days by keeping it clean and monitoring it.

I remarked to Arabella, "Much like the previous occasion when I sealed the breach in the castle, I experienced a similar bright light." I paused momentarily before continuing, "Although it wasn't as dazzling as the initial time. It's either that, or I was better prepared for what awaited me, unlike the first time."

Arabella said, "Out here, we didn't observe anything resembling what we witnessed in the castle's dungeon during your previous attempt. It was only after they assisted you that we noticed any changes."

Puzzled by the disparity, I pondered aloud, "That's quite intriguing. I wonder why it was so intense the first time but barely noticeable this time."

"I'm not entirely certain about this, as the whole situation remains a mystery to me at the moment," Arabella admitted.

I added, "While closing the portal, I had another vision that resembled my previous experience."

Curious, Arabella inquired, "What did you see?"

I painted a picture of the past: "This area was once a thriving village, home to several hundred people who led content lives. There were quaint shops where they could buy, sell, and trade goods, which helped sustain the community. It was secluded from the kingdoms but close enough for trade and inventory updates."

Arabella, intrigued, asked, "That sounds like a vibrant environment, but how did they manage their food supply?"

I explained, "Not far from here lies a sizable lake, where some villagers fished for food while others hunted in the surrounding area. Many villagers maintained farms where they sold and traded items at the market."

Arabella remarked, "Interesting."

"As far as I could discern," I continued, "everyone appeared to be living their best lives. People were happy, smiling, and children played games."

Arabella couldn't help but ask, "So, what happened to the village?"

I shared with Arabella, "The creatures, strikingly similar to the ones we encountered earlier, both here and in the castle dungeon, were responsible for the village's destruction. Initially, the villagers repelled the occasional small-scale invasions, but as time passed, the onslaughts became overwhelming."

Arabella responded with empathy, "That's truly terrible."

I continued, providing historical context, "I concur. From what I could gather, the initial malevolent attacks originated in this vicinity well over a thousand years ago. Regrettably, without a sufficiently large army or support from any kingdoms, the village met its demise."

Arabella anxiously inquired, "Please tell me that some of them escaped safely?"

I explained, "Based on the vision, most women and children were evacuated from the area. The men capable of fighting remained behind, along with a few women who contributed by providing meals for everyone."

Arabella found solace in this information, saying, "Well, it's heartening to know that not everyone here perished at the hands of those evil creatures."

I continued the story somberly, "Yes, that was a glimmer of hope, but not long after, a horde of these nasty creatures descended upon them. The remaining villagers were vastly outnumbered, probably at a ratio of ten to one. They had no walls or substantial defenses, so they stood no chance."

Arabella expressed her sorrow, saying, "That's truly horrifying."

"I concur, Arabella. This unexpected event has likely caused enough delay, so it's a good idea to resume our journey and try to reach Serendell according to our original schedule," I suggested.

Arabella agreed, saying, "You're right. Take a moment to rest while I give the orders to get the Army back in motion."

I expressed my gratitude, saying, "Thank you, Arabella, for your assistance."

She responded with a light-hearted tone, "No problem at all. I was just about to inform them that the King is eager to resume our journey," accompanied by a slight chuckle.

I chuckled in agreement, saying, "Sounds like a solid plan."

While Arabella went to rally the twenty thousand soldiers under our command in the vicinity, my thoughts involuntarily returned to the haunting vision I had witnessed when closing the portal. I had spared Arabella the gruesome details, not wanting to distress her, but I couldn't escape the visceral impact it had left on me.

What had occurred here a millennium ago was nothing short of a brutal massacre. The villagers had been utterly defenseless, standing no chance against the relentless onslaught. The evil creatures had struck just hours before dawn; their sinister figures shrouded in the cloak of night. The unsuspecting night guards had failed to detect their presence until it was too late, leaving no time to raise the alarm. Not only were they outnumbered, but they were also ill-prepared for a confrontation.

The creatures had advanced as though nothing could hinder their progress. They mercilessly stabbed, slashed, or hacked at any signs of life, reducing the once-thriving commerce area, with its bustling trade in goods, to a desolate ruin. Nothing remained to hint at its past prosperity.

As the morning sun finally broke over the scene, the ground was stained with the blood of the fallen, and there was no trace of life left. The evil had descended upon this place and obliterated it without mercy as if it were inconsequential.

I couldn't shake the foreboding sense that if the numbers of these nasty creatures continued to grow as I had seen in my previous vision, our chances of survival appeared increasingly uncertain.

"Valaric! Valaric," Arabella shouted.

Still lost in the thoughts of the vision, I incoherently answered, "What? What is it?"

"Come quick, you need to see this," Arabella excitably replied.

"Are we under attack? What's going on," I asked.

"I can't quite put it into words. It would be best to see it for yourself," Arabella insisted.

Despite the discomfort of my injured shoulder, I hastened to mount my horse, though it was neither quick nor graceful. We rode past the location where we had initially spotted the creatures during our journey before our soldiers engaged them. When we reached the spot Arabella wanted to show me, disbelief washed over me.

"We believe this is the aftermath of the creatures we vanquished earlier," Arabella explained.

I stood there, rendered speechless by the scene before me. The ground was drenched in blood, and what had once been a thriving village now lay in ruins, as if it had never existed. Lifeless bodies littered the ground, victims of an attack that closely mirrored the vision I had witnessed while closing the portal.

"We arrived too late. What if we had come just a day earlier? Could we have prevented this?" I wondered aloud.

Arabella replied, "We couldn't arrive a day earlier, considering we only returned to Thalondor yesterday."

Frustration welled within me as I responded, "I know, but we must find a way to get ahead of this situation before history repeats itself. Right now, what I saw in that vision at the cave portal is almost a replica of what stands before us."

"We must set out immediately and increase our pace to reach the Kingdom of Serendell as swiftly as possible before it's too late," I urged.

Arabella offered a practical suggestion, "How about we dispatch a select group of soldiers as an advanced party? They can travel faster than our entire contingent of twenty thousand soldiers."

"That's a sound plan," I agreed, "it will enable them to notify Queen Amelia of our impending arrival and relay the details of our recent encounter."

Arabella concurred.

I turned to a nearby soldier and asked, "Can you arrange for that to be set in motion?"

The soldier responded promptly, "Yes, Your Highness," and hurried off to carry out the orders.

"Let's also prepare ourselves for departure," I instructed.

Arabella nodded, saying, "Alright, we can return to where we've been stationed to make our way from there."

I had a different idea: "No, we're returning to the castle to confer with the elders about what we've witnessed here. Perhaps they have information to help establish a timeline or shed light on this situation."

Arabella inquired about our route, "Are we traveling the old way? Do you even remember where the entrance is?"

I smiled confidently, replying, "Ah, but of course, the entrance is right over there."

Upon the soldier's return, I directed him to advance with the army, leaving Princess Arabella and me behind. The soldier agreed and began organizing the troops for their journey towards the Kingdom of Serendell.

"Before you depart, can you estimate how many days it will take to reach the Kingdom of Serendell?" I inquired.

The soldier responded respectfully, "Yes, Your Highness, it should take a couple of days."

"Very well, that gives us a couple of days to investigate. We will rendezvous with you just outside the Kingdom," I announced.

Perplexed, the soldier asked how that would be possible.

"Don't worry; I'll explain later. For now, proceed towards Serendell, but maintain a safe distance to avoid provoking any hostilities," I instructed.

The soldier acknowledged, saying, "Yes, Your Majesty."

As the soldier set out to follow my orders, Arabella and I made our way toward the entrance of Glimmering Caverns. I looked up and called out for Scorch to descend so that I could stow him in my bag. He was growing quite large and would soon outgrow his current accommodations, but that was a concern for another day. Arabella and I dismounted our horses and ventured into the caverns, heading back to Thalondor for information.

Chapter 13 The Traitor

"Lucas, be careful," Aria cautioned as she shot a lightning bolt beside me.

"How about a bit more warning next time?" I shouted in response.

"There wasn't much time for a longer warning. That spider was nearly on you," Aria explained.

"I understand, and thanks," I acknowledged.

We are currently facing a challenging situation because we have intruded into the territory of the Gloomspawn Spiders. I assume these spiders migrated into the forest after the kingdom was restored. I had encountered these specific arachnids before while exploring the ruins of Thalondor.

Even though they're not poisonous, these spiders are still pretty impressive. They're as big as a large dog—that's how big they are! They're brown, which helps them blend into the forest backdrop. As long as they do not move, people can practically step on them because they do not see them.

What makes them attractive is their webs. These spiders make incredibly sticky webs, like glue. They're like the superglue of the spider world! But what's even more fascinating is how they design their webs. They build them in a specific pattern that's like a clever trap. Any unlucky animal or person caught in this web doesn't stand a chance. This intelligent design isn't just for trapping food; it's how these spiders do most of their hunting. So, they're not just big; they're also crafty hunters!

Some soldiers got tangled in a super sticky spider web as we strolled along a forest path. Suddenly, we couldn't go left or right anymore, and the web directed us to where we are now, facing a tricky situation. The soldiers who weren't trapped had to use their swords to slice through the web, but it was challenging. They had to protect the caught soldiers from the approaching spiders. At the same time, other soldiers were busy trying to free their trapped comrades from the web.

"Aria, what if we instruct the soldiers behind us to go right and flank around?" I called out.

"Right now, it's worth a try. They aren't very active behind us; the soldiers in front are seeing most of the action," Aria responded.

"Not to downplay our current situation, but can you imagine if Valaric were here? He'd be heading the other way already; you know he hates spiders," I remarked.

"I know, that would be pretty amusing," Aria said with a slight chuckle.

I made a quick decision and positioned myself toward the rear of our formation, directing the soldiers at the back to veer right. They had to find a way around the webs or cut through them to reach the rear side of the entangled area. We weren't sure about the extent of the webbing, but at the moment, we felt trapped in a funnel of webs, vulnerable and exposed. This was our best and perhaps only option.

Dealing with the spiders was a twofold challenge. First, their size alone posed a significant threat. However, the greater challenge lay in their overwhelming numbers in this location. We remained puzzled about where they were all coming from, but it felt like spiders were everywhere we looked. This tactic, a massive swarm of spiders combined with their intricate webbing, was designed to overpower any opponent. Having over a thousand soldiers with us was reassuring, as it increased our chances of survival in the face of this daunting threat.

I understood that the soldiers trying to outflank our present location would need time to navigate the impressive sticky trap. So, we had to hold our ground and protect ourselves until we could even beat the odds. We considered having Aria use fire spells to burn away the sticky webs, which would risk harming the soldiers trapped in the gooey substance. We were engaged in close combat, with no alternative but to defend ourselves until the soldiers on the flanking mission made their way around.

"How are you holding up over there, Aria?" I inquired.

"I'd be doing better if spiders weren't closing in from every possible direction," she replied.

"I understand what you mean. I managed to redirect a group of soldiers to flank around us, but I'm concerned it'll take them a while to reach us, considering the clever trap the spiders have set," I explained.

"That was a clever move, but you might be right; it could take longer than we'd like," she remarked.

"Let's not lose hope just yet. By the way, remind me to tell you a story about the guy who made scrolls when we get through this," I mentioned.

"Let me guess, he always found himself in sticky situations?" Aria asked.

"So you've heard that one before," I replied.

"No, it seemed fitting for this situation," she chuckled.

While I chatted with Aria, my main activity for the day was practicing my sword-swinging skills. I could barely take out one spider before another one closed in. What made things even more challenging was that we were positioned toward the center of our formation. We still had a few soldiers nearby who had yet to get stuck in the web. I strongly suspected that we'd spend quite a few hours freeing soldiers from the sticky webs when this ordeal was over.

The positive side was that they were easy to defeat. However, the downside was their sheer quantity; they could overwhelm us and close in rapidly, catching us off guard. Their advantage lies in their numbers rather than individual strength.

Just when the situation seemed dark, the soldiers in front of us successfully broke through the barrier. This opened a path for us to move forward through the carefully constructed trap, giving us more space to defend ourselves. Another positive aspect of this situation was that when the soldiers flanking from the right side arrived, they would approach from behind the spiders on that side. Looking back, I only wish we had also sent a flanking team to the right side as a precaution.

"Move ahead!" I yelled to the troops. "Let's advance beyond the blocked area and circle back to the sticky trap to widen the opening."

The soldiers moved ahead on the path confidently. After getting past the first obstacle, they began spreading out to both the right and left sides of the blockade. This enabled them to remove the sticky substance from the outside, allowing us to expand our formation and level the playing field against the quite sizable spiders.

Our odds of defending ourselves had improved. I noticed fewer spiders approaching my position, indicating that the soldiers on the outer edges of our formation were doing a better job of stopping them from advancing towards us. Well, that was the situation until just two seconds ago.

"What on earth is that thing?" I wondered aloud.

"What's what?" Aria inquired.

"That enormous creature coming this way, pushing spiders aside to reach us," I explained.

"Oh, that thing. I'm not certain, but it doesn't seem very friendly," Aria replied.

The most enormous spider I've ever seen appeared when I wondered about that. It was the leader of this spider gang, maybe the queen or the top spider. This one was twice as massive as all the others and let out a screech that could shatter your eardrums.

"What should we do about that thing?" I inquired.

"I'd suggest running the opposite way to create some distance, but they haven't cleared enough web for us to move," Aria explained.

"Yeah, I suppose our only choice is to confront that enormous creature. Can you focus your lightning spell on it?" I asked.

"I can, but my lightning spell might not be strong enough against such a massive creature," Aria pointed out.

"It doesn't necessarily have to defeat it; as long as the lightning can annoy the spider, it will be helpful," I reasoned.

Without thinking, I boldly moved toward the colossal creature, urging my fellow soldiers to join me in attacking it. Aria started using lightning spells on the giant spider. However, as she mentioned earlier, these spells didn't hurt it much. But we were determined to give it our all.

Sadly, the creature was much stronger than all of us combined. It could quickly grab soldiers and toss them over its back like they weighed nothing. This was a much bigger problem than we had expected.

But that wasn't our only worry. The spider could shoot out a lot of silk at once, which could completely trap a person. This was going to be a really tough challenge, especially with smaller spiders, still as big as large dogs, coming at us, too.

Once I reached the giant spider, the soldiers in front of it kept the thing distracted. This distraction allowed me to deliver a debilitating blow to one of the spider's legs. Unfortunately, all the blow did was irritate the spider even more, plus it still had seven other legs to walk on.

Without hesitating, I moved toward the gigantic creature, calling my fellow soldiers to join me in attacking it. Aria started using lightning spells on the giant spider. However, these spells didn't harm it much, just as she mentioned. But we were determined to give it our best shot.

Unfortunately, the creature was much stronger than all of us together. It could quickly snatch up soldiers and toss them over its back as if they were as light as a feather. This turned out to be a much bigger problem than we initially thought.

But that wasn't our only concern. The spider could shoot out a massive amount of silk at once, completely trapping a person. This would be a tough challenge, especially with smaller spiders, still as big as large dogs, advancing toward us.

Even though the spider could still trap soldiers with its silk, we now had more people. After the soldiers removed two more spider legs, the giant spider couldn't move. This allowed us to get to its body, and the soldiers quickly destroyed it. The battle that seemed really tough was finished in less than a minute. The giant spider wasn't a danger anymore.

With the bigger problem gone, we could now focus on dealing with the smaller spiders, which were still as big as giant dog breeds. Breaking through the blockage turned the situation in our favor. Where it once seemed like we were stuck in a complicated plan, we were now succeeding.

We had the advantage now that we could attack from all sides instead of just one narrow area. We kept getting rid of the remaining spiders coming toward us. At the same time, we continued to tear down the walls of spider webs that were directing us.

Once we were sure the attacks had stopped, we used this opportunity to rescue the soldiers stuck in the sticky substance. I knew this would take a while because many had been trapped. The giant spider had also caught some.

I asked Aria, "How's everything going?"

She replied, "I'm healing as many people as quickly as I can, but there are a lot of injured folks from this battle."

"Okay, keep doing your best, and I'll try to locate the Captain of the guard to restore some order," I said.

"Sounds good; I'll stay here and keep assisting people," she said.

"Thanks for your help, Aria. We appreciate it," I said.

I left where Aria was helping people and searched for the guard's captain. I wanted him to help us get organized again in case of another attack. Unfortunately, as I looked around, I was having a hard time finding him.

I started talking to some soldiers to ask if they had seen the captain of the guard. It seemed like no one had seen him for a while. Finally, word started spreading that they had found him, but he couldn't help us get back in order because he had died in the battle.

It turns out he was one of the soldiers trapped by the silk from the giant spider. But that's not what caused his death. One of the soldier's swords was sticking directly out of his back.

Chapter 14 The Execution

"Aria!" I shouted. "We've got a big problem here."

Sadly, she was too far away to hear me. I glanced around, trying to figure out who I could rely on. This situation was far from ordinary. A man had lost his life, but it wasn't because of the battle. There was a traitor among us, and I had no idea who it might be.

Turning to the nearest soldier I could spot, I asked, "Who's in charge now?"

"The Tribunus is in charge," the soldier replied.

"Thanks," I said. "Could you three please go and find the Tribunus?" I pointed toward three soldiers in the general direction. "Make sure you stick together."

"Got it," replied the soldiers.

They then asked, "Who should we tell him is looking for him?"

"I'm Lucas, the king's liaison," I answered.

I hesitated to send anyone to fetch Aria, not knowing who I could trust, especially with the possibility of an unknown executioner among us. By sending three soldiers to find the Tribunus, we'd reduce the risk of the Tribunus being attacked. Having three of them together also improved their chances of reaching the Tribunus safely, unless those three happened to be conspiring together.

My mind was racing right now, trying to make sense of it all. The attack might have been a lone incident, given that just a single sword was sticking out of the Captain's back. However, there could also have been a plot to overthrow the captain of the guard. The possibilities seemed endless.

As I waited for the Tribunus to arrive, my mind raced with different scenarios. There were a thousand soldiers, to begin with, and any one of them could be responsible for this betrayal. Could it be someone who disagreed with the Captain of the guard? Was it a plot to take over? Who stood to gain the most from the Captain's death?

I worried that the Tribunus might have the most to gain as he would become the new Captain of the guard. Had I unknowingly invited a dangerous person into our midst? We needed to devise a plan to uncover the truth, or else mistrust would spread among the ranks.

As I tried to think of our next steps, the Tribunus arrived with the three soldiers. Unfortunately, I had run out of time to devise a clear solution. I would have to figure things out as they unfolded.

"What's happening?" inquired the Tribunus. "The soldiers mentioned something about the Captain of the guard being dead."

"Yes, I asked them to find you so we can figure out what's happening here," I replied.

"Well, where is he?" questioned the Tribunus.

"Right over there, caught in the spider web," I pointed out.

"Why haven't we cut him down to show the proper respect for his rank?" the Tribunus asked.

"Because take a look here," I explained. "Isn't that one of the Army's swords sticking out of his back?"

The Tribunus took a moment to examine the situation.

"You're correct. That is indeed one of our swords," the Tribunus confirmed.

"Thank you. I didn't want to disturb him until we were sure," I explained. "I suppose we can cut him down now."

"I agree," the Tribunus replied. "Any ideas on how to find the person responsible?"

"What if I choose some soldiers randomly to conduct an investigation?" I suggested.

"Why you?" questioned the Tribunus.

"Because I'm a neutral party and don't have any prior knowledge about these soldiers," I responded.

"Well, what should I do then?" inquired the Tribunus.

"You'll be in charge of carrying out the punishment if we find the person responsible," I declared.

"Alright, that sounds like a plan," the Tribunus agreed. "Why don't you find some volunteers while we cut the Captain down? Once we have everything in order, we can give the Captain a proper farewell."

"Sounds like a good idea," I responded. "We also need to regroup and prepare for potential future attacks."

"I agree," the Tribunus concurred.

I headed back to where Aria was tending to the injured, making it appear as if I were searching for soldiers to assist with the investigation. I didn't want to converse with anyone because I wasn't sure what we were dealing with.

When I finally reached Aria's location, she was still busy tending to injured soldiers. It was clear that she had been working hard, which was good because she had saved many lives.

"Aria, I need to talk to you," I said.

"What's up, Lucas? I'm pretty busy right now," Aria replied.

"I understand, but it's important that we have a private conversation," I told her.

"Can't it wait?" Aria asked.

"I'm afraid it can't," I replied.

"Alright, just give me a moment to finish with this one," she said.

I moved away from the injured soldiers to ensure they couldn't hear our conversation. After Aria had finished healing the soldier she was working on, she walked over to where I was, and I explained the current situation to the captain of the guard.

"How? Why?" Aria inquired.

"That's what we need to figure out," I replied.

"What's our plan?" she asked.

"I'm working with the Tribunus to catch the person responsible," I explained. "However, it's possible that the culprit could be the Tribunus. He's the one who had the most to gain from the Captain's death."

"What's your plan then?" Aria asked.

"I'll choose seven soldiers randomly and have them conduct an investigation," I stated.

"But what if one of the seven you pick is the traitor?" she questioned.

"That would be unfortunate," I admitted. "But I feel that once the news spreads through the camp, someone will know or have seen something."

"Alright, I'll continue healing the soldiers while you select the soldiers," Aria agreed.

"I'll meet you in the makeshift healing area you've set up after I've chosen the soldiers," I said.

Aria returned to the spot where she was tending to injured soldiers, and there were quite a few of them, as far as I could tell. Judging by what I could see, those spiders had caused more damage than I had initially expected.

I began my search for random soldiers in the area. I avoided choosing anyone who seemed to be working or hanging out together. My goal was to select soldiers at random to minimize the chance of two of them being involved in the Captain's death.

The task took little time at all. I walked around and picked the first soldier, then the next one. In just a few minutes, I had selected seven soldiers who might help us bring the culprit to justice.

I quickly told the selected soldiers about the Captain's situation and instructed them to split into pairs, with one soldier staying with me. Their mission was to gather information and rendezvous with us in the medical area once they had any leads. I assumed that if someone had seen something, they would share the information with fellow soldiers. There was no way this could remain a secret.

The six soldiers dispersed to investigate while the remaining soldier and I returned to Aria's location. We hoped to gather information soon so that we could resolve this situation.

We waited near Aria as she continued to care for injured soldiers. If I had to estimate, there were at least fifty wounded soldiers, maybe more. In the grand scheme of things, the outcome could have been worse.

The spiders had set up a clever trap, and I made a mental note to remember this tactic for future battles. It was like a massive funnel system; we had been trapped without realizing it.

I was starting to feel anxious now. None of the soldiers had returned, and the afternoon turned into evening. I wanted to resolve this matter before nightfall, as I didn't want to have someone we couldn't trust in our camp during the darkness.

However, just when I was about to lose hope, two of the soldiers I had selected approached.

"Did you manage to uncover anything?" I inquired.

"We believe we did," one of them replied.

"What did you find out?" I asked.

"Well, Zebadiah is in that direction, bragging about how he stabbed the Captain," the other soldier revealed.

"What? Did he explain why he did it?" I inquired.

"From what I gathered, the Captain had an affair with Zebadiah's wife a long time ago, and this was his way of getting back at him," the soldier explained.

"Talk about holding a grudge," I remarked.

I asked the soldier who had been with me to stay put. The other two soldiers and I would head to where the Tribunus was stationed to share this newfound information with him. Hopefully, it was all true, and we could end this situation.

We made our way toward where I had last seen the Tribunus. Fortunately, he and a few other soldiers were still there preparing for the Captain's farewell ceremony.

"Tribunus, we have some information regarding the Captain's death," I informed him.

"Already? That was quite quick," the Tribunus remarked.

I asked the two soldiers to share the story they had heard with the Tribunus. They seemed to provide even more details than what they had told me initially. It's natural for soldiers to trust their fellow soldiers more than strangers.

I was curious to know whether they had told me the entire story. I wanted to resolve this matter quickly, as we still had another mission ahead. We couldn't afford delays like this, especially with a greater enemy on the horizon.

Two other soldiers arrived just as they finished explaining to the Tribunus. I also wanted to hear what they had to say, hoping their story would be similar to the first two. However, that would only complicate matters further at this point.

Fortunately, the good news was that the second set of soldiers confirmed what the first set had stated. News of this kind couldn't stay hidden for long. There was an assumption that someone would reveal the truth sooner or later.

"I've heard enough," declared the Tribunus. "Gather twenty soldiers and bring Zebadiah here."

"Yes, Tribunus," the soldiers acknowledged.

The four soldiers quickly departed to gather more soldiers as instructed. They took little time to return to our location, with someone in their group shouting. From what I could hear, the person shouting was Zebadiah, based on his comments.

"Can't a man protect his family?" yelled one of the group members. "I'd do it again without hesitation."

If that was indeed Zebadiah, he wasn't helping his case by yelling for everyone to hear across the camp. It appeared that this would be a swift resolution, as he had practically confessed to the Captain's murder.

As the guards approached, the Tribunus turned to face them. The twenty guards essentially surrounded the man to prevent him from escaping and ensure that no one harmed the accused. There was a possibility that he might be innocent and was being framed for the crime.

"Zebadiah, you are accused of stabbing the Captain of the guard in the back," the Tribunus declared. "How do you plead?"

"I was just protecting my family," Zebadiah responded. "That deceitful scoundrel had an affair with my wife before we entered Serpents Pass."

"I understand your grievance," the Tribunus acknowledged. "But what I'm asking is, did you stab the Captain of the Guard in the back while he was entangled in the spider web?"

"Yes, I stabbed him for taking advantage of my wife," Zebadiah admitted. "I'd do it again if I thought it would make a difference."

"Zebadiah, we have procedures for handling such situations," the Tribunus explained. "You didn't challenge him to a duel; you simply stabbed him in the back when he was defenseless. For this crime, I sentence you to death by beheading."

"What? Can you honestly tell me you wouldn't have done the same?" Zebadiah retorted.

"The Captain of the Guard may have been in the wrong for his actions with your wife. However, he was your superior officer. He didn't deliberately kill anyone, and he wasn't tried before his fellow soldiers. You acted as the judge, jury, and executioner."

"You know as well as I do that no one would have taken any action to bring the Captain of the Guard to trial," Zebadiah argued.

"That may have been the case, but we'll never know for sure now," the Tribunus remarked. "Is there anyone here who opposes the verdict rendered today?"

We all took a moment to look around. Nobody raised their hand or stepped forward. Most of us disagreed with what the Captain had done, but we also felt that he didn't deserve to be stabbed in the back for it. It was one of those situations where love could drive a person to do foolish things.

"Very well. Let it be known that the decision to execute Zebadiah by beheading was made, and no one opposed this resolution. The execution will take place immediately. Executioner, prepare for the task," the Tribunus declared.

"You coward. Don't you have the courage to carry out the execution yourself?" Zebadiah challenged.

"Understand this. There are formal procedures for situations like this. However, in this case, I will forgo the formalities and personally carry out the execution. The Captain was a dear friend of mine, and I am determined to see justice served for his murder," the Tribunus replied.

Before we could fully grasp what was occurring, the guards swiftly took Zebadiah to a tree stump. They made him kneel on the ground and positioned his head and neck on the stump. The Tribunus approached and picked up the executioner's long, heavy sword.

"After today, you will fade into obscurity," the Tribunus stated. "No one will utter your name. We won't place two coins upon your eyes for the ferryman. You will wander for all of eternity."

Suddenly, the Tribunus lifted the hefty executioner's sword above his head. With a rapid and forceful motion, he brought the sword down, cutting off Zebadiah's head from his body. Zebadiah's head rolled along the ground while his motionless body collapsed to the earth. Zebadiah had mercilessly ended a man's life, and now, by the laws that governed our land, justice had been administered.

Chapter 15 The Replacement

Arabella and I were quickly walking through Glimmering Caverns to get to the Kingdom of Thalondor. But our plan didn't go as expected because something strange happened in the caves.

"Valaric, did you hear that sound?" Arabella asked me.

"Yes," I replied.

I'd never heard that noise in the caves before. It was like a loud screech, maybe even scarier because of the way it echoed in the cave. We couldn't figure out if the creature making the noise were near us or far away. Even though glowing stones were around, it was still hard to see anything.

I reached into my bag and took out my trusty companion, Scorch.

"Okay, buddy, let's see if you can find that strange creature making all that noise," I said, setting him free in the cavern.

Arabella had her concerns, though. "Do you think he'll be safe in here?"

"Well," I replied, "I figure he can probably see better than us, and he has the power to breathe fire, so he's likely doing better than both of us already."

Scorch flapped his wings and soared ahead in the cavern. Suddenly, we spotted flashes of bright light up ahead, which made us think that Scorch had found something and was using his fiery abilities. The loud screeching noises had stopped. We wondered if Scorch had something to do with it or if the creature had hidden.

While Scorch led the way, Arabella and I cautiously moved deeper into the cavern. We quickly armed ourselves, just in case something was lurking nearby. We didn't want to be caught off guard in case anything managed to slip past Scorch.

I began to wonder what was happening in the caverns. More and more creatures were taking over the place. Every time we entered the caverns, we encountered more of these creatures. Our initial visit to the caverns didn't seem as dangerous. Yes, we had seen a few scorched animals from when Aria had passed through before, but there weren't as many as we're seeing now.

I started to question whether the Gem Golem had been able to keep the caverns safe from these creatures. I worried that the caverns might become overrun if we didn't deal with them. We needed more time to clear out creatures every time we entered. It felt like we needed to find a solution sooner rather than later.

"See that up ahead?" Arabella inquired.

"Yeah, it seems like Scorch has cleared this part of the cavern," I replied.

In front of us, a small fire burned inside the cavern. Scorch had encountered a creature and used his fire to deal with it. This made things easier for Arabella and me because we couldn't see as well in the cavern as Scorch could.

We noticed a few more small burning piles as we continued along the path. Scorch seemed quite effective at handling things in here, which was starting to give me an idea.

Once we made our way to where the Gem Golem had been defeated, we saw Scorch walking around the area as if he owned the place. The inscriptions remained the same as I glanced at the wall: "Victor of Glimmering Caverns possesses mystical abilities within the caverns. Protect the caverns, for evil lurks within the shadows."

I paused to consider the second inscription. What if I left Scorch in Glimmering Caverns to guard them? What if something more significant than what's here today enters the caverns? How will I find him if we need him in a fight on the surface?

"I'll be okay."

"What did you say, Arabella?" I inquired.

"I didn't say anything," she responded.

"It wasn't her speaking; it was me, Scorch," a strange voice explained.

I immediately looked down, feeling both amazed and a bit scared. Scorch stared back at me as if we were having a conversation. Without thinking, I blurted out, "You can talk."

Arabella swiftly faced me and remarked, "Yes, I can talk. We've been talking all along."

"Not you. Scorch can talk," I clarified.

"I didn't hear anything," Arabella responded.

"That's because I'm speaking to you through your thoughts," Scorch explained.

"It seems only I can hear what he's saying," I added.

"What? Animals can't talk. Are you okay?" Arabella inquired.

"I'm okay. I'm just as puzzled as you are right now," I replied. "Scorch mentioned that you're right; animals usually can't talk, but he's not a typical animal; he's a dragon."

"Now you're just making things up," Arabella remarked.

"He suggested that you whisper something to him, and he'll tell me what you said," I explained.

Arabella gave me a brief look, then shifted her gaze to Scorch. Afterward, she turned her attention back to me. I could see the puzzlement and skepticism in her eyes. She then approached Scorch and leaned down to whisper in his ear.

"Boudreaux, it is not made up," I quickly said.

Arabella gasped in surprise. "Oh my! You can communicate with him."

"Yes, that's exactly what I've been trying to explain," I affirmed.

Now that we had cleared up all the confusion, Scorch continued explaining how he'd safeguard the cavern. Thanks to the cavern's magical powers, he'd grow faster. He also mentioned that we could stay connected even when I wasn't in the cavern, using the same method. I quickly shared all this information with Arabella so she wouldn't be in the dark.

Of course, I had to ask if he could leave the cavern when necessary. He assured me that he could come and go freely once bound to the cavern. The cavern seemed like a good solution for Scorch's growth. Now, I had a place for him to stay as he got bigger.

"How do we bind you to the caverns?" I inquired.

"Just touch me and the wall simultaneously," Scorch explained.

Armed with this knowledge, I placed my hand on the wall while touching Scorch. Nothing seemed to change, so I wondered if the process had worked.

"Yes, it worked," Scorch reassured me.

I was slightly startled because I still wasn't accustomed to him communicating in my thoughts. I knew he could, but this was our first time talking like this. It was going to take some time to adjust.

Looking around, I noticed that only one inscription remained—the original about possessing mystical abilities. It seemed the binding had worked because the inscription related to protecting the caverns had vanished from the wall. As far as I could tell, the Gem Golem had been replaced, and the cavern's secrets would again be safe.

"Oh, I was getting used to having the little guy around," Arabella stated.

"He said he likes being around you as well. You give good head scratches," I said.

"Awe," Arabella said as she rubbed his head.

With the danger of creatures in the cavern now gone, it was time for us to make our way to Thalondor. We still needed to meet with the elders, hoping to figure out the creature's appearance pattern. This remained our top priority for the well-being of our land.

As we walked toward the entrance, Arabella and I glanced back at Scorch. He seemed entirely at ease as if this was his rightful place. Something didn't sit quite right about leaving him alone, though.

"I'm not alone. I'll always be in your thoughts and can talk with you whenever you want," Scorch reassured me.

Chapter 16 The Missing Manuscripts

Arabella and I exited Glimmering Caverns just outside of Thalondor. When we reached the gate this time, things were different. The guards noticed us and bowed as we approached.

"Your Majesty," the guard greeted.

"Hello once more. We can't stop talking now because we have important matters to attend to at the castle," I replied as we walked straight ahead.

We walked briskly through the busy streets toward the castle. I couldn't help but be amazed at how much this place had transformed in just a few days. It used to be a place of ruins, with plants growing everywhere. But now, there were people from different places doing business and talking to each other.

As we passed the open market, I reminded myself to visit it one day. I was curious about what the vendors were selling. Did they have fresh fruits and vegetables? Was everything in the market handmade? I'll have to save those questions for another time.

When we arrived at the castle, we went directly to where the elders gathered. Arabella and I went into the elders' room, and we were puzzled by the scene. Papers were all over the place—on tables, walls, and even on the floor. The elders were having intense, fierce discussions and didn't even realize Arabella and I had walked in.

"Hello there, respected elders. May we have a moment?" I asked politely.

There was no response. They were so focused on whatever they talked about that they still hadn't seen us. Arabella and I exchanged a glance and shrugged.

"Hey!" Arabella yelled as loudly as she could.

Well, Arabella's shout did the job because the room suddenly quieted, and everyone turned to look at us. They had blank expressions as if they didn't understand why we were standing there. After a few moments, one of them finally spoke up.

"Your Majesty! Princess! How can we assist you?" inquired the elder.

"What's happening here?" I inquired.

"Well, we got into a little discussion, you see," the elder explained.

"We noticed that. We were here for a few minutes, trying to get your attention," I replied.

"My apologies, Your Majesty," the elder said.

"So, what's all this about?" I asked.

"Well, Your Majesty, we seem to have a gap in history of about 100 years that we can't explain," the elder stated.

"Is this before or after the enchantment?" I inquired.

"It's before, Your Majesty," the elder answered.

"Please tell me that the missing information is not from 100 years before the enchantment," I said.

"I'm sorry, Your Majesty, but we're missing information from that specific time," the elder explained.

"That's unfortunate. Our goal here is to find a pattern from that time," I replied.

"What kind of pattern are you talking about?" the elder inquired.

"We're trying to figure out where these creatures came from, starting with the first place and moving on," I explained. "If we can discover that pattern, maybe we can close the portals in those areas before more creatures come through."

"That might be a good plan, but it could also be risky," the elder cautioned.

"Why do you say that?" I inquired.

"Whenever you close a portal, fewer creatures come into our world. But the creatures on the other side don't go away. This could mean that some portals we don't know about could suddenly release many creatures all at once, and we won't be able to stop it," the elder explained.

"I understand the reasoning, but we have to do something, or we'll end up in the same situation as a thousand years ago," I responded. "We must find a way to avoid repeating history."

"We agree, Your Majesty," the elder replied. "Unfortunately, our knowledge is limited without that last hundred years of information."

"I understand. Keep looking for those missing manuscripts. We'll stick with our current plan until you uncover more information," I said.

"Got it, Your Majesty," replied the wise person. "But before you go, may I ask what led you to this thinking?"

"As we were on our way to the Kingdom of Serendell, we came across a group of strange creatures," I began. "After our soldiers dealt with the ones we could see, we found the portal they were coming from. When I closed that portal, I had a vision of something that happened a thousand years ago, and then today, we witnessed a similar event," I explained. "We want to figure out if there's a pattern and if we can stop these creatures before they become a bigger problem."

"Thank you, Your Majesty. Now we have a clearer picture of what we're looking for once we find those missing manuscripts," the elder said. "Rest assured, Your Majesty, we will keep searching for those manuscripts," the wise person assured.

"Thank you," I replied.

Arabella and I watched as the elders started looking at old documents and talking about things that happened in the past. I couldn't stop thinking about the village that was destroyed by those terrible creatures. There was no warning this time, and the women and children didn't go to other kingdoms for safety. We had to do everything we could to stop these creatures before they ruined the land.

Then I remembered the two groups we sent out to warn the other kingdoms. I hoped they were doing well and had a few problems on their journey. They couldn't close the portals, but at least they could fight off the creatures as they came out. Hopefully, they could hold out until I made it there with the special dagger.

I worried about what would happen if we couldn't stop the destruction quickly enough. What would happen to the people and the land? Would it end up like my vision after closing the first portal?

There were so many questions we didn't know the answers to, but we had to find out if we wanted any chance of success.

"Valaric!" Arabella called out.

"What? Why are you raising your voice at me?" I questioned.

"I've been trying to get your attention for the past few minutes," she explained.

"You have?" I responded, looking puzzled.

"Yes, I started with 'your Majesty,' then 'King,' and finally just shouted 'Valaric.' I thought you were lost in your thoughts," Arabella clarified.

"My apologies, I was lost in thought. What did you want to talk about?" I asked.

"I was thinking we should call it a night. It's been a long day dealing with those creatures, the portal, and the Glimmering Caverns," she mentioned.

"I agree. It's been a long day, but there's still so much to be done," I replied.

"Yes, but you won't be able to do much if you're worn out," Arabella pointed out.

"I guess you're right," I conceded. "Let's get some rest."

"I also wanted to suggest that we head to Vindoria in the morning," she said.

"Vindoria? Is there a specific reason?" I inquired.

"I want to talk to my father and ensure the kingdom is okay. After what we saw in that village today, I want to be sure Vindoria is still safe," she explained.

"I get it. We can go to Vindoria then. It doesn't seem like we'll find much here, and we don't want to reach Serendell before the soldiers," I suggested.

"Thanks, Valaric," Arabella expressed her gratitude.

As we left the elder's room, a feeling of forgetting something important kept bothering me. It felt like there was more to this puzzle than I could see. Arabella may have had a point. I was too tired to figure things out now. Some sleep could help my brain work properly again.

Arabella went to her room, and I went upstairs to mine. Once I reached my room, I opened the door and dropped my things on the way to the bed. I was done for the day and laid down. I took a moment to reflect on today's events—getting injured in the shoulder, closing the portal, and witnessing the village's aftermath. Today was long and tiresome.

Chapter 17 The Treasure

Lying in bed, I tried to rest, knowing the following day wouldn't be more leisurely. Our journey to the Kingdom of Vindoria awaited, and Princess Arabella had made a valid point – we needed to inform her father, the king. Maybe he or the wise elders could provide valuable insights into our current predicament.

The possibilities for how this all played out were endless. I continued to wonder as I looked over at Whisperwind, who was sitting on the edge of the bed. He seemed pretty comfy as if he belonged in the castle.

I found myself reminiscing about better days to distract myself from the current troubles. Those were when we embarked on adventures; only our crew faced peril rather than an entire land.

My thoughts drifted to a specific event involving the crew of the Silver Serpent. It was the day our crew mates started vanishing near a waterfall. They had been innocently swimming in the pool beneath the cascade when they were suddenly pulled beneath the water's surface. Oddly, they hadn't uttered a sound, but Captain Stormrider had noticed their absence.

We had set out on a mission to track the missing crew members through the concealed caves behind the waterfall. However, the hints guiding us to the attackers' direction were diminishing, and the cave's darkness grew increasingly oppressive.

As we contemplated returning to retrace our steps through the dark and dangerous cave, an unusual sound echoed ahead. We exchanged glances to confirm that we all had indeed heard it.

Although it was faint, the noise was unmistakable, akin to a dislodged rock bouncing off the cavern walls. We wasted no time and moved toward the origin of the sound.

The cave's darkness posed a significant challenge, severely limiting our visibility. Nevertheless, as we pressed onward, a dim light began to flicker in the distance. Uncertainty loomed in the air, but our determination propelled us forward. The lives of our fellow crew members hung in the balance.

The faint light originated just around a bend in the cavern, curving to the right. We approached cautiously, swords ready, prepared for any potential threats. We remained in the dark regarding what awaited us in the glow of that light, but we were determined to defend ourselves should any danger arise.

As we approached the corner, Captain Stormrider cautiously peered around it. Whatever lay beyond that corner must have been incredibly disturbing; for the first time, it seemed as though the Captain himself might lose his composure.

Yet, the gruesome sight also ignited a fierce determination in the Captain. Whatever he saw filled him with fury. He signaled us to prepare our weapons and shields in silence, then commanded us to charge around the corner and confront the looming threat.

In retrospect, I was relieved that Captain Stormrider hadn't allowed us to glimpse what was around the corner before charging into battle. This decision was made for our safety and that of our missing crew members. Things might have taken a different turn if we had known what lay ahead.

Once Captain Stormrider determined that we were prepared to advance, he signaled us to move forward and eliminate anything that wasn't our missing crew members. With unwavering determination, Captain Stormrider took the lead, charging around the corner, and we followed suit, ready to confront any potential threats.

As we proceeded, our eyes fell upon a startling sight – two colossal worm-like creatures. These creatures were enormous, easily exceeding 20 feet in length and standing taller than the average person when lying flat on the ground. Their sheer size was awe-inspiring and daunting.

Without pausing to contemplate the consequences, we threw ourselves into battle. Our swords swung with purpose as we relentlessly attacked the colossal creatures. The air filled with the creatures' shrill cries and screams as our blades drew blood from the massive worms. We remained unwavering in our determination to locate our missing crew members and would not allow anything to obstruct our path.

One advantage of the cavern environment was that the sheer size of the worms limited their maneuverability. They were confined to moving forward or backward within the tunnel, granting us the upper hand. Despite their attempts to evade our assault, they made little progress. Our blades were beginning to inflict the damage they were designed for.

We didn't cease our relentless assault on the giant worm until we had cut entirely through its body. A greenish substance oozed from the severed sections, and we felt a sense of accomplishment, thinking we had eliminated one of the two menacing creatures. Or so we believed.

Our brief moment of celebration was swiftly shattered. Before we could fully comprehend the situation, both ends of the worm slithered away in opposite directions. It became clear that cutting through the worm hadn't killed it; instead, it had split into two separate worms. Now, the threat had tripled, with three worms in total.

Captain Stormrider quickly assessed the situation and shouted, "We need to focus our attacks on the heads of these worms! Everyone split up and concentrate your assaults at the opposite ends!"

In unison, we responded, "Aye, Aye, Captain!"

We all swiftly repositioned ourselves to the opposite ends of the worms, targeting what appeared to be the creatures' heads, determined to eliminate the threat. There was no time to waste, and we immediately resumed our relentless assault, inflicting as much damage as we could.

Our strategy was effective. On the worm I was facing, we relentlessly struck it with our swords, delivering one blow after another. Eventually, the worm ceased its movements and seemed to collapse. This time, we succeeded in our mission; the worm no longer displayed any signs of life.

Regrettably, there was no time for celebration because we still had the original second worm to contend with. We hurried over to the second worm, hoping that the end we faced was the one with the head. Technically, both ends now functioned as heads, as they operated independently after we had split the one worm in half.

Without hesitation, we launched a relentless assault on the worm. We swung our swords with determination, making a rhythmic sound as they slashed against the creature. We couldn't afford to take any chances; it was crucial to prevent this thing from escaping and posing a threat in the future.

After a few minutes of delivering powerful blows to the worm, it slumped over, much like the first one had. We had made the correct choice of which end to attack. This was a positive turn of events, considering the enormous size of these creatures. Attempting to defeat one of them with just one person might have been an impossible challenge, but we overcame the odds with three to four of us on each worm.

With the immediate threat now neutralized, we finally had the chance to look closer around the cavern. I'm grateful that our initial charge into battle had prevented us from seeing what Captain Stormrider had witnessed. We had been so focused on eliminating the threat that we hadn't noticed anything else.

As we surveyed the cave, a disturbing sight came into view. Bodies were hanging from the cave ceiling, enclosed within gel sacs that dangled from above. Numerous sacs containing human and animal remains were evident. The worms seemed to have been snatching bodies from the pool by the waterfall and storing them in these sacs for later consumption.

At this point, we couldn't determine which sacs might contain our missing crew members. Our only option was to start cutting these sacs down, but we needed to figure out how to do so effectively.

Captain Stormrider approached one of the sacs and created a small opening at its base, weakening its structure and causing it to open up. A mixture of liquid and the body of a creature resembling a deer spilled out from the sac.

"Men, just focus on cutting the bottoms of the sacs," Captain Stormrider instructed.

"Aye, Aye, Captain," we responded in unison.

Following his lead, we began puncturing the sacs to release their contents. The sound of liquid and goo hitting the cavern floor echoed around us. We worked diligently, hoping to find our missing crew members and praying we were not too late.

From the rear of the cavern, a crew member's voice rang out with excitement.

"I found them!" they shouted.

Captain Stormrider quickly inquired, "What's their condition?"

"They're still alive and breathing, albeit faintly," the crew member reported.

"That's excellent news," the Captain responded with relief.

Now that we had successfully located our crew mates, we briefly caught our breath. Some of our crew members couldn't help but comment on how this had been one of the wildest experiences they had encountered in a long time, and that was saying something considering their extensive travels.

As we prepared to leave the cave with our rescued crew members, one of our comrades noticed something in his peripheral vision.

"Captain, you might want to see this," the crew member called out.

"What is it?" Captain Stormrider inquired.

"Well, you might want to see for yourself," replied the crew member.

We all trailed behind the captain as he followed the crew member's lead. We were left in awe when we reached the spot where the crew member stood. Before us, in the dim light, a colossal mound of gold and ancient artifacts lay before us.

Our best guess was that this was the worms' discarded hoard, containing items found on their victims that were of no interest to them. Judging by its appearance, this pile had likely accumulated over centuries.

"Don't just stand there gawking; let's start hauling," Captain Stormrider commanded.

"Aye, Aye, Captain," we responded, filling our pockets with treasure.

For the first load, we carried as much as we could, retracing our steps through the caverns, past the pool near the waterfall, and back to the boats. Once aboard the ship, we unloaded our haul.

Afterward, we gathered chests, bags, and sacs to make our trips more efficient. In total, we made around twenty trips to transport the entire treasure. It was a day that would remain etched in our memories forever.

What began as an adventure on what we believed to be an untouched island had turned into the journey of a lifetime. Since no one had ever left the island, no one knew anything about it. That had all changed, and now we could share stories of the island, ensuring its legacy would endure for generations.

Recalling that story helped me unwind as I lay in bed. It offered a much-needed distraction from the current real-world events. It had always been one of my favorite adventure stories, and it did the trick. I was now prepared to drift into a peaceful slumber, getting a good night's rest before our journey to the Kingdom of Vindoria.

Chapter 18 The Challenge

"Roderick! What's happening? Why are they blowing the horns?" Ethan inquired.

It took me a moment to fully awaken from a deep sleep. I realized the horns were sounding on the north side of our campsite. I saw torches being lit in the area to make things more visible.

"It seems like we're facing an attack from the north side of the camp," I replied.

"An attack from what?" Ethan questioned.

"I'm not entirely sure right now," I admitted. "I need to speak with the Captain of the Guard."

I hurriedly paused to rub my eyes to help me concentrate. I had been sleeping soundly after a long day's activities. The big fish dinner we enjoyed at the end of the day sent me into a deep sleep. That dinner was the most delicious thing I'd had in a thousand years. I couldn't help but chuckle at that notion because, quite literally, it had been a thousand years.

While I set out to find the Captain of the Guard, my thoughts meandered back to the circumstances that had brought us to this location. During our journey, as we continued our westward path, we unexpectedly encountered an awe-inspiring lake. The sheer beauty of this lake had an enchanting quality, displaying a spectrum of blue shades that glistened under the playful touch of sunlight.

Ethan pointed to the lake. "Look at the beautiful view over there," he said.

I admired it and responded, "It's quite a stunning sight. Nature at its best."

Ethan suggested, "With the sun setting, how about we camp here for the night? Are there any objections?"

I replied, "I see no problem with a view like that. I'll speak with the Captain of the Guard to ensure the soldiers are okay with it."

I went to find the Captain of the Guard to discuss our plans for setting up camp. We briefly talked about the site while surveying the area. The spot had enough space for all the soldiers to rest comfortably for the night, and there were also trees nearby where the soldiers could set up makeshift hammocks.

We then talked about how we could protect ourselves if an attack happened. Usually, we prefer to defend from no more than two sides, but because the lake was behind us, we had to defend from three sides this time. It could have been a better spot, but it would work for a night.

The Captain of the Guard and I finished discussing organizing our camp. He ensured the soldiers were in their assigned spots and set up a system for keeping watch during the night. Then came one of the most critical tasks: getting dinner ready.

A group of our soldiers went hunting, hoping to find boar, deer, or really anything that wasn't pemmican. Pemmican was handy for eating while traveling and provided good nutrition, but when the chance came to have a different meal, most of us preferred something else.

Some of the soldiers improvised by making nets out of bags they used to carry things. They modified the bags to be wide open so fish could swim easily. They secured sticks inside the bags, forming a triangle shape, making it easy for fish to swim in but hard for them to swim out because of the sticks. They used pemmican as bait, and now we had a chance to catch some fish for our meal.

During our journey to this point, Lucas and I positioned ourselves in the middle of the formation. This allowed us to move in any direction in case of an attack. However, when we stopped for the day, we found ourselves by the lakefront.

Several fires were lit around the campsite. This provided light as the sun went down and allowed us to cook our food. Lucas and I didn't want to miss out, so we made our fire nearby. However, building a fire was more challenging than it might seem.

Don't get me wrong; making a fire is usually pretty straightforward. You arrange your kindling, place your wood, and add a spark. Those are the basic steps for creating a fire, typically. But when you have two competitive people involved, things can get tricky.

It might have been more practical to grab a lit stick from one of the other fires and use it to light our woodpile. However, we turned fire-building into a competition, which became a real challenge. People even started bringing us food because they knew it would take a while to get the fire going, and they didn't want us to go hungry.

"Roderick, how did you make a fire a thousand years ago?" Ethan inquired.

"I think it wouldn't be much different from what you do today," I replied. "We had flint and steel, just like you do now."

"What if you didn't have flint and steel?" Ethan clarified.

"We had various methods," I explained. "One way was rubbing sticks together on some dry materials until a spark started."

"How about the bow method?" Ethan suggested. "You know, where you tie a string to both ends of a stick, put the string on another stick, hold that stick on top with your left hand, and move the bow back and forth to make the stick rotate."

"What exactly are you getting at?" I inquired, which sounded like I was questioning his knowledge.

"Okay, let's turn this a challenge," Ethan proposed. "The first one to start a fire wins, and the loser has to do the cooking."

"Alright, you're on. Ready, set, go," I declared.

I dashed off and returned with the materials needed to begin. I gathered some dry wood that I could split and took a branch. I smoothed one end and rubbed the two pieces together using my blade.

On the other hand, Ethan did precisely what he had described earlier. He wanted to demonstrate that he knew what he was talking about. He held the top of one stick with the other end resting on a dry piece of wood while moving the bow back and forth, just as he had explained earlier.

Our ideas and techniques seemed flawless at first. We were confident that one of us could start a fire quickly. However, our execution was relatively poor—feeble. It was taking much longer than we had expected, and we were beginning to feel tired.

At a certain point, a crowd began to gather around us. The soldiers started cheering on both sides, some supporting me and others cheering for Ethan as part of a friendly competition. We were so focused on starting the fire that we did not notice the fire beside us was already burning.

The cheering suddenly stopped, and we looked to see what was happening. That's when we realized the fire was already lit. Neither of us had managed to light it. It turned out that at some point, the Captain of the Guard had walked over with a fire on a stick and ignited the fire for us.

At that moment, Ethan and I exchanged glances and shrugged.

"I guess we were taking too much time and being too loud," I remarked.

"I suppose you're right," Ethan replied.

"Should we consider it a tie?" I asked.

"Agreed, until the next challenge," Ethan replied.

By this time, we were hungry and began roasting the fish over the fire. Relaxing was pleasant, with the sound of crackling flames in the background. The aroma of fish cooking over an open flame only heightened my hunger.

"Have you ever been to this lake before?" Ethan inquired.

"No, I haven't visited this specific lake before," I replied.

"Oh, I see. I just thought you might have been around here at some point," Ethan remarked. "So, where exactly are you originally from in this unfamiliar land?"

"I come from a small village south of Thalondor," I explained.

"Is this the place you told King Valaric about in Glimmering Caverns?" Ethan inquired. "What happened there exactly?"

"Yes, it's the same area. The creatures began attacking our village so severely that they had to send the women and children to Thalondor for safety. My mother was one of the women who stayed behind to support our village's warriors. When I left that small village, it was the last time I saw my parents. Since then, the Army has been the only family I've known," I explained.

"Oh, I had no idea. I'm sorry," Ethan expressed.

"It's okay; there was no way for you to know," I reassured him.

"Let's go ahead and enjoy this fish; it smells good."

We continued our conversation while enjoying the fish brought to us. The fish tasted delicious, although almost anything would have been good compared to our usual rations. Before we realized it, we had finished our meal, and our stomachs were satisfied.

Sitting by the cozy fire with full bellies, we soon felt quite tired. We fell asleep without even noticing, only to be awakened by the sound of horns blowing.

I eventually found the Captain of the Guard to inquire about the situation. It was still a bit dark, so it took longer than expected.

"What's happening?" I asked.

"We've got some reports of attacks on the north side of the camp," the Captain of the Guard informed.

"Do we know who's responsible?" I asked.

"I haven't gotten all the information yet," the Captain of the Guard explained. "But I was told the attackers were around six feet tall and quite big."

"Okay, I'll go find Ethan and see if we can figure out what's happening," I said.

"Yes, sir," replied the Captain of the Guard.

He was returning to where Ethan was sleeping, which was much more straightforward than locating the Captain of the Guard. Despite the horns blaring in the background, Ethan was still fast asleep. He seemed so deeply asleep that I gave him a gentle nudge, but it rolled him over unexpectedly.

"Wake up, Sleeping Beauty. Let's go check out what's causing all the commotion," I said.

"You've been gone all this time, and you still don't know?" Ethan mumbled sleepily.

"Not exactly," I replied. "The reports say the creatures are about six feet tall and large. I thought with your sharp eyesight, you could take a few shots at whatever it is from a safe distance."

"Don't you have any archers in your group?" he inquired.

"Yes, but it's almost daylight now, and you're awake," I chuckled.

"Fine," Ethan reluctantly agreed.

We went to the camp's north side to investigate the situation. However, by the time we arrived, the horns had stopped sounding.

The soldiers had successfully dealt with the threat.

I asked one of the soldiers on duty, "What was the problem?"

"It appears there was a troll wandering around in the area," the soldier explained.

"What happened to the troll?" I inquired.

"The archers managed to take it out from here," the soldier explained.

I could sense Ethan's intense stare even without turning around. Slowly, I faced him, and I could now see his gaze piercing my forehead.

"How was I supposed to know it would be resolved so easily?" I questioned.

"I did try to tell you," Ethan responded.

"Well, what if the threat had been more serious than just a single troll?" I continued. "It's better to be prepared."

From what I gathered, Ethan didn't share that viewpoint.

"Look on the bright side," I remarked.

"What bright side?" Ethan asked.

"The sun is starting to rise, and you're already awake," I joked.

Unfortunately, Ethan didn't share my sense of humor, and he responded with a playful punch on my arm. I found the daylight joke quite amusing. It was a fact that the sun had risen, and Ethan was awake. However, he might not have been too thrilled about being up so early, but sometimes circumstances left us little choice.

Now that the threat had been dealt with and we were fully awake, we decided it was a suitable moment to start taking down our camp. Even though leaving the breathtaking beauty of the lake was hard, we realized the importance of continuing our journey. We still had at least one more day of travel to reach our destination, and it was essential to keep moving forward.

Chapter 19 Return to Vindoria

The following day, I was awakened by the pain in my shoulder. The injury didn't seem to be getting worse; it just hurt like a sharp ache. When you injure yourself, you suddenly realize how often you accidentally bang that area. I still couldn't believe that creature came out of the portal and stabbed me in the shoulder.

I looked around the room and noticed that Whisperwind was lying on the pillow next to me. He still looked adorable with his furry, colorful coat. It seemed like he was meant to live in a castle.

"You look comfortable," I remarked.

Whisperwind slowly opened one eye, almost like he acknowledged what I had said. However, he quickly closed his eyes again. It seemed like he either didn't really disagree with my statement or didn't care much.

I eventually decided to get out of bed and start my day. Some tasks needed to be completed, and they would need help. I could always hope, but I had a feeling they wouldn't.

After I dressed, I picked up my equipment and left the room. As I went down the stairs, I could hear Arabella talking.

"Good morning, Princess," I greeted her, smiling.

"Good morning, Your Highness," she replied sarcastically.

"Who were you talking to?" I inquired.

"Shadowfang was just listening to me ramble about some stuff," Arabella explained.

"Stuff?" I asked.

"Just things we need to try to accomplish and maybe find answers to life's mysteries," she replied.

"Oh, I get it," I said. "I was also thinking about that this morning."

Arabella suggested, "Should we get something to eat?"

"That sounds like a good idea," I answered.

After eating, we grabbed some things for our trip. We only needed a few supplies because we planned to return by the end of the day. Our visit to Vindoria should be quick. Our main goal was to update the king of Vindoria and see if their elders had any more helpful information.

Arabella, Shadowfang, and I departed from the castle and traveled through the kingdom. There were only a few people outside at this time, primarily vendors who were beginning to set up their shops, preparing for a day of buying and selling.

The reality of the situation was hard to believe. A few days ago, this place was in ruins, covered in vines and vegetation. It appeared as if the kingdom had never been in such a state. People were busy opening their shops, vendors were arranging their markets, and pedestrians strolled about.

We didn't have the chance to examine the goods they offered, as we were on a mission. However, I hoped to have the opportunity to see what everyone was selling and make a few purchases.

After reaching the gates, we made our way to the Glimmering Caverns. The caverns were close to the gate, so it only took a few minutes to reach the entrance. This time, we didn't delay and went inside. After walking a short distance, I decided to call out for Scorch.

"Scorch, are you here? It's Valaric," I spoke out.

"That's something I already knew," Scorch responded.

"You already knew? We just entered," I replied.

"I can hear your thoughts, remember," Scorch explained.

"Oh, right," I said.

I took a moment to explain the conversation to Arabella. She thought that ability was pretty cool and would come in handy. I agreed because we could communicate without really talking.

"Where are you?" I thought.

"I'm heading your way," Scorch replied.

A few seconds later, Scorch came around the corner of one of the many bends within the cavern. At first, Arabella and I were surprised by what we saw. Scorch had doubled in size overnight. He had been with us for days and grew like regular animals. However, overnight in the caverns, there was a noticeable difference.

"Wow," I exclaimed. "You appear much larger than when we left yesterday."

"Yes, I believe the magic in the cavern is helping with my growth," Scorch explained.

"I agree," I replied. "Unfortunately, we can't stay long to reach Vindoria. I just wanted to say hello and let you know we were coming in."

"I get it," Scorch said. "I knew you'd be in a hurry from your thoughts. If you need me, give me a heads up."

"Sure thing," I replied. "We'll catch up soon."

Arabella, Shadowfang, and I headed towards the exit of Glimmering Caverns, just outside the Kingdom of Vindoria. As we glanced around to check our surroundings, everything seemed unchanged since our last departure. The forest was still all around us, and the natural sounds within the forest could still be heard.

Judging by everything we saw, this area was shielded from the evil creatures currently causing chaos in the land. I couldn't help but wonder if the forest itself was responsible for keeping these creatures away. I asked what made this place so special: that it remained untouched by the darkness. That was a question for another time.

With no time to unravel the forest's magical secrets, we continued toward the entrance of the Kingdom of Vindoria. As usual, the guards were stationed at their posts, monitoring who entered and exited the kingdom. However, our reception was slightly different from when I was in this situation.

"Good morning, Princess," the guard greeted. "Good morning, your Majesty," he added.

"Hello," Arabella greeted back. "How is everything in the kingdom?"

"Everything is going smoothly in the kingdom so far," the guard replied.

"That's good to know," Arabella responded. "We've noticed significant attacks outside the forest, so please remain vigilant."

"Yes, Princess," the guard replied.

We pressed on through the Kingdom of Vindoria to find the King. It felt reassuring not to have to worry about creatures in the vicinity. At first glance, this place was functioning as usual, with no immediate threat of creatures taking over the world.

Upon reaching the castle, we entered and walked towards the throne room. Unfortunately, the King was nowhere to be found, so we approached a guard and inquired about his whereabouts. The guard then directed us to the king's chambers, and we proceeded in that direction.

As we entered the chambers, we knocked quickly on the door. Of course, Arabella took the lead since only she could enter without the King's permission. The King, busy with some parchments at his desk, paused momentarily to see who had come in unannounced. Instead of scolding, a huge smile lit up his face when he realized his daughter had entered the room. It was evident that he was overjoyed to see her.

"Arabella, you've returned earlier than expected," said the king with a smile. "It's wonderful to see you."

"Yes, Father," responded Arabella, returning the smile. "It's wonderful to see you too. We've returned to provide an update and inquire if you might have any information."

"Information? What kind of information?" inquired the king.

Arabella proceeded to describe everything that had transpired in the past few days. She recounted the messenger's arrival from the Kingdom of Serendell and the devastating attack on the small village south of Thalondor as Arabella narrated the gruesome details of the village assault, the king's face filled with horror and disbelief.

"So, that's why we've come to check if you, the elders, might have any information," explained Arabella.

"I honestly don't have the answers you're looking for on this matter," replied the king.

"Do you think consulting with the elders is a good idea?" Arabella inquired.

"Yes, let's go and seek their wisdom," replied the king.

We made our way toward Elders Hall to find some answers. Shadowfang and I followed behind the king and Arabella. They continued their conversation about Vindoria, discussing the usual responsibilities of monarchy. Listening to them made me realize that someday, I would have to deal with similar matters in Thalondor. I still felt uneasy about the idea of becoming a king.

We arrived at Elders Hall sooner than expected, probably because my mind was preoccupied with other thoughts. The king didn't hesitate and promptly opened the door to Elders Hall. As we entered, the elders welcomed us.

"What a pleasant surprise, your majesties," the elder remarked. "How can we be of service today?"

"We've come to inquire if you can aid us in recovering some forgotten knowledge," Arabella explained.

"What specific knowledge are you looking for?" the elder inquired.

Arabella then proceeded to brief the elders on everything that had happened in the past few days. The elders reacted the same way they had with the king. Their faces displayed shock as Arabella recounted the tale of the village attack.

Once the initial shock subsided, Arabella explained to the elders about the lost hundred years and our purpose.

"That's a remarkable story, and the amount of information is overwhelming," remarked the elder.

"Is there any possibility you can aid us in our mission?" asked Arabella.

"It will require a few hours, but we can delve into our history to see if we can uncover anything," the elder replied.

"Thank you for assisting us; the world's destiny might hinge on this information," Arabella concluded.

"You're welcome, Princess," replied the elder.

Arabella then asked me, "Valaric, what would you like to do while we wait?"

"I'm not sure. Maybe I'll visit the elemental springs for a little while and then head to the Ale House," I replied.

"That sounds like a plan. I'll stay here with Father to continue discussing matters in Vindoria. I'll meet you at the Ale House later," said Arabella.

"Hold on a moment," said the King.

"Yes, I understand. I require a guard to accompany me as I explore Vindoria. You'd think being a King, I'd have some perks. Perhaps you should send three guards for my safety in that case," I remarked sarcastically.

"You know, King Valaric, you might have a valid point," the king responded.

Chapter 20 The Parchments

I left Elders Hall to visit the elemental springs, where I had yet to experience the earth or water elementals. As the king had suggested, two guards were accompanying me. I glanced around and noticed only the two guards behind me.

However, to my surprise, two more guards suddenly appeared before me. With two guards in front and two in the rear, the king had played a little joke on me. But he still needed to finish; two additional guards, one on each side, joined to escort me.

The king had made his point, and I could almost imagine him chuckling at the sight of six guards surrounding me. I knew I had to remember this incident and find a way to return the favor when he visited Thalondor someday.

Accompanied by the guards, I moved through the castle's corridors. It was pretty amusing because I looked more like a prisoner than a king, and people couldn't help but give us curious looks. As we passed, folks stared at us silently, not saying a word. I couldn't help but find the whole situation rather humorous.

While strolling through the kingdom's streets, I took the opportunity to take in my surroundings. I still found it fascinating how the houses were constructed within the trees. The Victorians displayed remarkable skill in everything they undertook. I wondered if there was anything they couldn't build.

Our journey continued down the path, and I couldn't help but feel a sense of anticipation when we passed by the Ale House. I knew I would soon be able to join in and enjoy a sip of ale. The taste of that first drink was already on the tip of my tongue.

We continued along the path leading to the elemental springs. It all felt quite similar to the first time I had walked this route with Arabella—simple and unadorned but with a stunning view.

After a bit more walking, we eventually reached the elemental springs. I quickly looked around to appreciate the scenery and noticed we were the only ones there. With that, I decided to approach the earth elemental.

Taking a seat beside the earth elemental, I closed my eyes. Sitting there with my eyes shut, I focused on breathing, inhaling the fresh air and the natural surroundings. Gradually, I began to sense the vibrations emanating from the earth beneath me.

In my imagination, I envisioned earthy colors like brown and green, along with various textures. The solidity of the earth beneath me sent sensations throughout my body. It felt like I could perceive the land's geological processes and history.

It was as though ancient wisdom and the presence of a formidable force were flowing into me. I could sense the stability and firmness of the earth. Images of plants firmly rooted in the ground to stand tall flashed through my mind.

Water and air have shaped the earth's texture and shape over millions of years. All of this information appeared before me in a matter of moments. I could witness the earth's formation from its very beginning.

When the experience ended, I opened my eyes. It took a moment, but then I realized that Arabella was sitting before me again. She looked at me perplexed as though I had grown three heads.

"Let me guess, it's been longer than a couple of minutes again," I remarked.

"Yes. The guards mentioned you sat down for over five hours," replied Arabella.

"I swear, it feels like just a few minutes when I'm in there," I explained.

"I assumed you were still here when I stopped by the Ale House and couldn't find you," she said. "That, and considering your past experiences with the elements."

"I don't understand why it takes me hours while everyone else only takes a few minutes," I pondered. "I wonder if it would be the same with one of the ones I've done before."

"I don't know, and unfortunately, we don't have the time to find out right now," she said. "We need to return to Elders Hall."

"Oh, I was looking forward to the Ale House," I sighed. "Alright, let's go."

Without delaying any further, we made our way back to the castle. We hoped the elders had some positive news to share to aid us. We needed to devise a plan to defeat these creatures before they could take control.

As we passed by the Ale House, I couldn't help but feel a bit disappointed. My mouth watered at the thought of the delicious ale. I had been eagerly anticipating one of those drinks. I'll have to wait until our next visit to Vindoria.

Upon our arrival at the castle, we headed straight for Elders Hall. We pushed the door open and were greeted by the elders present in the room.

"Welcome back, Princess and Your Highness," one of the elders greeted.

"Hello," Arabella replied. "Did you happen to come across any information that could assist us on our journey?" she inquired.

"Regrettably, we have nothing in our records about that specific period," the elder replied. "The majority of our records begin after that time frame."

"Thank you for taking the time to investigate this for us," Arabella expressed her gratitude.

"Did all the manuscripts from Serpents Pass make it to Thalondor?" the elder asked.

"We would assume so. The elders in Thalondor were engaged in a heated debate, trying to unravel the mystery of the missing hundred years," Arabella explained.

"King Valaric, do you still have the manuscripts you discovered on the beach?" the elder asked.

At that moment, my mind raced. A flurry of thoughts flooded my mind immediately before I could respond. Was I searching for papers I had forgotten in my bag? Did I hold the key to what everyone was searching for?

"Yes, I completely forgot about those parchments in my bag. With everything else going on, I completely overlooked them," I admitted.

Arabella gave me a gentle smack on the arm, a small gesture that conveyed her unspoken thoughts.

I glanced at her and replied, "Yeah, I understand."

I reached into my bag and retrieved the parchments. There was quite a pile of papers; it was clear that one person couldn't read them all quickly.

"Maybe we should return these to the elders in Thalondor," I suggested. "They can divide them up and try to piece the story together."

"That sounds like a solid plan," Arabella agreed.

"Alright, let's make our way back to Thalondor before dark," I proposed.

"Let me bid farewell to my father, and then I'll meet you at the kingdom gates," Arabella said.

"That works. I'll see you there," I responded.

Both of us left Elders Hall. Arabella went in one direction to bid farewell to her father while Shadowfang and I made our way toward the gates. We patiently waited about ten to fifteen minutes until we spotted Arabella approaching. There was still some daylight left, so we were making good time.

We departed from the Kingdom of Vindoria and headed toward the Glimmering Caverns. We entered the caverns briefly but didn't linger as we were in a hurry. We emerged from the caverns just outside the gates of Thalondor.

Before we knew it, we had passed through the gates and reached the castle. We hurried over to where the elders were and handed them the parchments.

"Where did you discover these?" inquired one of the elders.

"Regrettably, I forgot they were in my bag this whole time," I admitted.

"In your bag? How did they end up in your bag?" the elder inquired.

I took a moment to recount the entire story of the beach, explaining how I had come across the chest and its contents. I clarified that I hadn't had the chance to read the entire parchment, only bits and pieces.

"May we examine the dagger?" one of the elders requested.

I handed the dagger to the elders, and they carefully inspected it, engaging in a conversation. From what I could discern, they had encountered the dagger before.

"This is remarkable," one of the elders exclaimed.

"In what way?" I inquired.

"Your ancestor, the king, had this dagger crafted to combat the creatures," explained the elder. "The king made it from the most resilient metal and imbued it with special abilities."

"Why didn't he use the dagger during his time?" I inquired.

"I had the same question," replied the elder. "My best guess is that too many creatures had already emerged through the portals by then. However, I now believe this was all part of a grand plan."

"How so?" I asked.

"If I had to speculate, the king sent these parchments with the prince," the elder began. "Since the king enacted the enchantment with the hope that someday, someone like you would return to defeat the creatures."

"That sounds like quite a risky plan to stake everything on," I remarked.

"Perhaps not," the elder replied. "If it seemed like the creatures were on the verge of taking over humanity, why not attempt anything?"

"I suppose," I conceded. "Well, the day is growing late. We'll return in the morning to check if you've found any helpful information."

"Yes, Your Majesty," the elder responded.

"Thank you for all your assistance," I expressed as we left the elder's area.

Arabella and Shadowfang made their way to their quarters for the night while I ascended the stairs to mine. As I walked, I couldn't help but reflect on the intricate plan that had brought us to this point.

Was the idea of an ancestor returning to save this region true? Would Thalondor be better if my grandfather had returned forty years ago? There appeared to be more questions that needed answers than the other way around.

Upon reaching my quarters, I had had enough for the day. The days were blending and felt exceptionally long. If we were to resume our efforts tomorrow, I needed some rest.

I took off my gear and changed into pajamas before climbing into bed. To my surprise, Whisperwind was sitting in the same spot where he had been this morning. Some days, having a day off and doing nothing might be nice. Unfortunately, that would have to wait until creatures weren't threatening humanity. For now, a good night's sleep suffice.

Chapter 21 The Attack

"Aria," I said, "the Tribunus told me we're not too far from our destination."

"Thanks, Lucas," she responded. "I'll be relieved to get off this horse."

"I understand how you feel," I replied. "It feels like we've been riding for quite some time."

We left our camp just before sunrise and kept heading north. Given the recent events, I wondered how much sleep anyone had managed to get. I think everyone was eager to leave that place behind us.

Considering the challenges we faced with the spiders, the traitor, and the Captain, most of us had experienced enough for one day. We were all tired, and the atmosphere in that place felt unsettling. We had no choice but to keep moving as the day slipped away before we knew it.

After the Tribunus had dealt with the traitor Zebadiah, nightfall arrived swiftly. Fortunately, they had made all the necessary preparations for the Captain's farewell ceremony. The event was a remarkable sight, unlike anything I had ever witnessed.

The Captain, dressed in his finest attire, was laid upon a stack of wood. Two gold coins were placed upon his eyes, a gesture for the ferryman to guide him to the afterlife. The others who had passed away were on smaller piles surrounding the Captain. The Tribunus then delivered the final words before bidding them farewell.

"Let us all bear witness to the lives and trials of these remarkable men," the Tribunus began. "Like the rest of us, they were human but defended their kingdom to the end. The Captain had helped and guided many of us along the way, and some had the privilege to call him a friend. For now, he leads his soldiers one last time into eternal rest. They may be gone from this world, but they will never be forgotten."

After the final words were spoken, the Tribunus lit the corners of the wood piles. We all stood there, watching as the piles gradually caught fire, enveloping the fallen Captain and soldiers in flames as they ascended into the night.

Everyone gathered around the final resting place of the Captain and soldiers, including those who were injured and able to stand. Aria and I could see the deep respect everyone held for the Captain and the fallen soldiers. It was evident how close-knit this group of soldiers was to one another.

As the fires gradually burned down, only about a hundred or so people remained standing. These were likely the individuals closest to the Captain and the soldiers during their lives. The rest had paid their respects and continued with their duties.

As more people departed the area, Aria and I approached the Tribunus to offer our condolences.

"We're sorry for your loss," I said.

"Thank you for being here and participating in this event," the Tribunus replied.

"From the brief time we spent with the Captain, he seemed remarkable," I mentioned.

"He was one of the finest," the Tribunus affirmed.

"We didn't have a chance to get to know the soldiers who have passed, but they will be greatly missed," I observed.

"This truly is a tight-knit family," the Tribunus remarked. "Sometimes, even in families, there are disagreements."

"I can see that," I replied. "We're going to return to the healing area. Aria still needs to attend to a few more wounded soldiers."

"I understand," the Tribunus said. "Once I'm finished here, I'll come to meet up with both of you so we can share information."

"Sounds like a plan," I agreed as Aria, and I returned to the area where she had been providing care to the injured.

Aria and I reached the wounded area in about ten minutes. It was a relatively small area. Aria immediately returned to check on the injured soldiers she had tended to earlier. From what I could see, she had done an outstanding job caring for them.

Shortly after our arrival, the Tribunus joined us.

"Thank you for caring for the men," the Tribunus said, looking at Aria.

"You're welcome," she replied. "Healing is my specialty, after all."

The Tribunus then turned to us and asked, "By my count, we lost twenty-six men in today's events. Do we have a count on the injured?"

"From my assessment, there are approximately sixty-four injured," Aria reported. "Most of them have minor injuries, but about ten or so will require assistance."

"I suggest we stay in our current position for the night and resume our journey in the morning," proposed the Tribunus.

We both agreed with his suggestion, partly because we were exhausted. The day's events had taken a toll on us, and it was evident that we were moving more slowly this morning.

We continued our northward journey for a while until we began to hear some murmurs among the troops. The talk was about a king up ahead, and Aria and I couldn't help but wonder which king they were referring to.

Curious, we made our way towards the front of the formation to see what was happening. After all, I had a message from King Valaric, so I needed to deliver this note if there was a king ahead.

Upon reaching the front of the formation, we were taken aback to see King Valaric and Princess Arabella casually present as if nothing unusual was occurring.

"What are the two of you doing here, and how did you manage to get here?" I inquired. "Never mind, I can figure out the 'how,' but I'm curious about the 'why.'"

"It's good to see you both, too," Valaric replied with a hint of humor.

"I don't know, it seems like they're not exactly thrilled to see us, Valaric," Arabella remarked.

"No, it's not that at all. We... weren't expecting your presence," I clarified.

"I understand. We were teasing you," Valaric reassured.

Valaric and Arabella then took a moment to explain their reasons for being in this location. It sounded like they had quite an eventful journey, encountering creatures that had destroyed a village and gathering information from the Kingdom of Vindoria. Knowing we weren't the only ones experiencing hardships was comforting.

"Wow, that's a ton of information," I commented. "But it still doesn't clarify why you're here."

"We were about to explain that part," Valaric responded.

"Oh, my apologies," I said.

Valaric continued, "This morning when Arabella and I woke up, we visited the Elders to see if they had discovered any patterns in the attacks. According to their research, the place you're heading to is the second location where unusual creatures have been reported."

"So, we might be heading into a challenging situation today?" I inquired.

"It's certainly a possibility," Valaric acknowledged. "How's the Army I assigned to you doing?"

"We've lost a few soldiers, and there are several more who are injured," I replied.

"Oh no, what happened?" Valaric inquired.

Aria and I took a moment to recount the events involving the spiders, the Captain's stabbing, and the discovery of the traitor, concluding with the departure of the deceased soldiers.

"Wow, that's been quite an adventure already," Valaric remarked.

"Yes, but we're managing as best as possible," I assured him. "We're hoping this next phase goes more smoothly."

"I agree. Let's hope for the best," Valaric concurred.

We stood and talked for a while as the soldiers passed by our location. Afterward, we mounted our horses again and continued riding in the center of the formation. It was comforting to see Valaric and Arabella, even though we had only seen them a few days ago.

Having both of them here would likely improve communication and garner more respect. We had a King and a Princess with us, which carried more weight than my simple memo.

While we chatted, the formation suddenly stopped, and we stopped our horses, continuing our light conversation. Arabella began telling us about Valaric's lengthy experience with elemental earth, which was unusual since most people spent only about fifteen minutes in such a trance.

Speaking of taking time, this pause lasted longer than usual. I assumed we had stopped because we were close to our destination, considering we had encountered Valaric and Arabella not too far from there.

Just as I was about to speak up, a soldier approached us and asked for our presence at the front of the formation. Valaric, Arabella, Aria, and I made our way to the front, hoping for the potential of forging a new alliance. However, instead of finding hope, we were met with a grim scene of death and devastation.

"No, no, no. Not again," Valaric uttered in disbelief.

"Again? What do you mean 'again'?" I inquired.

Valaric responded, "This is exactly what we encountered in the south. The story we shared with you earlier resembles what we witnessed there."

A heavy feeling settled in my chest as I looked around at the horrifying scene that stretched before us. I couldn't help but feel a profound sense of disgust at the sight. Lifeless bodies lay strewn across the ground, their contorted forms bearing witness to the agony they had endured. The brutality of the situation was evident, and it was painfully clear that most of these unfortunate souls had met a gruesome end, their vulnerability starkly apparent. Few weapons were scattered about, and they offered little evidence of a battle; it seemed these victims had been unable to defend themselves. From the looks of things, the slain could kill a few creatures before their demise, but the fight was one-sided.

We continued our search, desperately seeking clues that might provide insight into the terrible events unfolding here. We hoped to find something that could lead us toward rectifying this dreadful situation. However, as we pressed onward, the air was filled with the unsettling sounds of horns. These were not the welcoming tones of a friendly gathering; instead, they carried a foreboding warning of an impending attack.

Chapter 22 Defense

"We should retreat and organize ourselves into formation to brace for an impending attack," I suggested.

"I concur, Valaric," Lucas agreed.

We swiftly changed direction, away from the unsettling sound of the horns that heralded danger. I promptly issued orders to the soldiers, instructing them to establish a protective perimeter around us in anticipation of the impending threat.

Our soldiers wielded sizable shields at the forefront, each capable of being firmly planted into the ground. This setup allowed soldiers to take cover behind the shield, using it as a robust barrier to shield themselves from imminent peril. Positioned just behind this first row, the second line of soldiers brandished long pikes that extended beyond the front row of shields, forming a formidable defensive formation.

The third row, situated behind the second, comprised another line of shields, followed again by soldiers equipped with pikes. These arrangements formed the initial eight rows of our formation, strategically designed to accommodate various scenarios. In case of an enemy advance, the front row could retreat, seamlessly falling behind the final row of soldiers armed with pikes. This tactical approach ensured we could maintain a robust and adaptable defense against any approaching threat.

After our soldiers were armed with pikes, our skilled archers formed neat rows, ready to unleash a storm of arrows at any oncoming foes. Arabella, Lucas, Aria, and I positioned ourselves behind the archers, our gaze fixed on the horizon with growing unease. The unsettling sound of horns still hung in the air, casting a shadow of doubt over our circumstances.

As the imminent threat drew nearer, we dispatched our scouts, tasking them with venturing out to gather crucial information about the approaching peril. We hoped they would swiftly return bearing vital details that could aid us in our preparations. Our situation's uncertainty bore us heavily, as we needed to clearly know the enemy's makeup or the size of their force.

With bated breath, we awaited the scouts' return. We could ill afford to confront the grim prospect of facing an overwhelming enemy force of ten thousand strong with our modest contingent of fewer than a thousand soldiers. Such an alarming numerical disadvantage threatened to turn the tides against us. We hoped every advantage would be on our side in this uncertain and precarious moment.

"Has anyone spotted who might be sounding those horns?" Aria inquired.

"Not yet," I replied, furrowing my brow in thought.

"But I don't think it's the creatures themselves blowing those horns."

"Why do you say that?" Arabella inquired.

"In our prior encounters with them, we never saw or heard them using horns," I explained.

"True, but didn't you mention that battle horns sounded on both sides when you closed the first portal during your vision?" Arabella countered.

"Well, yes, they did," I admitted.

"Then, how did you come to this conclusion?" Arabella probed.

"I suppose you're right," I conceded, realizing that, at this point, we lacked concrete information to form a definitive conclusion.

Fortunately, as we conversed, the scouts returned to us. Their presence brought a glimmer of hope that they might have gathered information to shed light on the situation, potentially indicating that it wasn't as dire as we feared.

All eyes turned toward the hushed conversation between the scouts and the Tribunus, their words too distant to discern clearly. Nevertheless, judging by the Tribunus's demeanor, the news they brought appeared far from reassuring.

After their brief exchange, the Tribunus dispatched the scouts once more before making his way toward us, likely carrying unsettling news.

"What did the scouts uncover?" I inquired, my concern evident as the Tribunus approached.

"Your Highness, it appears there's a considerable military presence on the other side of that hill," the Tribunus informed us.

"How substantial are we talking about, and are they humans or the creatures?" I pressed further.

"They are human," replied the Tribunus, his expression grim. "If I were to hazard a guess, they might be connected to the village massacre we witnessed earlier. According to the scouts, the extent of the destruction we saw barely scratches the surface. Further in that direction lies even more devastation, with women and children bearing the brunt of the suffering."

"How numerous is 'substantial'?" I sought clarification.

"The scouts estimated that there are between fifteen and twenty thousand warriors," the Tribunus grimly reported. "We must get you and the princess out of here at once."

"Wow, I wasn't anticipating such a large force," I commented. "Before hasty retreat, let's explore the possibility of sending them a message."

"A message, Your Highness?" the Tribunus questioned. "I have reservations about that course of action at this juncture."

"Listen, we have to try something," I asserted. "I can't simply abandon all of you here to face certain slaughter."

As the Tribunus contemplated his response, I seized a moment to communicate with Scorch mentally. I conveyed to him the urgency of our situation and requested his assistance outside the cavern. Before the Tribunus could voice any objections, Scorch swiftly emerged from the entrance of Glimmering Caverns, causing quite a commotion and startling everyone with his sudden exit.

"What's the plan?" Scorch inquired.

"See if you can spot any groups of creatures moving away from here from up in the sky," I instructed.

Lucas struggled to articulate his thoughts, exclaiming, "What in the world? When did this happen? How?"

"I'll explain later," I responded. "Right now, Scorch is scanning the area for any creatures from above. This offers us three advantages: first, we may locate the ones responsible for the village attack; second, those sounding the horns will see that we have a dragon on our side; and third, by gathering information, we might be able to cooperate with them to seek retribution."

"I think I get it," Aria said. "I'll fetch you some parchment, ink, and a quill."

"Thanks, Aria," I replied.

As she hurried off to retrieve the parchment, ink, and quill, I began formulating a message. It was crucial to convey that we meant no harm and were willing to assist, even in the face of an enraged horde on the other side. I needed to determine the creatures' proximity to our position to achieve this.

"I've located them," Scorch reported.

"Excellent," I replied. "Where are they?"

"They're situated just east of our location," Scorch relayed. "I'd estimate there are a few thousand of them."

"That's too many for us to handle alone all at once," I observed. "Perhaps if I send a message, they can dispatch their scouts to confirm."

"Here's the parchment, ink, and quill," Aria said, handing me the necessary supplies.

I quickly took the items from Aria and began to write the message. There was a sense of urgency, and I knew we had only one opportunity to convey our intentions. The success of this message could determine the difference between a gruesome demise and the possibility of forging a new alliance.

My hand moved swiftly across the parchment as I composed the note quickly. Time was of the essence, and it was rapidly slipping away. When I completed the message, I sealed it with wax.

"Lucas, do you have the note I prepared earlier?" I inquired. "Right here," Lucas replied, handing me the parchment.

Turning to the Tribunus, I asked, "Could you dispatch a messenger under a white flag to deliver this message to the group we spotted?" "Yes, your Highness," the Tribunus confirmed. "Tell the messenger to remain there until they receive a response," I instructed. "Make it clear that it might take some time if our plan succeeds."

"Immediately, your Highness," responded the Tribunus.

Handing him the parchment, I added, "Ensure he delivers this one first. They'll likely request the second one once they've read the first message." "Understood, your Highness," acknowledged the Tribunus.

We all sat and observed as the Tribunus went to find a messenger. We held our collective breath, hoping that this plan would succeed. I had no desire to engage in a battle we needed to prepare to win, as it would not serve our cause.

On a positive note, Scorch had been able to track the creatures, providing us with a glimmer of hope. Yet, we remained in the dark about their point of origin. That was another puzzle we needed to solve. But for now, our hands were tied until we could determine the direction the opposing army was advancing.

The assembly remained alert, weapons ready, eyes scanning the horizon. Many among us wondered if the messenger had successfully crossed enemy lines and if our plea for peaceful communication would be received.

"This is dragging on," Arabella remarked with impatience. "What did you write in that note, Valaric?"

"It's a positive sign that they're taking their time," I replied, trying to remain optimistic. "It suggests that they're considering the message I conveyed."

Arabella was intrigued. "Explain how that works."

"Well," I began, "if they weren't giving it any thought, they likely would have attacked us already. The fact that they haven't indicates they're at least open to the idea."

Aria said, "I guess that's one way to interpret the situation."

"I requested them to send scouts eastward so they could witness the creatures themselves," I explained. "They should also find some dead creatures near the slain villagers who were brutally killed. Considering the time and what Scorch has observed, they're taking the allegation seriously."

Lucas raised an eyebrow. "What do you mean, 'what Scorch can see'?"

I clarified, "Scorch can see their scouts heading east to verify the note."

Lucas seemed puzzled. "How do you know what Scorch is seeing?"

"Well," I began, "I think it's time to explain a few things while we wait."

I took a moment to update Aria and Lucas on the latest developments concerning Scorch. They were finding it difficult to grasp how Scorch and I could communicate, not to mention that the dragon had grown significantly in size since their last encounter. I understood their questions, as I had struggled to comprehend them.

Life had taken a rather unexpected turn on this journey. Gone were the days of simple exploration in ordinary forests, encountering typical wildlife. Our path was filled with strange creatures, mystical caverns, dragons, and many other extraordinary things.

As I pondered these thoughts, we suddenly heard the horns again, emitting a different sound this time. If we interpreted it correctly, they were signaling their units to stand down. But, there was also the unsettling possibility that the sound signaled an impending attack, and we might soon find ourselves in a world of pain.

I shifted my thoughts towards Scorch, hoping to gather any information available. I conveyed to the team that the enemy scouts had returned, and I was eager to find out if they had verified the contents of my note.

Within moments, we spotted our messenger making his way back towards us. His unharmed appearance was a relief. When he reached our location, he handed me a parchment, a crucial puzzle piece.

"What's written on the parchment?" inquired Arabella.

"Just give me a moment to open it," I responded.

I unsealed the parchment and began to read its contents. After absorbing the message, I shared the information with the group. The village chief had verified the details I had included in my note and expressed a desire to arrange a meeting to discuss strategies and conditions for eliminating the creatures from our world.

"That's certainly good news," Aria remarked.

"Yes, but we can't let our guard down. We need a plan," Lucas cautioned.

"I think I might have an idea, but we need to locate the portal where these creatures are entering from so we can shut it down," I explained.

"Okay, what's the plan then?" Arabella inquired.

We gathered together, carefully crafting our plan after much discussion. Once confident in our strategy, we packed our belongings and shared our intentions with the Tribunus. This plan could strengthen our forces in the ongoing battle against the creatures. However, it came with significant uncertainty, as there was a chance it could backfire, resulting in our demise before the day's end.

Now that the Tribunus was informed of our plan, our group, consisting of Aria, Lucas, Arabella, and myself, embarked on the enemy's territory. We carried a white flag as a symbol of truce, a daring move that could either advance us toward success or lead to our downfall. Time was running out as the creatures continued to pour into our world at an alarming rate. We held a deep sense of responsibility toward the land and its people and were committed to taking every possible action to save them from the impending threat.

Chapter 23 Captured

"Wow, Roderick, that lake we just left was beautiful," Ethan mentioned.

"Yeah, Ethan, I agree with you," I answered.

"Do you think we can visit it on our way back?" Ethan suggested.

"Well, if things go as planned, we should be able to," I responded.

"Sounds like a plan," Ethan agreed.

We were farther into our journey than we expected because we left early. The troll we met might have helped us with that. We might have slept in longer today if the horns hadn't started blowing so early. We were so full of delicious food. I can still smell the fish cooking in my mind. It was a delightful meal.

We'll probably feel tired later in the day because of the lack of sleep. But who knows? We'll have to wait and see what the day has for us. If my calculations are correct, we should reach our destination around noon. Once again, leaving early was beneficial, allowing us to reach our destination sooner.

"I think we don't have much more to travel," I mentioned.

"What do you mean?" Ethan inquired.

"I think we'll reach the castle much earlier than we thought," I explained.

"That's great news," Ethan responded.

We can deliver the note, receive a response, and return to the lake today.

"It's a chance, but I wouldn't be too certain about it happening just yet," I cautioned.

"What farm?" Ethan asked, puzzled.

"Never mind," I said. "I was just saying that I don't know what will happen when we get to our location. Maybe we will give them Valaric's note, and maybe they will give us one to bring back."

"I understand," Ethan said.

"Although, I do share your sentiment as that fish was delicious," I replied, closing my eyes and licking my lips.

"Excuse me, General," a soldier stated.

Not paying attention, I quickly opened my eyes.

"Apologies," I said. "How can I help you?"

"The Captain sent me back here to inform you that we can see the castle up ahead," the soldier informed.

"Thank you for passing on the message," I acknowledged. "Tell the Captain we'll join him up there shortly."

"It seems we've arrived much earlier than we expected," Ethan observed.

"That's right," I concurred. "Should we make our way to the front of the formation?" I inquired.

"Absolutely," Ethan replied, quickening his pace as he moved towards the front.

"Why are you rushing?" I inquired.

"Let's hurry up so we can return to the lake," Ethan shouted behind me.

I couldn't shy away from a challenge, so I quickened my pace to reach the front of our formation. Ethan was already quite a bit ahead of me, but I was determined to catch up, confident that I would eventually close the gap.

Our journey to the front was relatively short. After all, our group only consisted of a thousand soldiers; we weren't leading a massive army with tens of thousands. This smaller contingent was carefully chosen to ensure our safe arrival at our destination, especially since we knew creatures were in the area. Being well-prepared was crucial in this unfamiliar territory.

As I arrived at the front of the formation, I took a moment to admire the kingdom ahead. While it might not have been as vast as Thalondor and Vindoria in terms of size, it possessed a unique and captivating beauty. The kingdom seemed like it had been frozen in time, a place of stunning natural beauty and intriguing mysteries.

A towering stone wall encircled the kingdom, adorned with intricate carvings and moss-covered stones. It stood as a testament to the incredible skill and craftsmanship of the people who had built it. The sight of ivy and wildflowers climbing up the sides of the wall added a touch of nature's artistry to the scene, enhancing the overall charm of the kingdom.

From where we stood, we had a remarkable view of a grand castle in the heart of the encircling wall. This castle boasted towering spires and turrets that reached for the heavens, resembling a magnificent masterpiece of medieval architecture. It was constructed using sturdy gray stone blocks that withstood countless storms over centuries. Atop the castle's towers, colorful banners bearing the kingdom's emblem gracefully fluttered in the gentle breeze, giving the illusion that the place was brimming with life and vitality.

A narrow moat encircled the kingdom's outer perimeter, providing an extra layer of defense. From our current location, we could spot only a single entrance, accessible via a drawbridge that spanned the moat's calm waters.

My curiosity was thoroughly aroused, and I yearned to draw closer to the castle, eager to scrutinize its intricate details. Even from a distance, I couldn't help but be captivated by the remarkable craftsmanship evident in its construction. I was excited and eager to examine the finer details up close.

It struck me that this was my first opportunity to visit this kingdom, not even having known of its existence in the past thousand years. The kingdom had remained hidden from my knowledge until this very moment, prompting me to wonder whether it had indeed existed for more than a thousand years or if it had emerged more recently, within the last millennium.

Whether it existed before or after the enchantment, there were more crucial things to consider now. What truly mattered was our collective effort to save the land today. We hope the people here will receive King Valaric's message and offer assistance.

"Roderick, are you lost in thought or something?" Ethan inquired.

"What?" I replied, snapping out of my daydream-like state.

"I've been trying to talk to you for a while," Ethan noted. "I noticed you seemed lost in thought and not responding."

"What did you say? I was off in my world," I admitted.

"I asked if you'd like to go to the castle and see if we can find out who's in charge," Ethan explained. "Maybe we can deliver Valaric's message and return to the lake."

"That sounds like a good plan," I agreed. "I propose we leave the soldiers here and enter as messengers from Thalondor."

"I agree, that sounds like a plan," Ethan said. "Why don't you inform the Captain of the guard about our plans while I prepare the horses?"

"I think I can handle that," I replied. "Let's aim to be ready to move in a few minutes."

"Sounds good," Ethan replied.

I went over to the Captain of the guard and informed him about our plan. I agreed with Ethan; it should take some time to deliver a note from the King and return to the lake. Perhaps Ethan and I could even have a rematch of our "start a fire" challenge, as I felt we were unfairly denied glory last time.

After speaking with the guard captain, I returned to Ethan's location. As promised, he had the horses ready, and we were all set to make our way towards the kingdom gates. I couldn't contain my excitement, eager to get a closer look at the kingdom that had looked so beautiful from afar. I could only imagine how stunning it would be up close.

Ethan and I approached the kingdom under the banners of Thalondor, hoping that this would permit us to speak with whoever was in charge. Traveling with just the two of us also made us appear less threatening.

As we drew nearer, the intricate details carved into the area near the gate became more apparent. I was genuinely astonished by what I was witnessing. It was evident that someone had poured their heart and soul into designing such ornate details, even near the gate.

Most gates I'd encountered were simple, square block formations with an opening. But this place was different. They had two impressive lion heads, one on each side of the drawbridge entrance. Even from a distance, you could see the intricate details. Clearly, someone had put a lot of effort into designing and sculpting this place.

Ethan and I were stopped abruptly by the guards stationed at the gate. While the guards themselves didn't appear overly menacing, we had no intention of causing any trouble. We couldn't help but notice the archers positioned on top of the wall, ready to unleash a volley of arrows in our direction if needed.

"State your purpose," the guard demanded.

"We are here to request a meeting with the ruler of this kingdom so that we can deliver an urgent message," I replied.

"What kind of message?" the guard inquired.

"It's a message of the utmost importance from King Valaric of the Kingdom of Thalondor," I explained.

"The Kingdom of Thalondor," the guard responded, wearing a puzzled expression. "Is this some joke? The Kingdom of Thalondor has been in ruins for centuries."

"There's no joke here," I affirmed. "A lot has transpired in the past week, and we'd be more than willing to explain. However, we must emphasize that time is of the essence."

"Wait here," said the guard as he sent a messenger off to deliver the message.

Our hopes of a quick encounter were swiftly dashed as we found ourselves waiting outside the gates of this kingdom for what felt like a couple of hours. Either their messenger was exceptionally slow, or they needed to be more prompt in extending courtesies.

In the past, I'd have been escorted under guard to the castle, where I could hand over the message and wait for a reply before departing. So, I could only partially fathom the issue with this kingdom.

Our association with Thalondor, a kingdom that had been in ruins for as long as anyone could remember, might be causing some hesitation. That could be contributing to the prolonged delay. We'll eventually find out, as we were being observed with great scrutiny from above and below.

"Is it just me, or does this seem to be taking longer than we thought?" Ethan questioned.

"It's funny you mentioned that because I thought the same thing. We've been waiting here for quite a while," I responded.

"Interesting," Ethan remarked. "Coming from Vindoria, we haven't had much contact with other kingdoms and are usually cautious about outsiders. I wondered if this place resembles Vindoria in not trusting outsiders."

As Ethan mentioned his observation, around thirty guards

appeared through the gate, each wielding menacing spears. Their stern demeanor made it clear that negotiation wasn't an option, and they promptly instructed us to dismount from our horses. We followed their orders precisely without hesitation, stepping down from our horses as directed. They then proceeded to search us, confiscating all our belongings and weapons methodically.

While I might have needed to be more rusty in my knowledge, messengers were typically accorded special treatment and recognized as emissaries of the king. The current treatment differed from what we expected, involving precautionary measures for outsiders like us. The reasons behind their actions remained unclear. Our connection to Thalondor might have raised suspicions, or perhaps they had their concerns and motives for their actions. Deciphering their thoughts at this point proved to be a challenge.

I clung to the hope that the Captain of the guard had witnessed the entire ordeal. If he had, he could relay the events accurately to the king, offering a comprehensive account of what had transpired. Nevertheless, I was optimistic that this reflected the kingdom's cautious approach when dealing with unfamiliar individuals and wouldn't escalate further.

Just as I was getting excited about the chance to see the kingdom's buildings up close, our captors suddenly placed masks over our heads. At that moment, my unease grew, and the situation took a disheartening turn. It felt like everything was falling apart.

On the bright side, they weren't physically mistreating us. However, their intentions were clear: they didn't want us to see where we were or communicate with each other. I couldn't even be sure if Ethan was still with me.

After a lengthy journey involving ascents and descents along staircases, they finally removed the masks. My relief was short-lived as I realized that Ethan and I were still together. Unfortunately, the dismal surroundings indicated we had been confined to the dungeons. It appeared highly unlikely that we would be returning to the lake tonight.

Chapter 24 The Note

I understood that as the newly crowned King of Thalondor, I was taking a significant risk by leading us into the unknown. However, I had only assumed the throne a few days ago and didn't carry the weight of responsibility that a seasoned king might have.

I firmly believed that a grave threat loomed over the entire land, one we couldn't afford to ignore anymore. These creatures' relentless rampage had to be stopped, and time was of the essence. We needed to take swift action before the situation spiraled completely out of control.

However, Lucas, Aria, Arabella, and I also had to ensure our survival in this high-stakes confrontation. As we made our way toward the location of the villagers, we encountered an advance party sent to guide us through the crowd. I assumed this was done for our protection, to shield us from potential anger and grief among the villagers who may have lost loved ones in the recent massacre.

They didn't even bother confiscating our weapons, which led me to believe they probably had archers trained on us, ready to react if we made any sudden moves. We had discussed this beforehand: no sudden movements. We were well aware that we were vastly outnumbered, and our chances of survival were slim.

I wasn't sure if their actions were meant to intimidate us or demonstrate their strength. They guided us through twenty thousand warriors to our intended destination. All we received were intense, unrelenting stares from these warriors. They wanted us to know how surrounded we were, to possibly understand that there would only be one way to survive this incident.

Finally, we stopped before a group of men, whom I presumed to be the village leaders. They didn't utter a word; instead, they stared at us. This might be an appropriate moment to introduce myself.

"Greetings, I am Valaric, King of Thalondor," I introduced myself. "Thank you for allowing us to converse with you during these uncertain times."

I wasn't sure what I had expected, but I hadn't anticipated such prolonged silence. They offered no response and just continued to stare in silence.

Glancing at my companions, I could see they had nothing to add. They all seemed somewhat bewildered, and a collective shrug was the only response I received. I decided to press on.

"These are my companions," I continued, gesturing toward each of them. "Princess Arabella, Lucas, and Aria from the kingdom of..."

"Silence!" one of the villagers shouted, cutting me off mid-sentence.

Initially, I had assumed they were open to a conversation, but now it seemed they were the ones who wanted to take the lead in speaking. I hoped that I hadn't inadvertently offended them with my introduction. All I had done was present ourselves to them, but it was clear they needed more interest in learning about us or our origins.

After several minutes of awkward silence, one of the men began speaking. In his hand, I could see the parchments we had sent over with a messenger. Perhaps he was the leader of the village.

"You mentioned in your message that you had a solution to combat this darkness," the man stated firmly.

"Yes, but I'm sure you're already aware that my people can't handle them alone," I responded. "I assume your scouts have already provided you with information about the number of creatures and our limited forces."

"The scouts did report a formation of creatures just east of here, approximately four thousand strong," the man confirmed.

"And as you know, we have barely a thousand people with us," I noted.

"Less than a thousand," he corrected. "So, what is your plan?"

"We need to locate the source of these creatures emerging," I explained. "This way, we can permanently eliminate the threat in this area. The key to stopping their relentless influx is to shut down the source."

"That's an interesting point you bring up," he said. "My men have discovered a location over the next hill."

"Could you show us this location?" I inquired.

The gentleman agreed, and we walked over the hill to the spot he had mentioned. The situation resembled the previous one, except this time, the source was not a cave. At regular intervals, a creature emerged from the opening.

I was relieved that they had already discovered this location. I made a mental note not to stumble upon the hole this time so I wouldn't end up with a spear in my shoulder again. The memory of that injury caused me to rub my injured shoulder instinctively.

The positive aspect was that the warriors effectively neutralized the threat as soon as the creatures emerged from the portal, helping prevent the creature numbers from increasing. However, the creature bodies were starting to stack up on the other side of the hill.

"This appears to be precisely the spot I was mentioning," I remarked.

"We discovered this location shortly before receiving your message," the man informed me.

"My people were fortunate that they did," I responded. "How frequently are the creatures emerging from the portal?"

"They don't seem to be emerging at a high rate," one of the warriors answered. "We've noticed a flicker of light through the hole just before one appears. When we see the light flicker, we prepare our weapons."

Right on cue, a flicker of light signaled the arrival of another creature. The village warriors swiftly sprang into action, efficiently eliminating the threat. Their combat skills were awe-inspiring to behold.

However, I knew I had to close the portal before the next creature emerged. I explained the process to the man we had been conversing with to ensure he and his people understood our intentions were not hostile.

After detailing the portal's closing procedure, the gentleman nodded in agreement. He instructed his people to step back from the portal, allowing me to approach it without risking being mistaken for an aggressor.

I reached into my bag and retrieved the ornate dagger. With the sword in one hand, I cautiously approached the portal. I carefully examined it to ensure no flicker of light, and then I plunged the dagger into the area where the creatures had been emerging. As expected, a blinding flash of light and a powerful shockwave knocked everyone off balance, sealing the portal and preventing more creatures from coming through.

"The area is now secure," I announced. "No more creatures will be able to come through that portal."

The man looked bewildered and asked, "What in the world was that?"

"That's what occurs when we close these portals," I explained.

With curiosity in his voice, the man asked, "How many of those creatures have you encountered so far?"

"This makes it the third one we've encountered," I replied.

His expression grew more serious as he asked, "How many of these creatures exist?"

"At this moment, I cannot provide an exact number," I replied. "We are striving to get ahead of this situation, but regrettably, we arrived too late."

The man's concern was evident as he asked, "How can we assist you in your mission?"

"I would request permission to bring my people here so that, together, we can eradicate the creatures responsible for the devastation of your village," I proposed.

The man's response was resolute: "I concur with your proposed course of action, as my people seek vengeance for the loss of their loved ones."

Upon hearing the man's agreement, I instructed Lucas and Aria to return and convey the message to the captain of the guard. This would enable us to join forces with the warriors and gauge how effectively we could collaborate in future endeavors. With the immediate threat of more creatures eliminated, we had only one task remaining.

As we waited for our companions to arrive, I casually conversed with the man we had been talking with. We still needed vital information, such as his name and the village's name.

"I don't believe I had the opportunity to learn your name," I mentioned.

The man introduced himself, saying, "My name is Cedric Blackhorn, and I am the leader of this village."

"It's a pleasure to meet you, Cedric," I responded. "We were informed by a messenger from the Kingdom of Serendell that this was Wynthrop. Is that accurate?"

Cedric confirmed, saying, "Yes, this is indeed Wynthrop. My great-great-grandfather was the founder of this village many generations ago."

"Being connected to such a long history is commendable," I acknowledged.

Cedric then asked, "Did you mention that a messenger from Serendell informed you about this place?"

"Yes, that's correct," I affirmed.

Cedric inquired, "Have you had the chance to meet the queen of Serendell yet?"

"I haven't had that opportunity so far," I responded. "However, I have soldiers en route to meet with her."

Cedric commented, "That's quite a distance to cover from here, about five to six days' walk."

"Yes, time is of the essence," I acknowledged.

Cedric concurred, saying, "I agree with you on that. Also, be aware that the queen is quite eccentric."

"I gathered that from the note she sent me a couple of days ago," I remarked with a slight chuckle.

At that moment, we received word that our group was on its way to join us. I felt a sense of relief and gratitude that we had successfully navigated a potentially dangerous situation, avoiding any bloodshed or unfortunate consequences, and the day had the potential to take a much darker turn.

Arabella tapped me on the shoulder and gestured to the left. I followed her gaze and spotted our people approaching. Seeing them filled me with hope and determination. Now, with our forces combined, our mission was clear: we had to come together and eradicate the creatures to the east of this location.

I turned to Cedric and proposed, "Shall we proceed east and address this issue before the threat escalates?"

"Indeed," Cedric responded.

I communicated with Scorch to check the creatures' current whereabouts. Fortunately, these creatures didn't possess great speed and had yet to stray far from their last known location. This was advantageous, allowing us to make up for lost time.

"If we set out immediately, we should be able to catch up with the creatures in less than a couple of hours," I informed Cedric.

"How do you have that information?" Cedric inquired.

"The dragon is still watching them from above," I explained. "Their slow movement works to our advantage."

Cedric nodded, saying, "I was curious if the dragon was accompanying you or if it was just a fortunate sighting."

"Yes, the dragon is with us," I confirmed.

I took a moment to provide Cedric with a comprehensive explanation of Scorch. I recounted how we had discovered the dragon egg in Serpent's Pass and how Scorch had hatched amidst the flames. I also described our unique mental connection, allowing us to communicate our thoughts effectively. As is often the case, this information was met with skepticism and disbelief, as it was not easy to grasp.

"We really shouldn't delay any longer and should start making our way towards the creatures," I voiced. "There's a lot to be done, and time is steadily slipping away."

"I wholeheartedly agree," Cedric concurred.

Cedric took a brief moment to rally his people, and we converged in the center of the warrior formation. Collaborating with another group was a satisfying feeling, and I hoped this would pave the way for a strong alliance, considering we needed as many allies as possible to confront the looming threat.

I briefly wandered to Roderick and Ethan, wondering if they were faring better in their efforts to ally. However, I quickly pushed those thoughts aside, recognizing the urgency of our current task.

The warriors accompanying us were fueled by a desire for vengeance for the loss of their loved ones. I hoped that this desire would allow them to stay focused. Our primary goal was to neutralize the threat while minimizing our losses. We would soon discover how effectively the warriors could work together when confronted with the imminent danger.

Chapter 25 Warrior's Battle

"Cedric, since we've got a bit of time, could you share some information about Wynthrop?" I asked. We had an hour or two left before we reached the creatures. This was a chance to gather more knowledge about our newfound allies and strengthen our connection with them on our journey to battle.

Cedric responded, "Well, Valaric, there's not much to say. Wynthrop isn't a large village but supports itself through farming."

"Farming?" Lucas questioned, "How does that work when you have so many warriors?"

Lucas said it quickly, but I had the same question. Based on our observations, they have fifteen to twenty thousand soldiers. I wondered how they supported so many fighters and where the farmers were.

Cedric explained, "The individuals you see here aren't warriors; they are hardworking folks who maintain our village."

Cedric continued to share more details about what life was like for the people of Wynthrop. He talked about how most villagers were farmers and skilled artisans. They worked diligently in their fields, growing essential crops like wheat, barley, and various vegetables in their village's rich and fertile lands. These crops were the primary source of their food and livelihood.

In addition to farming, Cedric also pointed out that there were talented artisans in Wynthrop. These craftsmen had honed their skills in various crafts like pottery, making fabrics, and crafting metal items. Their work was highly respected, and their creations were used within the village and traded with neighboring communities. This trade helped Wynthrop acquire things that couldn't be produced locally and built positive relationships with nearby villages.

Cedric also went on to describe the farming process in more detail. He explained that the men in the village were responsible for plowing the fields. They used livestock, like oxen, to assist them in this challenging task, which involved breaking up and preparing the soil for planting. Plowing was tough, physical work that demanded a lot of effort, and it had to be done multiple times throughout the year to ensure successful harvests.

"Where were all the men when the creatures came through?" Arabella inquired.

Cedric replied, "Twice a year, we embark on a week-long hunting expedition to gather meat."

According to Cedric, the hunting trip is a well-planned event that takes a week. They have a specific routine to ensure the hunt goes well and save meat for the village.

First, they walked for a day to get to the hunting area. Once there, they spend a few days tracking and hunting animals like deer and boar. They seemed to be skilled at this and knew the wilderness well.

After hunting, they prepare the meat to keep it fresh for a long time. They dried and preserved it to last for months and provide food for the village.

When everything was ready, they began the journey back to the village. According to Cedric, this entire process was essential for keeping the village fed and had been done for many generations.

Of course, most of the men on the hunting trip are the more physically fit men within the village to help carry the loads of meat back. The remaining men in the village are usually the elderly and those with injuries. This left the village unprotected, and the evil creatures took advantage of the situation.

As I look around, it's clear that things would have been very different if the hunting trip hadn't happened this week and the men were in the village. They could have defended the area from the creatures, and there would have been less destruction and loss of life. Unfortunately, the timing of the hunting trip and the appearance of the creatures was just bad timing for the village.

At the same time, I couldn't blame them for not being friendly towards us. It was all about bad timing. We showed up in their area just as they returned from their hunting trip. And to make things worse, in their eyes, their village had been attacked and damaged, and now they saw strangers on the other side of their village. Unfortunately, we were those strangers.

Think about how it might have looked to them. They probably thought we were somehow connected to the damage to their village, even though we had nothing to do with it. It was a miserable situation where they saw us as possible threats, and their unfriendly attitude was their way of being cautious in what they thought was dangerous.

"Valaric, how did you end up as the ruler of a kingdom that's been destroyed?" Cedric inquired. "Thalondor has been in ruins for many, many years."

"Thalondor isn't in ruins anymore," I replied.

"That's a story I'd be interested in hearing," Cedric remarked.

With plenty of time, sharing how Thalondor was rebuilt after being in ruins was a good moment. This tale might help them understand things better, especially when there were no creatures in the world, unlike now.

I began telling the story as we kept moving toward the upcoming battle. Now and then, I mentally checked with Scorch to make sure we were going the right way. Maintaining the correct path was crucial as we aimed to take the creatures by surprise.

Scorch's signals indicated we were nearing our destination. I passed this information to Cedric, who then shared it with his group. This led us to stop temporarily so we could discuss our next moves. It was a crucial moment, and we must plan our approach carefully.

"What's your plan for handling this situation?" I inquired as I turned to Cedric.

Cedric replied, "According to the scout reports, we have a five-to-one advantage over them. We could charge at them over the next hill."

"I don't disagree; you have the numbers on your side," I responded. "But have you considered how many casualties you might incur with that approach?"

Cedric asked, "Well, what do you suggest, then?"

"Why don't we allow the Captain of the Guard to organize our formation?" I proposed. "We could use our archers to take down a significant portion of their army."

Cedric agreed with the plan, and I promptly signaled the Captain of the Guard to take the lead in arranging our defensive setup. Trained soldiers swiftly responded to the signal, and in just a few minutes, our formation started to come together.

Most of Thalondor's soldiers assembled at the front, creating a solid shield wall to protect us. Right behind them, Wynthrop warriors armed with long pikes were strategically positioned, their pikes extending beyond the shielded front line. This arrangement offered an extra layer of defense and extended the reach of our combined forces.

The Captain of the Guard continued to organize the formation by filling in the third, fourth, and fifth rows with more Wynthrop warriors. Each row was strategically placed to support and back up the rows in front, forming a well-structured defensive line.

Following the infantry units, our archers took up their positions. This group included Aria, Arabella, Lucas, myself, Cedric, and the village leaders. This positioning allowed us to shoot arrows at the approaching enemy while being shielded by the soldiers in front of us.

This well-planned formation enhanced our defensive strength and demonstrated the strong teamwork and coordination between Thalondor and Wynthrop as we prepared to confront the impending threat.

Unfortunately, it became clear from the expressions on the faces of the Wynthrop warriors that they weren't used to this kind of defensive formation. As the formation came together, you could hear the murmurs among the warriors getting louder. Many shared their worries, feeling uneasy about being shielded by protective barriers. They thought this formation made them seem to be hiding, which didn't match their preference for open combat. Their hearts burned with a strong desire for revenge, especially for their lost loved ones.

The discontent and murmurs persisted among the ranks, but gradually, they quieted down as the first volley of arrows flew overhead. Just before the initial arrows hit their targets, the archers released another volley of arrows. These arrows filled the sky, forming a continuous rain of deadly shots that struck with accuracy and power. The timing of the arrow volleys was flawlessly synchronized, with another wave of arrows released just as the first batch started hitting their intended marks.

The continuous barrage of arrows had a significant impact on the Wynthrop warriors. Their initial hesitance transformed into a growing resolve as they recognized the importance of this defensive strategy in pursuing justice and protecting their people from further harm.

The murmurs among the warriors turned into cheers as the arrows found their marks. We witnessed the creatures beginning to fall as the arrows continued to strike. Meanwhile, on the creatures' rear, Scorch rained down flames upon them. The combination of arrows and flames took a toll on the creatures, significantly reducing their numbers.

The remaining creatures were getting closer to us, steadily advancing in our direction. As I looked at the battlefield, it was clear that their numbers had been significantly reduced, with about half of their forces still standing. This change in numbers put us in a significant advantage, with the odds now being ten to one in our favor.

Their first ranks clashed with our front lines as the enemy force approached. However, their ranks had no order or organization; it was pure chaos. In their desperation to break through our formation, they accidentally impaled themselves on the long pikes that extended beyond our shields as they tried to attack us.

The time they have had come for the Wynthrop warriors to seek justice for their loved ones. At the command of the Captain of the Guard, our front line shifted its position. The soldiers in the first row separated, with those on the outer edges moving forward and those on the inner edges moving backward. This new formation created a funnel-like opening, allowing the creatures to pass through so the Wynthrop warriors could confront them and seek revenge. It was a powerful and emotional moment as the Wynthrop warriors surged ahead, determined to hold those responsible for their suffering accountable for their actions.

The new formation worked well. Most of the creatures ended up in the funnel, slowly approaching defeat. This formation helped us fight the enemy more effectively. It kept our losses and injuries to a minimum, which was important because we needed as many fighters as possible to win the battle.

A few monsters went slightly to the right and left of our formation, but we quickly sent warriors to deal with them. However, our primary focus remained on steadily decreasing the number of creatures inside the funnel. Our goal was to weaken the enemy and maintain control of the situation.

Even Aria, who didn't want to stay in the rear of the formation, decided to get involved in the fight. She went toward the left to catch up with one of the stragglers, showing her determination and dedication to the battle, just like the other warriors.

"Wait, don't go alone!" I shouted toward Aria as she kept pursuing the creature.

"I'll go with her," Arabella declared as she quickly followed after Aria.

When Arabella decided to follow after Aria, I thought something else would happen. I anticipated a squad of soldiers heading off with Aria to eliminate the wandering creature. I understood Aria and Arabella were solid, skilled fighters who could handle themselves. However, seven against one is better than two against one. I assumed they would be fine and quickly returned to the battle before us.

The battle was progressing well, but it had its challenges. A strong desire for revenge drove the warriors, sometimes leading them to act recklessly and without discipline. Their eagerness to engage the creatures even caused them to accidentally harm their fellow villagers in their rush to get to the enemy. This reckless behavior was causing an increase in injuries, although not necessarily from direct attacks by the creatures.

Despite these challenges, the battle would be over soon. We would have to address some issues with the discipline of the Wynthrop warriors, but for now, they were working alongside our soldiers effectively. This was a promising sign for the future, as I believed a significant conflict was on the horizon, and we would need the combined strength of our entire community to overcome the looming evil threat.

Chapter 26 The Dungeons

"Hey, Ethan," I called out.

"Yes, Roderick," Ethan responded.

"Um, I think we won't be able to return to the lake today," I mentioned, speaking from within my cell.

"I think you're right," Ethan concurred from his dungeon cell.

The dungeon cells were not at all welcoming; in fact, they were grim and uncomfortable. They were situated deep underground, where the air was chilly and damp, making it feel consistently cold. The low ceilings made the space feel even more confined and tight, which could be distressing.

These cells had walls made of solid, unyielding stone. These stone walls witnessed numerous prisoners come and go, and spending time in this dismal place was a way of wearing down their hopes and dreams. Moisture seeped through cracks in the stone, leaving a perpetual sense of dampness in the air. The faint sound of dripping water echoed through the chambers, creating an unsettling rhythm that seemed to taunt those unfortunate enough to be held here.

Despite the harsh conditions, the captors provided minimal amenities for the prisoners. A bit of straw was scattered on the stone floor, serving as a basic but uncomfortable bed. It offered a small amount of relief from the unrelenting coldness of the stone beneath. In one corner of the cell, there was a simple bucket for personal needs, adding to the indignity of the situation.

As I sat in the cold and damp dungeons, time felt like it was dragging on, and I wasn't sure how long it had been since we were locked up. It might have been just a few hours, but it seemed like an incredibly long time in the gloomy darkness. I felt uneasy as I thought about what our captors had planned for us.

The situation was quite puzzling. I had imagined that our arrival and diplomatic mission would go differently. Usually, messengers in such conditions were treated with great respect and politeness, almost like royalty. Even if intentions of hostilities or an attack were planned for the next day, diplomatic customs were typically followed. This was not just for appearances but also to avoid alarming potential enemies.

"So, what's your guess on how they'll do it?" Ethan inquired.

"Do what?" I responded.

"Kill us. Do you reckon they'll go for hanging or beheading?" Ethan questioned.

"Well, at this moment, I was hoping they weren't even considering that," I replied.

The atmosphere felt quite sad as Ethan discussed those dark possibilities. Initially, I hadn't even thought about those as potential outcomes, but now they were on my mind, causing a lot of worry. I had so many questions about what our captors had in mind and why they needed to give us more information.

Suddenly, a group of guards entered the dungeon, catching my attention. They approached the cell where I was held and started unlocking it. They were here for me, but I needed to learn about their intentions.

They gestured for me to move closer to the cell door, and as I did, they quickly placed shackles on my hands and legs and covered my head with a hood. With these restraints on, they led me out of the cell and down a poorly lit corridor. I couldn't help but feel a deep sense of unease about what might await me.

In the background, I could hear Ethan's voice getting louder as he yelled and asked where they were taking me. He used strong language among his questions, though swearing could have helped our situation.

While we descended the stairs, the guards helped me, ensuring I had no trouble with the steps. They didn't treat me roughly or poorly, which was a relief. But they didn't say anything about their plans, leaving me uncertain.

When we reached the top of the stairs, we entered a complex network of hallways, and they started moving faster. I needed help keeping up as we turned left and right multiple times. I wasn't sure where we were going, but I had a sinking feeling that it might be outside the kingdom's walls.

We finally stopped in our tracks after navigating through a labyrinth of hallways. It was disorienting, and I had no clue where or what was around us. There were voices nearby, but the hood covering my head made it impossible to see anything. Being in this unfamiliar place with numerous people around me was unsettling, and I felt a growing unease.

As time passed, the room grew eerily silent, increasing my anxiety. With the hood still obstructing my vision, I could not know what was happening in the room. The voices had ceased, leaving me in a state of uncertainty. Even though I couldn't hear anyone anymore, I could sense the weight of their stares from all directions.

The guards then proceeded to take action, lifting my hands and securing the shackles to something nearby where I was standing. They repeated the process with the shackles on my feet, making it clear that they were determined to prevent any chance of my escape. It served as a stark reminder of my captivity, and the gravity of the situation sank in, sending chills down my spine.

Next, they lifted the hood from my head, allowing me to see my surroundings. I glanced around and noticed that, as I had suspected, I was surrounded by many individuals in the room. Everyone appeared more dressed up than I was accustomed to, but then again, I didn't own any particularly fancy clothing.

A man, a woman, and a child were directly in front of me. While I couldn't be sure of their identities, my initial assumption was that they were this kingdom's King, Queen, and Princess. However, rather than risk saying something that might offend them, I opted to remain silent and let the situation unfold.

Then, from my left, a rather thin-looking man began to speak.

"Kindly provide your name and place of origin," the man inquired.

"I am Roderick Ironheart, General of the Armies of the Kingdom of Thalondor, and I serve as a messenger for King Valaric of Thalondor," I replied.

Before I could finish speaking, I heard audible gasps from the people around me. I wondered if I had said something incorrectly or if my words took them aback. Then again, the entire situation had been quite unusual from the beginning.

"Did you just mention the Kingdom of Thalondor?" inquired the man at the side.

"Yes, that's correct," I replied.

"That's unbelievable. The Kingdom of Thalondor has been in ruins for centuries," the man asserted.

"You're right. The Kingdom of Thalondor remained in ruins until the sole surviving heir returned to our lands," I explained.

Once more, the gasps of the individuals surrounding me filled the room. Reflecting on everything that had transpired over the past week, the story likely sounded implausible. For these people, who had known the ruins as a part of their lives, the transformation into a functioning kingdom must have been difficult to grasp.

"Why do you insist on speaking untruths about clearly impossible things?" the man inquired skeptically.

"I do understand that this situation may be difficult to believe," I replied calmly. "But I assure you, I came here with no deceitful intentions. It was at the request of my king to deliver a message to the King of this Kingdom. If you kindly retrieve my suitcase, I can fulfill my duty by delivering that message and leaving."

"We've already discovered the message from your alleged king," the man informed me. "While you were held in the dungeon, we took the liberty of examining your belongings."

"Well, you must be aware that we came here without malicious intentions," I asserted.

"Don't be naive, young man. We are fully aware of the army stationed just outside our gates," the man countered.

"The army's presence was solely for our protection during our journey here," I explained.

"Yes, that's what you claim," the man muttered skeptically.

"I assure you, I am telling the truth," I began. "My companion and I arrived as messengers. You already know that our army is not substantial enough to pose a threat to your kingdom. I'm uncertain what more I can say to convince you."

"The document you were carrying mentioned creatures and ancient enchantments dating back a thousand years," the man inquired. "Can you explain the significance of this?"

I took a deep breath and did my best to recount the entire story, beginning with the battles that took place a thousand years ago and leading up to the present, as far as I understood it. While my knowledge about Valaric's arrival was limited to fragments, it was better to share what I knew than offer nothing.

"I realize this story may sound unbelievable, especially since none of you have encountered anything like it before," I began. "But I want to emphasize that we cannot overcome these creatures alone. We must unite and form a formidable army to defeat this darkness."

"This is all very..."

The man on the side attempted to interject, but he was promptly silenced by the man seated before me.

"You've shared an intriguing narrative," the man before me remarked. "It's almost too extraordinary to be fabricated, yet it's told so convincingly that it's difficult to dismiss as mere fiction."

I maintained my silence at this juncture. While I couldn't be sure of the identity of the man addressing me, I had a strong suspicion that he might be either the king or a high-ranking representative of the king. I believed that this was the moment to observe how events would unfold. In reality, the situation seemed to offer only two possible outcomes: they would choose to cooperate with us, or they would condemn us to a grim fate, perhaps by hanging us both.

"We will dispatch our messengers to Thalondor," the man before me declared. "At the very least, we seek confirmation that Thalondor is no longer in ruins, as you claim. If their accounts align with your story, we can discuss further."

"But Your Majesty," the man from the side interjected.

The man in front of me, whom I now presumed to be the king, lifted his hand to hush the other man. It seemed like a positive turn of events. All we needed was confirmation from their messenger returning from Thalondor, verifying that it was a prosperous kingdom, and we should be clear.

"For now, we will remove the shackles, allow you to keep your weapons, and relocate the two of you to better accommodations," stated the king. "Both of you will be closely guarded and restricted to your quarters until we can verify certain details, though."

"Thank you, Your Majesty," I acknowledged. "King Valaric is currently on his way to the Kingdom of Serendell at Queen Amelia's request, so he won't be available to greet your messengers."

"That's of no consequence," replied the king. "My primary concern is confirming whether Thalondor is no longer in ruins. We can address other matters later."

"I understand, and thank you, Your Majesty," I expressed my gratitude.

The king ordered, "Remove the shackles and escort him to his quarters. Retrieve the other individual from the dungeon and guide him to his quarters."

The guards followed the orders and took off the shackles from my wrists and legs. They escorted me through the castle and settled me into a room. While the room wasn't luxurious, it was a vast improvement from the dungeon.

Before long, Ethan was brought into the same room, and he immediately bombarded me with questions. I did my best to provide answers, but the inquiries came so rapidly that keeping up with them all was challenging.

I took a few minutes to carefully explain everything that had transpired, trying to provide Ethan with some much-needed reassurance. Well, as much reassurance as we could muster given the circumstances. We weren't technically prisoners, but our freedom was severely limited. At least we were spared the misery of the dungeon.

With a resigned sigh, I accepted our reality. There was no use dwelling on our current predicament; it was what it was. We needed to make the best of the situation, as it seemed we would be here for the foreseeable future. Our fate was inextricably tied to the return of the messenger, a process that we anticipated would take at least four days. Until that day arrived, this room would be our world.

Chapter 27 The Confrontation

Filled with determination, I urged my horse forward and galloped toward where I had spotted a creature or two. I was uncertain as I rode, not knowing precisely where these creatures were or how many lurked nearby. I did know, without a doubt, that I couldn't stand idly by while the men took all the action.

Gradually slowing my horse's pace, I scanned the area, hoping to catch a glimpse of the elusive creatures. Suddenly, a female voice called out from behind me. Given that Arabella and I were the only women on this quest, I assumed it was her. The urgency in her tone indicated something important, prompting me to turn my horse around and investigate swiftly.

"Aria, can you ease up a bit?" Arabella called out.

I responded, "I was trying to catch those creatures."

Arabella cautioned, "I get that, but Valaric stressed that no one should travel alone."

"I just couldn't stand being stuck behind all those men, watching them in action while I couldn't participate," I explained.

"I completely get it, and that's why I didn't waste any time following you. I wanted a taste of the action, too," Arabella replied.

I nodded and added, "Unfortunately, I don't see any creatures. Let's keep moving in that direction."

"Okay, let's do it," Arabella agreed.

With our determination pushing us forward, we kept searching for the creatures that escaped the trap. I should have paid more attention to where the creatures were precisely before I started chasing them.

Looking back, I wondered if I should have been more careful and checked their direction.

But I hoped we would spot them easily because these creatures were pretty big. That was our plan as we kept searching. As we continued, I realized I had gone more to the left instead of following my desired diagonal path. That led us up along the left side of the soldiers who were in formation.

We realized we had to turn to the right and head in that direction. We might have already gone past the creatures, so we'd need to go back a bit if we wanted to catch them. The good thing about that would be that we could surprise them because they'd be focused on the soldiers.

So, we turned our horses to the right to change direction. After riding on our new path for a while, Arabella started talking about what she was thinking or seeing.

"Aria, there's something I've wanted to discuss with you for a while now," Arabella began.

"I just haven't had the chance to speak with you privately."

"About what?" I inquired.

"I'm aware of what you did," Arabella declared.

"What do you mean?" I questioned.

"I know that you betrayed Valaric," Arabella stated firmly. "The real question is, does he know?"

"Betrayed Valaric? What are you talking about, betraying Valaric?" I inquired.

"Don't pretend, Aria," Arabella responded firmly. "I witnessed you sharing every little detail of the mission to save Sir Gregory's life with my father."

"You saw and heard me?" I asked, puzzled. "How? What do you mean you saw and heard me?"

"It doesn't matter how I saw you," Arabella replied. "The important thing is that I witnessed you providing my father with all the information about that mission. I knew my father had an informant on that mission, but I was surprised to discover that the informant was you."

"What do you expect from me?" I inquired.

"What do you mean?" Arabella questioned.

"Your father, our King, tasked me with gathering every piece of information about the newcomer for the sake of our kingdom," I explained. "What other choice did I have? Betray our King and our kingdom? All for someone we knew nothing about back then?"

"I can see why you did what you did," Arabella acknowledged.

"I don't think you truly understand," I responded. "We're not all alike."

"What in the world are you implying?" Arabella demanded.

"We're not princesses," I explained. "If we attempted even a fraction of what you do, we'd wind up in the dungeon."

"I find that difficult to believe," Arabella replied. "You have no idea the daily challenges I face to safeguard the kingdom."

"Perhaps I don't understand what it's like to be in your shoes, but in any case, I had no other option," I responded. "My king gave me an order, and I followed it."

"When do you plan to confess your actions to Valaric?" Arabella inquired.

"Why should I do that?" I questioned. "What purpose would it serve, aside from creating discord within the group?"

"To ensure there are no hidden truths among us," Arabella replied.

"I'm not sure that's prudent, as it could create unnecessary turmoil," I responded. "Furthermore, if you overheard my conversation, you know I didn't say anything derogatory about Valaric. I conveyed the facts."

"Well, either you confess, or I will inform him," Arabella declared.

Unfortunately, a rock hurtled through the air before I could respond, striking Arabella squarely in the head. The impact knocked her off her horse, and in a panic, the horse bolted away from the danger. My gaze shot in the direction from which the rock had come, revealing one of the creatures preparing to hurl another projectile, this time directly at me.

It became painfully evident that we had become so engrossed in our argument about past events that we had forgotten the primary purpose of our expedition: hunting down these elusive creatures. Regrettably, the animals hadn't forgotten about us.

With swift reflexes, I maneuvered the horse out of the line of fire and dismounted to confront the creature on foot. I was acutely aware of my diminutive stature and the futility of engaging the beast in a physical brawl. Instead, I began by casting fire and lightning spells to fend off the looming threat.

In a desperate bid to protect myself and take down the advancing creature, I unleashed a relentless barrage of lightning spells. The crackling energy surged from my fingertips, striking the creature with a brilliant burst of electricity. But, just as quickly as the spell hit, I was already summoning my fire spell, hoping to engulf the creature in searing flames.

Unfortunately, my powerful spells weren't quite potent enough to subdue the creature alone. This was precisely where Arabella's or Ethan's arrows had always proven invaluable. The creature responded by hurling larger rocks in my direction, forcing me to utilize everything within my reach as makeshift shields to either slow down or soften the impact of the incoming stones. Having witnessed the devastating effect of these rocks on others, I couldn't afford to be struck by one, or there would be two of us incapacitated on the ground.

Despite the difficult situation, I attacked the creature with a relentless onslaught of lightning spells. The surrounding area echoed with crackling and popping sounds as each spell struck its target. The lightning was indeed causing some damage, evident from the creature's jerky movements, but it wasn't enough to halt its relentless advance.

Frustrated by the creature's resilience, I switched tactics and created fiery rings around it. However, even these passionate barriers didn't inflict significant damage. It was as if everything I threw at the creature harmed it but didn't quite deliver the killing blow. I couldn't help but wonder if I was facing some super creature or if I needed more practice. In all likelihood, it was a combination of both factors.

Desperate to end the encounter, I focused a few more powerful lightning charges onto the creature. This time, the combination of fire and lightning had the desired effect. The creature staggered and fell face-first to the ground. Not taking any chances, I promptly dropped several firebombs onto the fallen creature to ensure it wouldn't rise and pose a threat while I was distracted.

With the creature finally subdued, I wasted no time and rushed over to where Arabella lay motionless on the ground. Kneeling beside her, I carefully examined the damage caused by the rock that had struck her in the head. As I picked up the offending rock, it became painfully clear why the princess was now unconscious.

Regrettably, my timing couldn't have been worse. Just as I was tending to Arabella, Lucas and Valaric arrived on horseback, accompanied by a group of soldiers. The situation had taken an unexpected turn, and I could only hope they wouldn't jump to conclusions about what had transpired.

"Aria, drop the rock," Lucas instructed.

"I need to explain," I protested.

"Just drop the rock and step away from the princess," Lucas insisted.

I quickly released the rock the creature had hurled and distanced myself from the princess. Valaric rushed to her side, tending to her injuries.

"She's still breathing," Valaric reassured us.

Then he proceeded to take some bandages and wrapped them around her head, covering the area where she had been struck.

"I need you soldiers to create an improvised stretcher so we can transport her back to the healers," Valaric ordered. "You three, take Aria into custody."

"But you don't understand," I pleaded. "Please let me explain."

"You will have your chance to explain," Valaric replied. "Once we return to Vindoria."

"Why were you holding the rock over her body?" Lucas inquired.

"I was inspecting the rock to assess it better," I explained. "The creature threw the rock at her."

"Why didn't you begin healing her?" Lucas inquired. "Why were you holding the rock over her instead of attending to her wounds?"

"You should pray that she recovers and supports your account," Valaric warned. "Based on the evidence, I doubt her father will be inclined to trust you."

I found myself in a precarious situation. Valaric, Lucas, and the soldiers had arrived just as I held the rock over Arabella's still form. I couldn't deny the unfortunate timing and how suspicious it looked. Yes, I had been upset with her earlier due to our argument, but it was a far cry from wanting to harm her.

Regret gnawed at me as I wished she had never followed me into this area in search of the creature. She would be safe and sound if she hadn't, and I wouldn't face potential charges. I hoped she would pull through and provide her account of the events, corroborating my story and clearing me of any wrongdoing.

"Lucas, return and inform Cedric of the situation," Valaric instructed. "Check if he and the warriors can join you on the journey to Thalondor."

"Understood, but what will you be doing?" Lucas inquired.

"I will escort the princess and Aria back to Vindoria," Valaric replied. "The guards will accompany us to transport the princess and ensure Aria's security."

"Roger that," Lucas acknowledged.

With the guards carefully carrying Princess Arabella on the makeshift stretcher, we embarked on our journey back to Vindoria. Valaric scanned the surroundings briefly before leading the way toward the entrance of Glimmering Caverns. We entered the caverns, retraced our steps, and emerged on the other side, suddenly finding ourselves outside the Kingdom of Vindoria.

The journey back was uncertain, and my mind raced with worry about Arabella's condition and the consequences of my actions. As we made our way toward Vindoria, the weight of the situation hung heavily in the air, leaving me anxious about what lay ahead.

Chapter 28 The Balance of Life

We immediately headed toward the entrance of the Kingdom of Vindoria. I led the way before the soldiers carrying Arabella and escorting Aria. Once we reached the guards at the kingdom, they halted us.

"Look, we need to go through immediately," I said.

"King Valaric, what is your business here," the guard asked.

"Look, I need to get Princess Arabella to the healers," I stated.

The guards took a moment to look on the other side of me, seeing that the princess was lying on a stretcher. Then they looked at Aria, escorted by the soldiers behind the princess. I could tell they were trying to put the entire scenario together.

However, we don't have time for that right now. We needed to get the princess to the healers. Plus, I wasn't sure what had happened either. We just happened to ride up on a set of events.

"Alright, follow me," one of the other guards stated.

We rushed toward where the healers were located. We didn't want to waste more time, as time was of the essence. I realistically didn't know how long the princess had been knocked out.

Once we arrived at the healer's quarters, we walked right in. I took a second or two to find one of the healers as they were in the back portion of the room.

"We need some attention over here," I said.

"What seems to be the rush," the healer said without looking up.

"The Princess had been badly injured, and we need medical attention," I said.

The healer no longer looked at whatever he was looking at. Once I stated that the princess needed assistance, he jumped up immediately. Whatever he was doing was no longer critical.

He immediately rushed over to the soldiers' carriage, where the princess was. He looked over her and started removing the bandage from her head.

"What happened?" asked the healer.

"We believe she was struck in the head by a rock," I said.

Then he looked around at the soldiers holding Arabella and surrounding Aria. I could see the wheels spinning in his head as well. He was also trying to figure out what had happened. Unfortunately, I was not even sure what had happened.

"Gently place her on the table over here," the healer said.

He continued looking over her to see if he could see any other identifiable injuries. Based on what he said, other than the usual bumps and bruises one gets, the head seemed to be the only location of serious injury. Unfortunately, he was concerned because the injury was to the head.

"There seems to be some swelling on her head," the healer stated.

"Well, what do we need to do?" I asked.

"Nothing can be done at this time," said the healer. "Right now, all we can do is care for the wound and see if she wakes up."

"Are you sure?" I asked. Is there no particular plant or bush we can get that will help?"

"Not in this case," said the healer. "Right now, she just needs rest."

"Alright. Please send word should her status change," I said.

"Will do," the healer said.

We needed to find the king to tell him what had happened. Although I suspect by now, he has already been informed. Just as we were walking out of the healer's quarters, the king could be seen coming down the hallway.

"Valaric, what happened," asked the king.

"Arabella was hit in the head by a rock," I said.

The king took a quick second to look around me and saw Aria surrounded by my soldiers.

"What is the meaning of this?" asked the king. "Why do your soldiers have Aria contained?"

"We found Aria holding the rock above the princess's head when we rode up upon them," I said.

"What?" questioned the king. "What happened?"

"I do not know," I said. "We immediately started caring for the princess. Detained Aria and headed to this location."

"Head over to my chambers; I will meet you there in a few minutes," said the king.

We left the area and followed one of the king's guards toward the king's chambers. When we arrived, the guard let us in. I took the liberty of sitting at the table the king had once seated at.

This gave me a few minutes to stop and think about what had all transpired. I didn't have time to think as I rushed to get the princess to the healers. I don't exactly know what happened; I only know what we saw when we rode up.

I was having difficulty believing that Aria could do such a thing. Although, when people are pushed, there is no telling what they can do. The entire scenario was bizarre.

Just as I contemplated this some more, the king walked in. He walked over to his usual spot and sat down. He took a second to look at me and then at Aria.

"What happened?" asked the king.

I took a moment to explain the details I knew about the situation. I described the whole incident with the village, the creatures we encountered, and how we worked with the village warriors to battle the creatures.

I explained that Aria had taken off after some stray creatures had escaped our trap and that Arabella followed her. As I said the entire piece, I again reminisced that letting them go alone was wrong, although this wasn't the scenario I thought would happen.

Then I explained that as we were finishing up the battle with the creatures, we saw Arabella's horse show up alone. Lucas and I immediately took off in the direction that her horse had come from. Along the way, we passed Aria's horse, which let us know we were on the right track.

I further explained that when Lucas and I arrived at the ladies' house, we saw Aria holding a rock over Arabella's head. I told him we didn't have the time to figure out what had happened or if Aria was even to blame. We just headed here to get medical care for Arabella.

"Is this true?" yelled the king as he looked at Aria. "Did you strike the princess, my daughter, with a rock?"

"No, Your Highness," Aria stated. "This all happened to be bad timing."

"Explain yourself then," bellowed the king.

She began explaining the entire chain of events as they occurred. She told how they took off after the creatures. Then, they became distracted and were caught off guard by one of the creatures they were trying to find.

She explained how the creature threw the rock at the princess and then how she had to battle the beast—followed by the part where we showed up with her holding the rock above the princess's head.

Unfortunately, I did not see the creature in the area. Although, I hadn't looked for one either. I was primarily focused on getting the princess to the healers. I didn't have time to figure out what had happened.

"That is a pretty lavished story," the king said. "Unfortunately, the only one that can collaborate on the story is lying unconscious on a bed in the healing station."

"What will you do?" I asked.

"Soldiers, escort Aria out into the hallway, and don't let her speak to anyone," said the king.

I quickly looked at the king to ensure he knew those were my soldiers. He looked in my direction and nodded. I looked at the soldiers and gestured for them to do as the king asked.

"The healers said Arabella may be out for a few days," the king said. Unfortunately, the rumors will get out that Aria struck the princess in the head, regardless of whether they are true. We cannot release her; if she did it, we must take action. However, if she did not hit the princess with a rock, people will believe she did until Arabella can prove her innocence."

"I agree," I said. "What can I do?"

"Nothing," answered the king. "I will place her in her living quarters under guard, with strict instructions that nothing shall happen to Aria until I say so."

"Alright, that sounds like a plan," I said. "Sorry, I didn't have more information. My priority was to bet Arabella to the healers."

"You were right to do so," he said.

"Look, I have to run; I was supposed to be at the Kingdom of Serendell today," I said.

"Kingdom of Serendell?" questioned the king.

"The kingdom is south of Thalondor," I said. "The Queen there is quite eccentric, from what I gathered from her note."

"What about the King?" he asked.

"I don't know," I said. "The note was from the Queen of Serendell."

"Interesting," the king said.

"I would imagine so," I said. "I have to leave, but I will check back in a few days to see how Arabella is doing."

"Alright, I will have a couple guards accompany you and your soldiers to the gate," the king said. "Thank you again for bringing my daughter back."

"You welcome," I answered as I left the room.

Just as the king stated, the guards escorted my soldiers and me right out of the gate. There was no hanging out, stopping at the alehouse, or stopping for something to eat. They walked as quickly as they could to get us out of the kingdom.

It didn't really matter as we had to get to the Kingdom of Serendell. Hopefully, the twenty thousand soldiers are staying far enough back not to cause any issues. We had sent the messenger back, stating we were taking the queen up on her invitation to visit.

The visit will be less adventurous than the last few days. Hopefully, the creatures haven't merged in that area yet. If they have, though, we will have to do our best to defeat them.

I was thinking about all of this while we headed toward the entrance of the Glimmering Caverns. Before we entered the caverns, though, I glanced back at the Kingdom of Vindoria. I wish you a quick recovery for the Princess. Hopefully, when I returned in a few days, she would at least be conscious. Only time will tell.

Chapter 29 The Arrival

We didn't spend much time in Glimmering Caverns as we needed to get to the Kingdom of Serendell. I realized Scorch had returned to the cave when we were in the cavern. Mentally, I already knew that Scorch was in the cave, but his presence was verified as I heard soldiers yelling and screaming about a dragon in the cavern.

They had never been that close to a dragon before. In reality, I can't say that I blame them. If I were walking inside a dark cavern where a dragon lives that I didn't know, I imagine I would also be a little nervous. Imagine if the dragon unleashed fire through the cavern. There would be no possible escape. However, watching all the soldiers freak out made me chuckle slightly.

Once all the excitement died down, we exited Glimmering Caverns. I took a moment to look around the surrounding area, as I was unfamiliar with this location. This was an area that I had never been before. I wasn't sure that I was even in the right place.

However, I looked over my left side and found where our soldiers were. Not wanting to waste any more time, we headed toward the soldiers. Now, we needed to find the Captain of the Guard so I could get an update on the current situation.

I didn't take long to find the Captain of the Guard. The soldiers in the area pointed me in the right direction so that I could see him. He was in the middle of the formation, handling some business. So, we headed in that direction.

Before we arrived at the location of the Captain of the Guard, he had already noticed me. I wasn't sure how he knew I had returned, but he did. I imagine that word spread throughout the camp rather quickly. At this point, anything was possible.

"Your Highness," said the Captain of the Guard.

"What's our status?" I asked.

"We are just outside the Kingdom of Serendell, Your Highness," he said. "The scouts said the kingdom is over in that direction."

"Have we made any contact with them yet?" I asked.

"No, Your Highness," said the Captain of the Guard. "We have only arrived shortly ago. We were following your last set of orders. We were setting up camp and awaiting your arrival."

"Did you run into any issues from when I left?" I asked.

"None worth mentioning, Your Highness," he said.

"Alright, that's good news," I said. "Let's prepare to send a messenger to alert them that we have arrived."

"Right away, Your Majesty," said the Captain of the Guard.

I drafted a parchment note to let the queen know we had arrived. There was no secret that we were coming, but no one knew when we would arrive. I didn't want to visit a kingdom with twenty thousand soldiers. That would send the wrong message.

No one would question that a king is traveling with twenty thousand soldiers. They may ask the intention but wouldn't find it unrealistic. Sending a message just made things easier. They would know we had arrived and now have the opportunity to prepare stuff for my arrival.

Once I completed drafting the note, I rolled the parchment up and put my seal on the outside. I wanted to make this look as official as possible to gain other allies. Thus far, we have built a relationship with Lord Cedric Blackhorn of Wynthrop Village. Hopefully, by now, Roderick and Ethan will also be making a relationship with those people.

We would need as many allies as possible, based on the information we had received from the past. If we didn't act fast and work together, we would be overpowered by the creatures. These meetings and negotiations had to work, as failure was not an option.

While deep in thought, a messenger showed up at my location, letting me know that the Captain of the Guard sent him. I handed him the parchment and asked that he deliver the message to the Queen and await instructions. He took the parchment, bowed, and exited to deliver the message.

Now we wait. I could only imagine how this meeting was going to happen. Just from the Queen's note alone, I could tell she was eccentric, if nothing else. I wished that Arabella had been here for this event. She could smooth things over with little to no effort.

Of course, this made me wonder how she was doing. Hopefully, she will be alright and recover quickly. Her injury was not insignificant, but it wasn't as bad as Sir Gregory's. Hopefully, she will have a speedy recovery.

I still don't know how I felt about the situation with Aria, though. Could Lucas and I show up at the wrong time? Again, why was she holding the rock instead of healing Arabella? Some things about the entire scenario didn't make sense. Hopefully, Arabella will recover and confirm Aria's story.

The messenger finally returned and handed me a parchment in the middle of the night. I assumed he wouldn't have shown up shortly after leaving, but I didn't expect he would return in the middle of the night. After all, the day had already been extended. I was exhausted and sleeping by this time.

I started opening the parchment to read what the Queen had sent. Based on her last note, I had no idea what to expect from this one. Her previous note was quite elaborate, and I am still in shock. I couldn't wait to see what this particular note entailed.

Once I had the parchment fully open, I began reading. Just as I suspected, her note did not disappoint. It was written very similarly to the previous one. After I read through all of the rhetoric about how she is happy that we have finally arrived to meet her, the meeting details are outlined in the lower section.

In a lot less words, she will send an entourage to greet us in the morning. I do not know what I expected, but why couldn't the note be more straightforward? I want to apologize for being late. I will send an entourage in the morning and get some sleep. One would think that would save time in the long run. However, I suppose she wouldn't be who she is if she didn't do it.

The fact didn't matter now. Unfortunately, I was awake and would have trouble sleeping. My mind began to race as I started to think about everything, from how I arrived in this strange new land to how these creatures were trying to overrun the land.

I wish I could remember how I ended up in this land. This made me think about the ship remnants on the beach I awoke on. I didn't want to know the answer, but were those the remnants of the Silver Serpent? Where was Captain Stormrider and the crew of the Silver Serpent? Where did the trunk that was holding the dagger come from?

There were still too many unanswered questions for any of this to make sense. In my first vision, there was a massive army on both sides. Based on what I read in the parchments, Thalondor's army was grand. However, the armies in the vision seemed much more significant than what I read in the parchments.

Was that army so big because it did the same thing I am doing now? Am I repeating history only to suffer the same fate? These questions and numerous others continue to keep me up at night. There has to be something I am missing that would solve this issue.

So many things are happening right now, and it is impossible to keep up with everything. We are spread across the land, trying to keep this thing under control, but we are slowly losing ground. We must find a way to get to an area before the creatures to save the people within that area.

Right now, I seem to be one step behind the creatures and can't be everywhere at one time. We need to find a way to contain them at the portals. However, we have to find the portals first. Maybe after talking with the queen, we can call the elders to pinpoint locations. We understand this would only show the ones documented a thousand years ago.

Keeping the people of the land separated is not the answer. We need to be united to have more numbers to defeat the creatures. Then what do we do? Do we move everyone around Thalondor? What about Eldoria Forest? What's north of Serpents Pass?

Perhaps tomorrow's discussions will develop some new ideas. If nothing else, they should at least be interesting discussions. However, maybe they have information from the last thousand years that may benefit our quest. They must have different perspectives, as their people were here before the enchantment.

We will see what tomorrow brings. It was pretty late, so I needed to get some rest. I had a feeling that tomorrow wouldn't be a typical day, per se. Only time will tell, but it was time to rest for now.

Chapter 30 The Procession

If you have never been abruptly awakened to the sounds of horns blowing in the distance, let me tell you, it is quite the experience. That's exactly how my morning started. I was abruptly awoken from a deep sleep. Feeling as if I had closed my eyes a few moments ago, I struggled to open them. At the same time, I was jumping up to figure out what was going on.

Lucky for me, I was surrounded by soldiers because, at the moment, I had no clue where I was, what I was doing, or what was going on. However, I quickly figured out a few of those questions once I started waking up. However, the part about what was going on was still vague.

If I wanted to know what was going on, I needed to head towards the direction of the horns. So, I set off in that direction while also trying to locate the Captain of the Guard. If anyone knew what was happening, I assumed it was him.

As I headed toward the direction of the horns, I could see many soldiers interested in what was going on as well. At least I knew I was heading in the right direction, as numerous soldiers were heading the same way. As each passed, they gave a cordial Your Highness.

I finally made my way to the Captain of the Guard's location. Hopefully, he can fill in the details. Please let me know if we are under attack or something. That may be a good thing to know, as I was unprepared for battle this early morning.

Don't get me wrong, the sun was up, technically. By up, I mean I could see the initial illumination of the sun, signifying morning.

However, I don't think the sun was up enough even to alert the roosters yet.

"What's going on?" I asked the Captain of the Guard.

"Good morning, Your Highness," answered the Captain. "We still don't know."

"Well, are we under attack or something?" I asked.

"I don't think so, but we still aren't certain," he answered.

"Well, what is all of this noise?" I asked.

"That is what we are trying to find out, Your Highness," the Captain of the Guard said. "I have positioned scouts closer to where the noise originates."

"Alright. How long before you think we will know something?" I asked.

"Hopefully, real soon," the Captain said.

I was starting to believe that he was as lost as I was. Of course, he was not wrong. Just as we finished speaking, a scout showed up. The scout let us know that the sounds were coming from above the walls of the Kingdom. He went on to say that they had just opened the gates, and the scouts could see a line of soldiers starting to march out of the gates.

Of course, we had asked if they looked like they were preparing for battle. The scout didn't think so, as they would have never opened the gates. He said that based on their appearance, they looked as if they were performing some type of ceremonial piece.

Ceremonial piece, I thought to myself. Here, the conversation would be the only eccentric piece today. This sounded like we were about to see many things we needed to prepare for today. I was wishing for an easy day.

"What do you want us to do, Your Highness?" asked the Captain of the Guard.

"At this moment, nothing," I replied. "Be prepared, but they are showing no signs of aggression at the moment so that I wouldn't show any either."

We finally started seeing the initial part of the formation as they headed toward us. The scout was right; they seemed to be dressed up in more ceremonial gear. From what we could see, the personnel in front of the formation had colorful breastplates with what looked like feathers atop their heads. They looked as if they were dancing more than marching toward us.

Followed behind them were horns and drums. They were playing some tune, and the people in the front seemed to be dancing and walking, too. I had never seen such a display in all my life. If they were going to attack, this would be one of the weirdest ways to attack.

Thirty to forty soldiers were behind the horns and drums, fully dressed in golden armor with white capes flowing down their backs. Against the rising sun, they were pretty shiny-looking. I wasn't sure if this was a display of wealth and power or just a display.

When I thought we had seen everything, we saw ladies walking big cats. The ladies had lions, tigers, pumas, and other relatively large felines I didn't know the name of. How did they get them to walk on leashes like that? If nothing else, this was quite the spectacle all in itself.

At one point, I looked across our formation and saw everyone staring at the elaborate display. Not one of our soldiers was prepared for any potential threat. They were all too engrossed in the spectacle in front of us.

Following the big cats were people riding elephants. There were only about ten to fifteen of them, but elephants aren't particularly small. As I watched this elaborate show go on, I started to think about how I had not seen any of these types of animals in my travels in this area. Did they hoard them all here?

Next were horses with chariots. The chariots had two people on them. One controlled the horses, and one shot fire out of their mouths. I was still determining if this was a kingdom or a traveling entertainment piece. This was my first time seeing something like this back in Aurelia. At most, we saw something strange coming off of the ships now and then.

I was wondering if this show was going to end at some point. However, the archers were following. They had gold breastplates and golden helmets. Other than being overdressed, nothing seemed out of the ordinary. That was until they shot arrows into the air with streamers attached, which decorated the skyline.

Behind the archers were about nine palanquins, carried by two men each. Maybe the queen was in one of these. I didn't know and probably wouldn't find out any time soon as the front part of the formation hadn't even made it to our location yet. We were still seeing all of this from a distance, so I imagine once it became closer, the spectacle would be larger than life.

After the palanquins, there were more soldiers, but this time, they were in silver armor. This is more fitting to the traditions that I had seen in the past. At least something in this formation finally looked a little normal. I started to wonder if this was the end of the show.

As luck would have it, that was not the show's end. Following behind the armored soldiers were soldiers on horseback. This entire procession was quite vast, but I didn't think they were going to put their entire army into this show. Now, I started wondering if this was how they met everyone they had invited or if this was something special just for me.

Don't get me wrong, this was quite the show, but the entire thing was way over the top for what we needed to do. We merely needed to speak, become friendly, and help each other for the sanctity of humanity. I don't think we needed this type of presentation to start with. However, this explains what she wrote in her message a little better.

Now that I think back to her original message, I may need to understand the message. Based on this spectacle, she may not believe she is better than everyone else. However, she is a lot more elaborate than others. After watching this show, this will be one of those moments I will remember for the remainder of my life.

Right about now, the show's first part is starting to reach us. I imagine that they will have to keep on walking until the palanquins get to our location. Maybe once the palanquins arrive, we can start talking. I would have assumed we would be invited into the kingdom for these discussions, but this also works.

A few moments more, and I figured that I was only half right. The procession did stop once the palanquins reached our location; however, the queen was not in any of them. Instead, an elaborately dressed man in colorful, fancy robes exited one of the palanquins. He asked where the king was, and then he automatically followed all the fingers pointing in my direction.

As the man drew closer, the soldiers stepped around me, blocking his advancement. Then, the elaborately dressed man began to speak.

"Your Highness, my name is Ezekiel," he said. "I have a note from

Queen Amelia."

"A note; you mean to tell me she was not in this procession?" I asked.

"No, your highness," Ezekiel said. "I was tasked to deliver this to you and only you."

I took a quick look at the Captain of the Guard, and we both shrugged our shoulders. Neither of us knew what to do with all of this, so I motioned for the note to be sent forward.

I quickly read the note, which was just as elaborate as the last. Of course, after watching this procession, I couldn't expect anything less, as the procession was merely used to send me a note. I took a moment to consider what type of person Queen Amelia was. Thus far, everything she had done was quite extraordinary.

"What did the note say?" asked the Captain of the Guard.

"We are to get into the palanquins so they can take us to the queen," I said.

"Couldn't we have just rode our horses there, Your Highness?" the Captain asked.

"I was thinking the same thing," I said.

Unfortunately, riding our horses was too late. If we refused to ride in the palanquins, we would be showing disrespect to the queen. However, if we rode in them, we would also be giving her the upper hand, as we would be doing exactly what she wanted us to do.

This could be her way of showing respect to us. Instead of just allowing us to walk in like common folk, she had this elaborate procession, which not only was made to impress us but also used to let her people know that dignitaries had come for a visit.

After taking the time to contemplate things, I looked at the Captain of the Guard and then Ezekiel and nodded. Then, I told the Captain to gather about five hundred soldiers to accompany us into the kingdom. They could walk around the palanquins just for show.

I figured if we weren't going to be able to stop the silliness, we might as well join in it. This also protected me as I couldn't imagine what would come next. Thus far, I couldn't guess what would come next.

We started walking towards the palanquins, and Ezekiel quickly tried to escort me to one of them. This particular palanquin was a little larger than the rest. I figured it was easier to follow his direction than try to resist. Again, I wanted to get this show on the road so we could start talking.

However, when I opened the drapes to enter, I quickly noticed that two rather beautiful, underdressed ladies were already occupying the palanquin. I quickly glanced at Ezekiel, who nodded and made a hand gesture to enter. In an effort not to delay this any further, I jumped into the palanquin so we could get to the kingdom.

At this rate, we would lose half the day trying to get to the queen's location. I was starting to wish things were a little bit simpler. Currently, there is a lot at stake for the land. We didn't have time to be fancy and elaborate at this point.

Chapter 31 The Kingdom of Serendell

As we made our way through the gates, I couldn't help but notice the ornate details around the gate itself. They spent a lot of time and effort building an aesthetically pleasing structure. Which made me wonder how ornate the remainder of the kingdom would be.

Thus far, I wouldn't put anything past the queen. Everything has been quite elaborate in this process. Nothing has been less than over the top from the initial message to this point in time.

As we entered through the gate. People were lined up as far as I could see on both sides of the road. Is this how all visitors were treated, or just the ones invited by the queen? Did the people even know who I was or who was walking through the gates? Did they even care, or were they forced to be out here?

These and numerous other questions crossed my mind as we continued the parade of events. However, I was glad that I had our soldiers directly around us. I know I initially put them around the palanquins as a joke, but now, with this many people around, I didn't want to get rushed by numerous people, either.

Once I looked past people, I couldn't help but notice the building structures. Even though the buildings were not part of the castle, they were still built with character and contained ornate detail. People lived in and did business in these weren't ordinary square buildings.

The buildings exuded an aura of grandeur and splendor. Towering spires adorned with intricate carvings stretched towards the heavens, their facades covered in glistening marble and golden accents. Elaborate archways and ornate columns framed entrances, leading into majestic structures adorned with stained-glass windows depicting epic tales of the realm's history.

The streets were lined with elegant townhouses, each featuring meticulously landscaped gardens and elaborate wrought-iron gates. Imposing mansions stood as testaments to wealth and power, their facades resplendent with balconies, domed roofs, and intricate stonework. Lush ivy and vibrant flowers cascaded from the balconies, adding a touch of natural beauty to the urban landscape.

The city square, a bustling hub of activity, boasted a magnificent palace at its center. This regal edifice featured towering spires, shimmering golden domes, and expansive courtyards adorned with fountains and statues. Gilded accents glinted in the sunlight, giving the impression that the entire city was bathed in the warm embrace of affluence.

The elaborateness of what I could see continued to impress me. I was starting to understand why and how the notes had been delivered. Thus far, from what I have seen, more needs to be done.

We arrived at the palace, and our soldiers, except my immediate guards, were asked to stay outside. They were allowed to accompany us into the castle.

I exited the palanquin and started ascending the palace stairs. However, I took a moment to view and admire the beauty outside the castle. The ornate details and craftsmanship were unbelievable.

The castle's exterior walls were a work of art featuring intricate carvings, delicate filigree, and decorative motifs that celebrated the kingdom's rich history and culture. The castle's stone walls bore the weight of centuries, yet they seemed timeless in their grace and luxury.

As we proceeded to enter the castle, the views did not change. Massive, oak double doors adorned with golden handles entered the castle's grand foyer. As one stepped inside, they were greeted by breathtaking splendor. The walls were decorated with priceless tapestries depicting heroic sagas, and the marble floors gleamed beneath magnificent crystal chandeliers that bathed the room in a soft, golden glow.

Every corridor and chamber within the castle bore witness to masterful craftsmanship. Vaulted ceilings featured intricate frescoes painted by renowned artists, while elegant stained glass windows filtered the sunlight into a breathtaking dance of colors. Gilded moldings adorned with precious gemstones traced the edges of walls and archways, shimmering with regal magnificence.

As we entered the throne room, I was so taken aback by the beauty and grandeur that I almost forgot why we were there in the first place. The throne room was the epitome of grandeur. A massive, intricately carved throne sat atop a dais adorned with silk draperies and velvet cushions. The ceiling was a masterpiece of painted frescoes depicting the kingdom's history, and enormous mirrors framed in golden filigree adorned the walls, creating an illusion of endless luxury.

However, I was abruptly brought back to reality as I heard Ezekiel announce my presence to the queen. I assumed the queen was the lady sitting on the throne directly before us, but I needed to figure out what I had seen thus far. Either way, I could feel the eyes around the room staring in my direction, so I knew I needed to say something.

"Greetings, Queen Amelia and the noble people of the Kingdom of Serendell," I started. "My name is King Valaric of Thalondor. I have traveled all this way to inform you of our troubles within the land."

As I was talking, I noticed out of my peripheral vision that this lady had now walked up to my side. The encounter was a little uncomfortable as she was now on my right side, staring directly at me. I didn't want to offend the queen I was addressing then, so I didn't dare turn my gaze to look at this woman on my right side who was nearly touching me while blatantly staring at me.

This entire situation was quite uncomfortable, but I didn't know what else to do, so I continued with my speech.

"There are creatures plaguing this land from centuries past," I said. "I have traveled all this way to see if we can collaborate to rid this world of the evils.

As I finished my sentence, the lady beside me asked what type of creature. The lady was so close I could practically feel her breath on my face when she said that. At this point, I was still determining what I should do. Should I turn and face this woman or continue talking like I am answering the question directly in my ear?

As I continued staring forward, the lady on the throne showed no emotion. She wasn't asking any questions. She showed no sign of alarm when I mentioned the creatures. She did not indicate that she was listening to what I was saying. This complete scenario was quite awkward, but I continued talking.

"The creatures are rather large and slow-moving, but they have great strength," I said. "They come through portals in which they were imprisoned a thousand years ago by our ancestors."

Without skipping a beat, the lady on my right asked, "That sounds far-fetched. How do we know that they were imprisoned a thousand years ago?"

Now, this was turning from awkward to downright annoying. I have never had anyone stand that close, talking in my ear, while I was addressing someone else. At this point, I was becoming irritated and willing to address the point.

I turned to the right to face the lady speaking directly into my ear. We were so close that our lips were merely an inch apart. I addressed her by answering her question while staring directly at her.

"Because we have the ancient parchments that tell the story, Queen Amelia," I said.

The odd thing was she didn't move. I assumed she would have stepped back when I turned to the right. She continued standing in the same spot.

"Well, that was a bold move," she said as she stared at me.

I stared back at her, looking into her beautiful eyes. They were the only part of her I could see clearly at this close distance. They were a deep, vibrant shade of blue with a slight sparkle.

I answered without missing a beat, "I am bold. I figure we either talk face to face, or we don't talk at all."

"Interesting," she said as she turned to her right, her golden blond hair smacking me in the face. "Follow me."

So I followed her—a little further back than she had been standing beside me. I didn't want to make her feel uncomfortable. However, after that display, I wasn't sure that was possible.

As I followed her, I couldn't help but notice that her physical appearance was undoubtedly striking. She had a lovely hourglass figure with golden blond hair halfway down her back. If I had to guess, she was probably about five foot, seven or eight inches tall, and she carried herself well.

She led me down a few hallways, which allowed me to continue taking in the view. I found myself staring on more than one occasion, to the point that I was sure I wouldn't be able to find my way back to the throne room. I was still utterly amazed by the beauty and finesse put into this kingdom. Even the hallways didn't skimp on the ornate details.

We finally reached a room at the end of one of the hallways. The room continued with the exact ornate details of the rest of the kingdom. There was a table with chairs in the middle of the room, with some bookshelves along one wall and windows on the other.

Queen Amelia sat at the table and gestured for me to sit across from her. I sat down, hoping we could begin discussing what was happening. I knew the longer we delayed, the larger the enemy force grew, and based on the visions from a thousand years ago, there would be no defeating them if this occurred.

"Queen Amelia.." I started but was quickly cut off.

"Just call me Amelia if you are alright with me calling you Valaric," she said.

"Alright, Amelia," I said.

"So, what stories were you telling about creatures and portals," Amelia asked.

I proceeded to tell Amelia everything that had happened up until this point. I watched her face change from delight to morbid horror as I explained the details about the villages. I let her know that we had the villagers of Wynthrop joining us and were looking for others to aid us in our quest.

"We have traveled all of this way because we cannot stand idle and continue to allow the creatures to take over the land," I said. "Will you aid us in our quest?"

"Before I answer that question, you might want to follow me," Amelia said as she stood up and walked out of the room.

Uncertain what she was doing, I had no choice but to follow her. She led me down some more hallways, and we descended some stairways. I thought she was intentionally trying to lose me as she continued moving through areas.

We finally stopped at a door down this one particular walkway. I wasn't sure where we were in the castle, but I hoped to find out soon. She slowly shoved the door open, and we walked into the area.

"There is something I have to show you," she said.

I took a quick look around the area we were in. I assumed it was their version of a dungeon, but that was only because we descended so many stairways. As I looked around, I saw a familiar setting: soldiers aligned on two sides, with a portal in front of them.

"How long has this been going on?" I asked.

"Only about a week or so," Amelia answered.

"How often are they coming through?" I questioned.

"At first, they were only coming out about once every twenty minutes," she said. "However, we have noticed an increase, and they have started popping out every ten minutes."

I couldn't help but wonder why the creatures were coming through at a quicker rate. In a relatively short time, the creatures came through twice as fast as they had initially. Could that be because of the length of time or because I had closed the other three portals?

"Watch yourself, my Queen," said one of the soldiers.

Shortly after the soldier made that statement, one of the creatures came through the portal. Just as with the others, the soldiers immediately eliminated the creature as it went through the portal. The good news was that the scenario was the same, but the bad news was that they were coming through faster.

We would soon find ourselves making difficult decisions without knowing the risk. We needed to understand better how this initially unfolded a thousand years ago. If we continued to attack this unthinkingly, we would undoubtedly repeat history.

Chapter 32 The Bath

"Amelia, I have an idea, but we are going to have to leave this like it is at the moment," I said.

"Valaric, what is your idea?" Amelia asked.

"Currently, it appears your soldiers have this under control," I said. "Why don't you and I head back to Thalondor and speak with the elders? "Before we close another portal, I want to see if the elders found anything out."

"Wait, you can close the portals which will stop the monsters from coming through?" she asked.

"Essentially, yes. However, that may cause an influx in another location," I said. "Your increase may have been because I had closed another one within the land."

"Well, close this one; I don't want these things taking over my kingdom," Amelia shouted.

"Look, I understand your frustration," I started. However, we need to find a centralized point from which to attack, surround them, and hit them as they come out by the second."

"Well, I surely do not like this plan, especially when I can save my people," Amelia said.

"Look, I know you are frustrated and want to do the right thing," I said. "We can go to Thalondor in the morning and return the following day."

"How is that possible, as the trip takes a few days to get there," She asked.

"I have a much quicker way of getting us there and back, but you must trust me," I said.

She nodded, agreeing, but I still didn't think she trusted me. It seemed like most had that same reluctance in these unnerving times. A lot was going on, and yet none of us knew the actual reality of the situation.

We left the dungeon area to head back up the stairs. At this moment, the soldiers standing guard had everything under control. If the creatures continued at their average pace, the soldiers would have no issue eliminating them—well, that is, until they started coming through much faster.

We must find that magic spot to align the area with warriors. However, the pace at which the creatures come through may be at a rate none of us can handle. This is likely the place of doom where true evil meets the light of day.

"This is your room," Amelia said.

"What?" I asked as I looked around to figure out where I was.

"I said this is your room for the night," she said.

"Sorry, I kind of got lost in thought on our way here," I said, not even realizing we were walking back up the stairs.

"I understand that, as I do the same often," Amelia said. "I assumed you must have been lost in thought as you hadn't said much."

"Yes. There has to be a key to solving all of this," I said. "Unfortunately, I don't know how to solve the issue yet."

"Well, get some rest," Amelia said. "Maybe a good night's rest will help solve some riddles."

"That sounds like a plan," I said as I entered my room. "I will see you in the morning."

"Alright, I will see you in the morning. Have a good night's sleep," she said with a slight mischievous giggle.

However, as I shut my door, I was quickly greeted by two gorgeous women. They immediately started helping me get ready for a good night's sleep. Before I knew what was going on, they had removed my sword, shield, bag, and garments. I still wasn't sure I knew exactly what was happening as they moved quicker than expected.

The next thing I knew, I was escorted to another room wearing only an elegant robe. The ladies walked me down some stairs to get to some other location. I couldn't help but notice the details that surrounded the area.

The outside featured a grand facade made entirely of pristine white marble. The walls were detailed with carvings depicting scenes from mythology and history. Above the entrance, a finely sculpted marble frieze showcased graceful figures in various states of relaxation and indulgence.

As we walked through the door, I couldn't help but notice the towering marble columns. The columns went up to a dome ceiling with a mesmerizing mosaic depicting celestial bodies. At the bottom, the columns surrounded a beautiful rectangular marble pool filled with crystal-clear water.

While I was busy gazing upon the intricacies of the room, I hadn't noticed the two beautiful women had now disrobed. I realized that they were naked when I saw them removing my robe. Now, my gaze went from the intricacies of the room to the beautiful women standing before me.

The ladies each grabbed a hand and led me into the marble pool. The water was hot to the touch and felt incredible on my skin. I was starting to wonder if I was dreaming or if this was reality. In either case, I would enjoy this as much as possible.

We walked to the far side of the pool, where the ladies sat me down on a bench. Then, they proceeded to rub sponges with soap across my body. They started with my hands and arms before moving onto my back and chest. Everything felt incredible as I hadn't had the opportunity to wash in what seemed like forever.

At this moment, I couldn't tell you what felt better—getting washed up in a soothing hot bath or being in a hot bath with two beautiful ladies. Either way, I didn't want this moment to end, as the entire scenario was unbelievable.

Once the women finished with my chest and back, they each grabbed a foot. They gently massaged and washed each foot, then slowly started working their way up my legs. The ladies ensured that they scrubbed and cleaned all sides of my leg as they worked their way to my upper thigh.

By now, there was no way of containing things. As they went up my inner thigh, I had an erection that could easily be seen. The lady on my right continued moving up my inner thigh and decided to clean my rather intense bulge. She even gave an intense "oh my" as she continued washing.

At that moment, I thought this would turn into an incredible night. I was sitting in a hot bath with two beautiful women who just rubbed my entire body, and we were all naked. I couldn't have dreamed of a better scenario than this one. All we needed to do now was have a little more fun, and I would have one of the most incredible nights' sleep since I had arrived in this place.

Unfortunately, that little more fun idea never happened. The ladies went from rubbing sponges all over my body to sitting on the outer edges of the bench. I wasn't sure what was going on now. I looked to the right and left; both were staring forward.

Now, this entire situation was awkward. Was I just supposed to handle business myself, with both just sitting there? They did everything to get me in this current position, then abandoned me. I wasn't sure what was happening, but my perfect night started getting dragged down.

I looked to the left and right to see if they were still sitting there but noticed they were now bowing their heads while looking forward. Looking forward, I could now see why the ladies were bowing. Queen Amelia was standing at the entrance of the marble pool.

Now, the entire situation was awkward as the queen had just shown up, and here I was, sitting naked in a hot bath with two naked, beautiful women with an erection. I don't know if things could have gotten any worse.

"So, how is it?" Amelia asked.

"How is what?" I asked as I tried to shield myself from this embarrassing moment.

"The bath, of course," she said with a slight chuckle. "Is the bath warm enough for you?"

"Yes, the bath is quite warm and very nice," I said.

"Great," she said, dropping her robe to the ground.

At this point, my jaw nearly hit the water. I couldn't help but stare as she slowly walked into the water I was sitting in. Nothing was left to the imagination, and she just walked in as if this was a regular everyday occurrence.

She moved over to the side wall and sat on the bench on my right side. The two ladies immediately went to where she was sitting and started washing her with the sponges. Again, everything about this place was utterly abnormal.

"I hoped my ladies treated you well," Amelia said as the ladies were cleaning her arms.

At this point, I was still determining where I should look. Was I supposed to look in her direction while talking? Did I look straight forward, hoping that I don't strain my neck muscles trying not to look? This was all quite confusing.

"They did a good job," I replied as I continued looking forward. "I haven't had the opportunity to get a bath in a long time."

"I assumed as much as you sounded like you were doing a lot of traveling," she said.

"You were correct," I said. "The bath was an excellent idea."

"Why do you not look at me while we are speaking?" she asked. "Am I so grotesque that you must avert your eyes while talking to me?"

"What?" I asked, with a bit of drool coming out of my mouth. "The exact opposite. You are quite stunning."

"Then why do you look away?" she asked.

"I wasn't exactly sure where I was supposed to be looking," I said.

"Being naked is a perfectly natural thing," she said.

"True, but you are the queen," I quickly said.

"Are you not a king?" Amelia asked.

"Yes, of course, but.." I started to say.

"No buts. We can be adults and have a natural, normal conversation while sitting in warm bath water," she followed up with.

"I suppose," I said as I slowly looked in her direction.

We may both be adults, but I wasn't sure about conversing while naked in a bath. I felt like I was staring more than looking in her direction while talking. Usually, a tub would be relaxing. Unfortunately, this situation was not that relaxing.

However, we did talk a little more as the ladies continued washing her body. I talked a bit about the creatures and what I had seen thus far, but nothing severe. I still was uncomfortable and wanted to move on from the situation.

"I suppose that is enough chatter for tonight as we have a journey tomorrow," Amelia said.

"The good news is that it will not take us long to get to Thalondor," I said.

"If you say so," she replied as she stood up. "Well, are you getting out of the bath?"

I knew this situation was going to arrive eventually. One of us had to get out before the other, and it would not be me in my current state. Of course, her getting up first didn't make matters any better, as the water flowed down her perky, voluptuous breasts, making them glisten in the candlelight.

"In a minute," I replied. "You go ahead. I am going to relax here a little more."

"Ok, suit yourself," she said. "My ladies will ensure you return to your room when ready."

"Thank you for the warm hospitality," I replied.

"You are quite welcome. See you in the morning," Amelia said as the ladies helped put on her robe.

After a few moments, Amelia finally left the room. I was still slightly uncomfortable with the other ladies present but felt less awkward than when Amelia was here. Again, every situation around here was more over the top than I was used to.

Eventually, I decided to get out of the bath and head to bed. As I exited the tub, the ladies dried me off and helped with my robe. At least now, things were de-escalated, and I wasn't pointing at everyone.

The ladies placed their robes back on and escorted me back to my room. I assumed they would go their way when we arrived at my quarters. However, that didn't happen. They came into the room and stayed with me the entire night.

I was not disappointed, but I now knew that sleep was optional.

Chapter 33 The Cavern

The very next morning came entirely too soon. I wasn't unhappy with my current situation as I woke up with a beautiful woman on each side of me. Although I was a little tired, I was pretty satisfied with being a bit tired.

However, simultaneously, I couldn't help but wonder how Arabella was doing. Hopefully, by now, she would have awakened. Maybe she could tell how Aria was on top of her with a rock above her head. I took a moment to contemplate the entire scenario as I lay in bed.

Although laying around all day seemed nice, I knew we had to get moving. I decided to get up and gather my things to start the day. Once fully dressed, I headed out for something to eat.

When I arrived in the kitchen, I noticed the queen eating breakfast. As I walked in, she looked up at me and smiled.

"Good Morning, sleepy head," Amelia said. "I trust that your accommodations were more than adequate?"

"Yes indeed. There were no issues with my accommodations at all," I said with a slight grin.

"That is good to hear," she replied. "We can start our journey as soon as you finish eating."

"Sounds like a plan," I replied. "Any issues with traveling with only twenty-five guards a piece?"

"Only twenty-five guards," she exclaimed. "Didn't you travel here with twenty thousand guards?"

"I did, but that was different," I replied.

"How is that different?" Amelia asked.

"Can you just trust me?" I asked.

"Alright, but if anything starts to feel funny, we are turning around immediately," she exclaimed.

"Understood," I answered.

Once we completed eating, we gathered our things and mounted our horses. We started towards the gates of the kingdom. The trip out was not as elaborate as the trip in. However, that was probably because I needed more guards.

Even though we had a smaller procession, the kingdom's people still noticed us leaving and saw us off. She honestly had her people's attention. They all seem to want to be part of this society from appearances.

We exited the gate and headed to the location of my remaining soldiers. I assumed the entrance to the Glimmering Caverns was still near there. At least, that was my assumption, as that was the location I arrived in from Vindoria.

My assumptions were correct as I quickly spotted the entrance. I gave the signal to dismount, but I could see that Amelia couldn't understand why. After all, we just started our journey and were already taking a break.

"We are here," I said.

"Here? Where is here?" Amelia asked.

"The entrance to Glimmering Caverns," I said while pointing at the ground.

"I've never heard of Glimmering Caverns," she said. "I thought we were going to Thalondor."

"We are going to Thalondor, but at a much quicker pace than normal," I said with a sly grin.

"I still don't understand," she said with frustration. "How does this get us to Thalondor quicker?"

"I really can't explain the how. You have to see for yourself," I said.

"You know I am not really into surprises, right," she said.

"Really? I believe you have surprised me the entire time I have been here," I replied.

"Those aren't surprises; they are elaborate plans put into motion," she laughed.

"Well, while we are on the subjects of elaborate plans, don't be alarmed by what you see in the cavern," I said. "I better let everyone know."

"I don't believe I like that sound," Amelia replied.

Assuming the others didn't know the story of Glimmering Caverns, I took a moment to gather everyone who would be entering. I explained the story about the Gem Golem and the battle and why the cavern is called Glimmering Caverns.

"Well, that is an interesting story, but that still doesn't tell me how we get to Thalondor quicker," Amelia said.

"I am getting to that piece, but first, I figured I better explain one last thing before I show you how we get to Thalondor quicker," I said. "This is probably better for everyone to see out here than in a dark cavern."

"Well, now you have piqued my interest," Amelia stated.

Sooner than Amelia could finish talking, something incredible happened before our eyes. Scorch burst out of the Caverns with unbelievable speed. It all occurred so quickly that Amelia couldn't take her next breath before Scorch soared above.

A chuckle escaped me as I watched the reactions of the people around us. Whispers of panic, surprised gasps, and wide-eyed stares filled the air. Scorch's sudden appearance had taken them by surprise.

Throughout the moments when I shared the story of Glimmering Caverns, I silently communicated with Scorch through our special mental connection. Together, we crafted a complex plan that unfolded right before everyone.

"Was that a damn dragon?" Amelia said excitedly.

"That was indeed a dragon," I replied with a grin. "His name is Scorch."

"That thing has a name?" she replied.

"Yes, he is my friend, so I gave him a name," I said. "We can also communicate mentally and hold conversations."

"How in the world did you gain the ability to have a dragon as a friend?" she asked.

"The short answer is, I was there when he hatched out of the egg," I said.

"Where did you get the egg?" she asked.

"That is the longer story that I will be more than happy to share later as we have to get going," I said.

"Well, can we at least get a closer look at him?" Amelia asked.

Just then, Scorch landed right in front of me. Everyone backed up, even though they wanted to see the dragon. People can be funny at times. They want to know more, but at the same time they don't.

Amelia eventually walked up to Scorch to be able to touch him. She was intrigued and yet a little terrified all at the same time. The entire situation was quite interesting to watch. Here was the queen who made every attempt possible to make everything she did elaborate but didn't know what to do in this situation.

"Alright, we need to get going," I remarked. "We have a long day ahead of us."

"I thought you said we would get to Thalondor quicker?" Amelia asked.

"Yes, but we have much to do once we get there," I replied.

I quickly pat Scorch on the head and motioned for him to lead us into the cave. At least with Scorch leading, I knew nothing was lurking in the caverns. He would eliminate them if there were before we arrived in that location.

We followed behind Scorch, a mixture of the two kingdoms soldiers before us and a few after Amelia and I. I wasn't worried about anything in the cavern, but I never knew what we might see once we arrived at Thalondor. I hoped that nothing out of the ordinary was there, but one never knew in this world.

Amelia was automatically drawn to the illuminated stones within the cavern. We discussed how a few of us carried them as they also work in other areas. I went to grab the one out of my bag when something else caught my eye.

When I arrived on this strange land, I found the crystal buried in the sand. I had almost forgotten about it, as I still didn't know its importance, and I still couldn't figure out why it was buried in the sand.

"What is that beautiful thing?" asked Amelia.

"Some crystal I found when I first arrived in this area," I replied.

"You just found it?" she asked. "Where did you find such an alluring item,"

"It was on the beach under a large rock," I said. I was attempting to find a rock to cook on and noticed the crystal underneath the rock."

"Well, what is it for?" she asked.

"I still hadn't figured that part out just yet," I replied.

As we continued to walk and talk about the crystal, I took the opportunity to place it back in my bag. I needed to figure out the significance of the crystal. It seems odd for a crystal like this to be abandoned on a beach.

Maybe someone stole it and hid the crystal until a later time. Perhaps it was just something that washed up on the beach. Either way, I was confident I would not find the solution in this cave.

With my concentration solely on the crystal, I had lost track of where we were in the cave. As I looked up, I noticed we were in the area we had got our butt kicked by the Gem Golem before I got the lucky blow. I took this opportunity to share the story's details with Amelia and showed her some remnants still on the ground.

"Well, I went a little further into the cave than I intended," I said as I motioned for us to go back in the direction we came.

"What do you mean?" Amelia asked.

"We need to head back towards the entrance," I replied.

"I thought we were heading somewhere that would reduce our journey," she said.

"We are, but not how you think," I said.

I could see the confusion on her face. I took the opportunity to explain the history of Glimmering Caverns as we walked towards the entrance. I further explained how we could travel from one location to the next based on my ability to think about a place once the Gem Golem was defeated.

Once we arrived at the cave's entrance, I sent twenty-five soldiers just in case. Amelia and I followed behind them and exited Glimmering Caverns. The remaining soldiers followed behind us.

I could hear the initial gasps as we exited the cavern. They couldn't believe that we had entered a cavern and then exited the same cavern in a completely different location. Everyone didn't know where we were, but they knew we were not in the exact location.

"Where are we exactly?" Amelia asked. "I thought you said we were going to Thalondor, but all I see is forest."

Upon hearing Amelia, I took a quick second to look around. She was correct; we weren't in Thalondor. However, I could see where we were immediately. We were in the Kingdom of Vindoria, and they couldn't see the kingdom.

Chapter 34 Strange Noises

"Roderick, do you think everyone else is having this much trouble on their mission?" Ethan asked.

"Hopefully not," I replied. "I would hate to think that every one of us is locked up and none of us are getting any closer to our objective.

"I know. Could you imagine Valaric locked up in the Kingdom of Serendell, based on the initial note she sent to Thalondor?" Ethan asked.

We both chuckled at that thought for a moment. However, Ethan's question did raise merit. I did wonder if everyone else was having this much trouble or worse. Since we had no way to communicate, everything was a mere guess.

What if some of them ran across a more significant force of creatures? Which means they never made it to their objective. When one takes a moment to think of all the possibilities, we weren't doing that wrong.

Being locked up in a castle wasn't getting us closer to accomplishing our tasks, but we weren't doing too badly. I mean, we did have these cushy quarters to hang out in. Unfortunately, there wasn't much to do while we were sitting here.

"I could see Valaric's face now, as he has to listen to things she was saying," I said.

"That's a funny thought," Ethan replied. "Hopefully, she hadn't locked him up as well."

"If that is the case, then things may be much worse for him than for us," I said.

"Hopefully, Lucas and Aria are doing better than us," Ethan said.

"Yes," I replied. "Hopefully so."

To pass the time, Ethan and I played different games we knew. Of course, my games were a lot older than his. I was surprised to see that a couple of them still existed today. They were a different version, but the concept was essentially the same.

One of the games was where you had to make gestures and motions using just your body and no words. The other person had to guess what you were trying to say. Some of the clues Ethan gave were horrible, but at least they helped us pass the time while we waited.

In reality, we didn't have much else to do to the point where we saw who had the fastest hands. One person would place their palms facing down on top of another person's palms facing up. The person whose hands were on the bottom would attempt to slap the person's hands on top. If that person missed, then the two people switched their hand positions. Now, the other person had to try to smack the other person's hands.

After a few hours of doing that, the back of our hands was red. A couple of the hits could have broken bones if we had misconnected. Ethan was a lot faster than I would have thought. I got a few good hits in as well, though.

"What in the hell was that?" asked Ethan.

"I don't know," I replied. "It sounded like screams of terror."

We heard screams from the hallways as we attempted to devise something else to pass the time. We quickly headed towards the door to see if we could figure out what was going on. The guards were still at the door and wouldn't let us proceed into the hallway.

"What is going on here?" I asked. "What is with all the screaming."

"We don't know," answered the guard.

"Well, don't you think you ought to find out, as the screaming seems a little serious," I said.

"We have been given strict orders to stand here and ensure you don't leave this room," the guard answered.

I looked at Ethan to see if he had any ideas, but he seemed as confused as I was. Since the guards wouldn't let us pass, we would just shut the door to muffle some sounds.

"You don't think our soldiers started attacking the castle?" Ethan asked.

"Not likely, as we didn't have enough soldiers to get past the gates," I replied.

"Well, what could be making the people within the castle scream like that then?" he asked.

"I believe that is the question we need to find out to provide answers later," I said.

Then, out of nowhere, we heard a commotion just outside our door. We slowly opened the door but didn't initially see anything as we looked out the door through a small crack. Then we saw the blood run up under the door, which made us both look down.

From the looks of things, the two guards assigned to our room were now dead, laid out on the floor. Something had just ended the two guards' lives, and neither of us knew what it was or if it was after the two of us. Based on this new knowledge, neither wanted to sit around and wait to be killed.

"Shall we?" I asked.

"Yes, we shall," Ethan answered as he gathered his things.

Once we had everything we needed to move, we opened the door and stepped over the guards. We looked in both directions but saw nothing in either direction. Then we heard screams coming from the hallway on the right.

We immediately dashed down the hallway to see if we could figure out where the screams were coming from. Then we saw the reason for the screams. One giant, green, large creature was standing right before us.

However, the creature wasn't making any screams. The screams were coming from the Queen and Princess. The King was the only thing in between the beast and his family.

Without thinking, Ethan fired an arrow into the back of the creature. The arrow didn't do much damage but did cause the rather large creature to turn around to see what just hurt him. This allowed the king and his family to escape harm's way.

Not wanting to waste time, I drew my sword and plunged it into the creature's soft flesh. Ethan continued to unload a few more arrows into the beast. The king even buried his sword into the creature's back, which seemed to be the final blow.

We watched as the creature fell to the floor. Then, looking up, we saw the king staring right at us.

"What was that?" asked the King.

"That was one of the monsters we warned you about," I said.

"Where did it come from?" the King asked.

"If I had to guess, there is an open portal in the dungeon," I replied. "When we went to Thalondor, still in ruins, we found a portal in the dungeon."

"That doesn't explain how the thing got up here," said the King.

"I can't explain that now, your Majesty," I said.

"If there is a portal, can you close the portal?" asked the King.

"Unfortunately, we cannot," I replied. "King Valaric can close the portal, but we should be able to contain the creatures as they come through with the right setup."

"Will you help us contain them then?" asked the King.

"Yes," I said. "Ethan and I, with a few of your soldiers, can search for the portal while the rest deal with any more that may have come through."

"You think there may be more?" asked the King.

"Based on the screams in the other direction, I would say it is a safe bet," I replied.

Soldiers showed up at the King's quarters as if on cue. Based on their looks, they still weren't sure what happened; they just thought that something had happened. I assumed their guard duties would soon change because one of those creatures arrived at the King's quarters.

The King quickly divided the soldiers into groups. He sent a few out to gather more soldiers, and then he left four soldiers here with instructions for the other soldiers who arrived to search the castle for any other creatures.

He sent the remaining soldiers with us to find the portal. Just when we were about to leave to start searching for the portal, the King asked us to hold up while he grabbed his gear. He didn't want to sit on the sidelines while his kingdom was attacked. He wanted to see the stories we had already told him with his own eyes.

Once the King was ready, we headed down the hallways. We placed a few soldiers before the King, Ethan, and me to lead the effort. We did this mainly because we knew we had to protect the King, but we also needed to figure out how to get to the dungeon.

We could hear screams in the distance, which let us know that at least one other creature was in the castle. The other band of soldiers could handle that one. We needed to find where these things were coming through to contain the situation before we found ourselves in a situation similar to Thalondor.

As we walked down the hallways, we passed bodies slain on the floor. The only good thing about that sign was that we knew we were headed in the right direction. We assumed the portal might be in the dungeon, so we started heading down the stairs toward the lower floors.

I couldn't help but think how far away the dungeon was from the King's quarters. Based on the time it was taking us to get to the dungeon led me to believe more creatures were lurking around.

The guards let us know we were at the stairs to the dungeon. The door was wide open, and a slain guard lay out on the stairwell. We had to be careful from here, as there may also be more lurking.

We started heading down the stairs, uncertain of what we would find. Then, we saw the portal at the far end of the dungeon. It looked the same as the portals I had seen over a thousand years ago.

We took a moment to look around but didn't see any other creatures in the vicinity. This meant one of two things. Either no other creatures came through the portal, or they were roaming around the castle.

"How did this get here?" asked the King.

"We aren't sure how or where these things appear," I replied.

Before we could say anything further, another creature emerged from the portal. At first, the King's soldiers looked at each other as if mesmerized. This delay allowed one of the creatures to grab hold of one of the soldiers and practically choke him to death.

I quickly pushed the King back out of the way and started to attack the creature. Ethan released two arrows into the beast before I could slash it with my sword. I took a step back in preparation to stab the beast, and before I knew it, the King had plunged his sword into the beast.

Due to the King's sword, the creature swung his arm around and hit the King square in the chest, knocking him off balance. Ethan released another two arrows into the beast and delivered the final blow. The beast fell to the ground motionless after that.

We took a second to look around to ensure everyone else was alright. Other than the one soldier, everyone else seemed to be okay. Everyone was a little shaken up but alright physically.

"How long before another creature comes through the portal again?" asked the King.

"We don't know at this point," I replied. "However, I suggest we prepare for the next one that walks through."

The King sent a few soldiers to gather more people so we would be better prepared for the next creature to emerge. We all stood around the portal, awaiting the next one. The good news was that there wasn't one popping through every other minute.

"I guess we should have listened better," said the King.

"We did not know when or where a portal would appear," I replied. "There is no way we could have foreseen this coming."

"We could have prepared better for the incident had we listened, though," answered the King.

"Possibly, but there is no point in worrying about the past," I said. "We now know where the portal is located and where they are coming through."

"Yes, that is true," the King replied. "By the way, I don't think we have been formally introduced. My name is King Matthias."

"Glad to meet you, your Highness," I replied. "This is Ethan, and I am Roderick."

"Thank you for coming to my aid and assisting us tonight," said the King.

"We must help each other. Otherwise, we won't survive," I replied.

"Yes, but unfortunately, we did not treat the messengers of Thalondor fairly," the King answered. "You could have just as easily ignored the screams."

"I believe you treated us fairly enough," I said. "We could have still been down here in these dungeons when those things started coming through."

"I suppose you are right," said the King with a slight chuckle.

We turned as we heard a noise at the top of the stairs. The soldiers the King sent for started coming down to the dungeon. This put us in a much better position because we could have the soldiers surround the portal with a little distance so they were prepared for the next attack.

We briefed them on what would happen to prepare them. Nothing can prepare anyone for creatures coming through a portal, but we did our best to explain.

We initially put the soldiers before us because they had already seen what had happened. We placed some archers further back so they could bombard the thing with arrows. Hopefully, this will be enough to manage the beasts coming through until the portal is closed.

Chapter 35 The Princess

"Valaric, I thought you said we were going to Thalondor?" said
Amelia.

"We are, but we took a little detour," I said.

"A detour? To some forest," Amelia said with tone.

I was here two days ago, so I doubt there was much change in
Arabella's condition. Unconsciously, I must have been thinking about
her. I wanted to know how she was recovering and if she had regained
conscientiousness.

Unfortunately, now we are outside the Kingdom of Vindoria with
strangers. I can hear the King now as he cannot stand having
strangers in his kingdom. I understood his rationale, but you have to
move forward in life at some point.

"A forest per se, but not exactly," I replied.

"Care to elaborate on that statement?" asked Amelia.

I took a moment to explain how Arabella and I were headed to the
Kingdom of Serendell and how we assisted the Wyntrhop village. I
also included the part where Arabella was knocked unconscious and
then brought home to the Kingdom of Vindoria.

Of course, I had to explain how Glimmering Cavern moves from one
location to another. I knew we needed to go to Thalondor, but I must
have thought of something else. Of course, if I made this mistake too
many times, I would end up in the wrong location, which could be
detrimental to the entire crew.

"I am following you so far, but that does not explain why we are in
the middle of nowhere in the woods," Amelia said.

"Well, we aren't exactly just in some woods," I replied.

Amelia looked around before saying, "Looks like we are in the middle of the woods."

Now that I can see things, I understand Arabella's frustration when I first came to this area. I was having difficulty explaining how things could be present even though you couldn't see them. If Arabella could only see me now, trying to explain what she had explained to others, she would probably laugh at me.

"Just because you cannot see anything does not mean the thing is not there," I said.

"You aren't making any sense," she said.

"I understand things are hard to understand, but would you be willing to hang out for about an hour right here?" I asked.

"Where are you going?" Amelia asked.

"I am going to check on Arabella quickly to see if her status has changed," I said.

"So, you want me, Queen of the Kingdom of Serendell, to just hang out in the woods while you go galloping," Amelia said.

"Come on, it isn't like that at all," I said. "I just need to go check on a colleague."

"I can see you're not going to give up on this charade," she said. "If you want to run off into the woods for some alone time, be my guest."

"Thanks," I said. "Stay right here; these woods tend to shift paths."

"What?" Amelia questioned.

"Nothing, just hang out here for a moment, and you will be fine," I said. "Take a moment to take in the wilderness around you by listening to the sounds in the forest."

"We have forests around Serendell," Amelia stated. "I already know what the sounds of a forest are based on my trips to the forests."

"Yes, but Eldoria Forest is quite different and may surprise you," I replied.

"I doubt that, but let's get on with it so we can get to Thalondor," she said.

"Alright, I will be back shortly," I replied.

I headed towards Vindoria, which, of course, I could see. I am confident that if Amelia or the soldiers watched me, they could see me vanish into thin air. I would have to explain this little trick later. Right now, I want to find out about Arabella's well-being.

At least this visit will be different from the last two. The one before, I ended up in a dungeon, and the last one, we delivered a Princess, unconscious and hanging onto life. This should be smoother, as all I am coming to do is find out how Arabella is doing.

The guards were on point, as usual. You couldn't just walk in; there were always questions. I wondered if the King of Vindoria was treated the same way as everyone else. Of course, that would mean he must go outside the kingdom.

Actually, at this moment, I didn't care. I just wanted to check on the Princess and see how things were going. I didn't have much time to waste as Amelia would probably get into something she shouldn't have if left alone for too long.

The guards took a moment to grill me about the fifty soldiers and the strange lady. I tried to explain that they were from the Kingdom of Serendell and that peculiar lady was the Queen of Serendell. Of course, just like their King, they were more concerned with me bringing strangers this close to the kingdom.

I explained that they couldn't see the kingdom and would hang out in Eldoria Forest. Of course, I knew what this meant. They probably already sent word to the King that there are a bunch of strangers outside the kingdom, which means I would have to explain everything again.

If I had to guess, I would see the King before I could see Arabella. To hear the same complaints about how I endangered his people. At some point, he would have to come out of his sheltered way of thinking, as things in the world were more dangerous than most strangers.

Finally, after giving me the third degree, the guards let me into the kingdom. Of course, they had to have at least one accompany me while I walked through the kingdom. By now, I was becoming familiar with Vindoria. The guard was to ensure I didn't do anything wrong, more than telling me where things were.

Since I had little time, I headed straight for the healing room. Of course, I didn't exactly get to that location before being intercepted by the King. Based on his scowl and walk, I would guess he was not pleased.

"Valaric," the King Yelled. "How dare you bring more strangers to the Kingdom of Vindoria."

"Relax, they can't see the kingdom," I replied.

"Makes no difference," he replied. "You inadvertently put the Kingdom in danger."

"Look, I am sorry," I said. "I didn't intend on bringing them here; I was headed to Thalondor."

"Well, how exactly did you end up here?" asked the King.

"I suppose subconsciously, I just wanted to check up on Arabella," I replied.

"I fail to understand how you ended up here if you were headed to Thalondor," said the King.

"We were traveling through Glimmering Caverns," I said. "We planned to head to Thalondor to meet with the elders to figure out our next move, hopefully. Unfortunately, my mind must have wondered about Arabella's well-being, so the cavern brought us here."

"While I appreciate your concern for my daughter, I do not like it at the expense of the kingdom's safety," said the King.

"I understand your concern, but they have no idea where we are exactly," I said. "They wouldn't even know where to enter Eldoria Forest or which direction to travel."

"Well, as King, I don't have the luxury to believe that no harm can come from this visit," he said.

"Alright, I understand," I said. "However, the more you sit here and hound on me about this issue, the longer we stay in the area. How about you let me see the Princess so those people and I can go?"

"Fine," muttered the King. "She will be happy to see you."

"She's awake?" I asked.

"Just this morning," said the King.

"That is wonderful news," I replied. "At least with her better, I shouldn't unconsciously show up in the future."

"Wouldn't that be something," he replied.

"If you have nothing further, I want to see her now," I said.

"Very well," he replied.

I didn't waste another moment checking on her. I headed toward the healers to see Arabella's smiling face. I hoped her injuries were not too severe and that she would be moving around soon.

She had been an excellent traveling companion, and we had become closer as we gathered more information. I hated that this incident happened to her. I knew I should not have let Aria and her go alone. If anything, I should have sent soldiers with them.

After navigating through the hallways in the castle, I finally made it to where Arabella was being monitored. I walked through the door and took a moment to look around. There she was, laying in bed reading over some parchments.

She hadn't even taken the opportunity to look up. That was her, all business, no matter what was happening around her.

"Arabella," I said with excitement.

Rather than putting it down, she looked over the paper and said, "Valaric. How nice to see you."

"How are you doing?" I asked.

"I am better now than yesterday," she said.

"That's good to hear," I said. "I have been worried about you. So much so that I inadvertently ended up here when I was headed to Thalondor."

"Well, that is quite interesting," she said. "Thank you for getting me to the healers as quickly as possible."

"You are welcome," I replied. "I am just glad to see you awake and talking."

"So am I," she said with a chuckle. "Why didn't you just let Aria heal me, though?"

"When Lucas and I arrived, we weren't sure what was going on," I stated. "All we saw was that she was holding a rock over your head."

"You didn't think that she did this, did you?" Arabella asked.

"She said she didn't, but we didn't know what to think," I replied. "The only thing we knew was you were laid out on the ground, and she was holding a large rock above your head when we arrived. So what did happen?"

"We were discussing an issue while looking for the beasts that missed the trap, and the next thing I knew, I was struck from behind," she said.

"So her story was true," I said. "I honestly didn't want to believe she had anything to do with you being laid out on the ground, but unfortunately, the situation needed more facts."

"I can understand your confusion," Arabella said. "Did you get a chance to meet with Queen Amelia?"

"Aw crap," I blurted out. "She is in the woods outside the Kingdom of Vindoria."

"You brought her here!" She exclaimed. "You know my father will be furious about that."

"Oh, I know. He already caught up with me and gave me the third degree on my way here," I replied.

"Well, tell me all about her," Arabella said.

Over the next few minutes, I tried to explain everything that had happened over the last two days, from the fancy procession to get us from the woods to the castle to the ornate details throughout the kingdom. I attempted to do my best to explain everything and elaborate that Amelia's boldness isn't just in her letters.

"Wow, that does sound a little bit elaborate," Arabella said. "What was your next move?"

"I was planning to return to Thalondor to meet with the elders to figure out our next move," I said. "However, I ended up here instead."

"What about Lucas, Ethan, Roderick, and Aria?" She asked.

"Lucas should be close to returning to Thalondor, hopefully with villagers from Wynthrop. Hopefully, Ethan and Roderick are on their way back to Thalondor as well, with some good news from the kingdom they went to," I said. "Aria should be here. Your father had her quarantined to quarters until we could figure out this mess."

"Quarantined?" she asked.

"Yes. Since none of us could explain what happened, your father quarantined her to her quarters under guard," I said. "Did you tell your father the same story you told me so that he can release her?"

"I did, but I didn't know she was quarantined to quarters. I thought she was with you or Lucas," she said. "I will have to follow up on that so we can make sure she is released."

"Alright, that sounds like a plan," I said. "Look, I have to go to ensure the Queen out there doesn't get herself into trouble."

"I understand, based on what you told me," Arabella replied. "Let me grab my things so I can come with you."

"I don't think that is a good idea, as you just woke up this morning," I said. "Besides, your father wouldn't let you come in this condition. Take a few more days to heal, and I can come back to check on you."

"Oh, alright," she exclaimed. "I don't have to like the decision, though.

"Alright, talk to you in a few days," I said.

I stood up from the chair I was sitting in and headed to the door. However, before I exited the area, I looked back and gave her a wave. She just smiled and waved back at me. I was happy to see her up and moving again. At least now, I could focus on what needed to be done.

As I traversed the castle hallways, I thought about how much we needed to accomplish in the coming days. However, I needed to focus on the things directly before us if we wanted any chance of survival. We needed to get back to Thalondor quickly to develop a strategic plan.

Chapter 36 The Messengers

I took longer than intended in the Kingdom of Vindoria, but at least now I knew that Arabella was better. It was time to get serious on the mission again, as we had many things to do. Of course, I would have to deal with Queen Amelia, whom I had just left in Eldoria Forest.

As I started to exit the kingdom, I could see her out in the forest, just pacing back and forth. I wasn't sure that I wanted to go out there to deal with that at this moment. There were plenty of other things to deal with, and I wasn't prepared to hear this nonsense.

"Did you miss me?" I said as I exited the kingdom.

"Where did you go?" Amelia asked. "And how come you left me alone in this forest."

"As I explained, I needed to check on Arabella," I said. "I also didn't leave you alone, as fifty soldiers are standing around you."

"But you didn't go anywhere. You just vanished into thin air," Amelia said.

"I know this is hard to understand, but just because we cannot see anything does not mean things are not there," I said.

"I don't understand what you are saying," Amelia said.

"Listen for a second," I replied. "Do you hear the babbling brook in the distance?"

"Well, yes, but," she replied.

"No, buts," I said. "You can't see the brook, but you know it is there because you can hear it. You can also hear the animals around us, yet you cannot see them."

"I get the analogy about hearing the brook and animals," Amelia stated. "However, I understand those because I can hear them. I don't hear anything that sounds like a kingdom. People don't vanish into thin air either."

"Yet, before today, you didn't know you could move from one place to the next, spanning vast areas of land, in a matter of minutes, by walking into a cavern," I replied.

"That still doesn't explain why I can't see the kingdom," she said. "Why can't you just bring me with you into the kingdom?

"Look, maybe another time," I answered. "I have already received enough crap about bringing you just outside the place. The king here is suspicious of strangers because someone took advantage of them."

"Why would anyone ever be suspicious of me?" Amelia said.

"Look, we can sit and talk about this for the rest of the day or get moving to Thalondor," I replied. "Which would you like to do?"

"Fine then. If you refuse to tell me your little secret, let's go to Thalondor," she said.

"Alright then," I replied.

The discussion would go nowhere, as I could not show her the Kingdom of Vindoria, especially since the king didn't want to see strangers. He would have to overcome not seeing strangers at some point in history. The world was changing, and we would need each other regardless of past histories.

I was done worrying about the issue, as we had many other problems. We headed back towards the cavern so we could get to Thalondor. I knew the conversation Amelia and I were having was far from over, but I wanted to head to our original destination.

We walked back into Glimmering Caverns. Amelia was not particularly happy with me, based on how she stared at me with her arms crossed. I assumed this would be a long day, but I figured eventually, she would have to get over the ordeal. There was little I could do to fix the issue.

After a couple of minutes passed, I instructed our soldiers to head back outside the cavern. I followed behind them, with Amelia and her soldiers taking up the rear formation. As we exited the cavern, I could see Thalondor from our position, which let me know I was thinking of the correct place this time.

"You know, a girl could get used to traveling like this," Amelia said.

"I agree; the cavern has allowed us to get across the plains with little effort, which has allowed us to get to places quicker than intended," I said.

"I wish I could," Amelia started before suddenly stopping her sentence mid-sentence.

I glanced back at Amelia and saw that she was taking everything in. Thalondor didn't have the elegance and attention to detail that Serendell did, but it was much larger than Serendell. Amelia just took a second to take everything in for a moment.

"The last time I saw Thalondor was when I was a little girl," Amelia said. "The place was in total ruins and looked like pure death."

"I remember the first time I could look around after the transformation," I replied. "When we came here originally, the place looked exactly like you described. However, once we closed the portal, the change happened instantly. Before we knew what had happened, it was as if the place was never in ruins."

"Now that it has returned to its formal glory, Thalondor looks massive compared to what I remember," she said.

I sent the soldiers ahead to get us through the gates faster. No one knew we were returning yet, nor did anyone know we would return with a Queen and her soldiers. I didn't want any engagements happening because people were unaware.

We continued heading towards the gate and eventually ended up in the kingdom. We had to keep stopping because Amelia kept stopping to look at different things. Unfortunately, I didn't notice she had stopped until I was a few paces ahead of her, which caused us all to stop.

I shouldn't complain, as she no longer glares at me with her arms crossed. Now, her attention and focus are on the kingdom itself. The sad part was I couldn't be much of a tour guide, as I didn't know much about the area either. I needed to get with Roderick and learn the history of this place.

We walked our usual path to the palace, which, of course, brought us right past the marketplace. At that point, Amelia darted towards the market with soldiers in tow. As usual, we trailed them to ensure nothing happened.

I didn't mind that we were going to check out the market. We had a lot of stuff to do, but I also wanted to check out the market. I never allowed myself the time to do so with everything going on. We didn't have the time either, but I thought, if not now, then when.

When I previously passed by the market to and from the castle, I always took a moment to glance at the market, but I never knew how intense it could genuinely be. As soon as we arrived in the marketplace, vendors were trying to sell us wares from start to finish. They had everything from food to weapons to jewelry.

"Well, have you found anything you just can't live without," I asked.

"Maybe not live without, but," she started. "I want a lot of things they have to offer."

"I can understand that," I replied.

We continued working our way through the market. I was starting to feel a little sorry for her soldiers, as they were now having to carry the things she was beginning to buy. I didn't even know she had brought along that much currency. Where did she have that much currency?

I guessed that the soldiers were carrying her money for her. Of course, now they would be taking the things she had purchased, which was inconvenient.

"How come you aren't buying anything?" Amelia asked.

"I don't need anything at this moment," I replied.

"Regardless of whether you need anything or not, you should buy things from the people within your kingdom," replied Amelia.

"How come?" I asked.

"Because it is a great honor for the King to purchase things from the merchants and allow them to say the King bought this same thing," she replied. "This increases sales amongst your people because people will want to buy what the king has purchased."

"I suppose I have never looked at things that way before," I said.

Of course, shortly after she pointed that out, I started looking like her. I bought a few things and had my soldiers carrying them. However, I didn't buy half as much as Amelia, as I was still trying to get us to the castle.

After making our way through the market this time, we finally started returning to the castle. However, this was the most extended trek from the gate to the castle in history. Amelia continued to take in the sights consistently. She seemed to want to take in every detail and didn't want to miss a thing.

I wish I had that fortitude to stop and take in the details like her. I took the time to review the things in her kingdom, but I doubt I did it to this detail. I know I didn't take this time within the Kingdom of Thalondor.

As we walked and talked, the castle finally came into view. She paused momentarily to admire the view but never took her eyes off the castle the remainder of the way. She grabbed the opportunity to point out some of the architecture and details of the castle that I had never seen before, which allowed me to gain a different perspective on things.

Once we reached the castle, we climbed the stairs and headed to the main hall. Everyone knew we were in the kingdom because everyone I didn't understand was trying to tend to us. However, I only wanted to get to the elders to see if we could figure out our next move.

I quickly instructed our soldiers to accompany Queen Amelia's soldiers to the barracks, except for those who would be accompanying us. Then, we continued through the great hall towards the elder's area. However, before we made it any further, one of the advisors stopped me to inform me that two messengers had arrived from where Ethan and Roderick had gone.

This information quickly grabbed my attention as it seemed odd that two messengers were here instead of Roderick and Ethan. I had expected them to return by now, but two messengers showed up instead of my people. The elders would have to wait for the moment, at least until I figured out what was going on.

I called for the two messengers to come to our location. I wanted to find out what their message was from their King. In the back of my mind, though, I wondered if Roderick and Ethan were alright or if they were currently sitting in the dungeons.

Instead of doing the formal thing and sitting up on the throne, I just went for a discussion in the main hall. Amelia stood near me, although she didn't understand the breadth of the situation at the moment. I quickly attempted to tell her how I sent Roderick and Ethan to the kingdom east of Thalondor to gather more information while we awaited the messengers.

Once the messengers showed up, I was anxious to hear what they said. They quickly bowed formally to Amelia and me, although I wasn't sure how they knew who we were. I assumed my people told them they would speak to the King, and we happened to be the ones they were standing in front of, merely separated by guards.

"Why are you here, and where are my people?" I asked.

"Your Majesty, King Matthias merely wanted us to collaborate on Sir Roderick and Ethan's story that Thalondor was no longer in ruins," said the messenger.

"So, where are my people?" I asked. "Are they locked up in the dungeons?"

"Your Majesty, they are not locked up in the dungeon; they are quarantined to quarters within the castle until we return," the messenger replied.

"I understand," I said. "What exactly were your plans now?"

"Your Majesty, we merely arrived this morning after two days of travel," the messenger stated. "We planned on starting our return trip in the morning."

"Alright, have you had the opportunity to eat yet?" I asked.

"Not just yet, your Majesty," the messenger replied.

I motioned for my people to get the messengers some food. This would buy us some time while we spoke to the elders to see our next possible move. We knew that the creatures were coming through a portal in Serendell, but we knew little more about other places.

Now that the messengers were occupied with being cared for, Amelia and I headed to the elder's location to see if they had found any more information to help our cause. Unfortunately, all we did know was that the creature's presence was increasing, and I unfortunately didn't understand how to stop the past from repeating itself.

All I knew was that if we didn't do something fast, the past would soon repeat itself, even though everyone had long forgotten what had happened to this place. I was starting to feel as if the weight of the world was resting upon my shoulders, and the fate of the people was in my hands.

Chapter 37 The Skies Above

Now that we aided the Kingdom of Thaloria, Ethan and I had a little more free range of the kingdom. The King had removed the confined to quarters he originally put on us, as we had proved ourselves now. Unfortunately, we weren't free to go yet, but we were no longer constrained.

Although we wanted to get back to Thalondor, this wasn't too bad of a compromise. Well, except for the fact that Ethan wanted to go back to that lake for a day. I couldn't say that I blamed him, as that was a beautiful sight.

"Well, what is the plan?" Ethan asked.

"I didn't have much of a plan," I replied.

"We have been locked up in this room for a couple of days now, and now that we have the option to do something, you don't have a plan," Ethan replied.

"Well, what is it that you want to do?" I asked.

"Let's go check out the kingdom," Ethan said.

"Sure thing, but first, let's go check out the dungeon to ensure the soldiers have everything under control," I replied.

"Oh, alright," he replied. "I could have gone a day without seeing those creatures, but if we must."

I couldn't help but chuckle at Ethan because we hadn't seen the creatures yet. Well, not compared to a thousand years ago, when there were more creatures than the eye could see.

So far, we have only seen a few here or there. I wondered how he would react when seeing an entire battlefield of the creatures. Based on what I could see, things were returning to that scenario.

However, that was neither here nor there at this point. Putting that aside momentarily, Ethan and I left the room to head towards the dungeon. As we walked down the hall, we took the time to admire some of the paintings that adorned the walls.

"My niece painted those paintings," came a voice from the side.

Both Ethan and I turned our heads in the direction of the voice. Neither of us had seen anyone else walk or even heard anyone walk up. However, we relaxed when we noticed the person speaking was the King.

"Your Highness, you shouldn't sneak up on people like that," I said.

"Especially after events like last night," Ethan replied.

"I didn't mean to startle you; I was merely heading to check on our issues in the dungeon when I saw you admiring the paintings," replied the King.

"We were also heading to the dungeon to check on the situation," I replied. "May we accompany you, your Majesty?"

"Yes, please do," answered the King.

As we walked down the hallways, the King talked about the kingdom. The kingdom wasn't that old in comparison to Thalondor. It had been around for a few hundred years but not a couple thousand.

The Kingdom started as a small village and continued to grow over time. Before everyone knew what had happened, the village became more prominent, and the villagers had just started building walls around it for protection. From there, everything we see now is there.

As we continued walking, he pointed out a few more paintings his niece had painted. Like the others, they were spectacular and vibrant with colors. Each one we passed was a little different than the other but similar in style.

As we walked towards the dungeon, the discussion with the King made the time pass quicker than usual. The walk down the hallways and the stairs wasn't that far away, but the discussions and history made the time pass faster. Well, it's better than being drug down to the dungeons in chains.

Once we arrived at the dungeon, we descended the stairs. At first glance, the scene looked exactly like we had left it last night. The guards surrounded the portal, awaiting the next thing to pop out.

"How are things going down here?" the King asked.

"We have everything handled from this end, your Highness," answered the guard.

"How often are the creatures coming through?" asked the King.

"Right now, there seems to be one coming through about every twenty-five minutes or so, your Highness," the guard stated.

"Have we been able to neutralize the threat?" asked the King.

"Yes, your Highness," answered the guard.

The guards controlled everything based on how things were going down here. Hopefully, the creatures' arrival pace will remain the same, and the guards can continue neutralizing the threat.

As we discussed the portal scenarios, we started to hear numerous screams. We looked over everything in the dungeon but saw nothing coming through the portal. The screams weren't coming from within the dungeon but inside the castle.

Had we missed a creature that came through last night that no one had noticed until now? Where were the screams coming from exactly?

The King, Ethan, and I quickly climbed the steps to exit the dungeon. We drew our weapons in preparation for what we were about to find.

We walked through the hallway, prepared to engage in battle, but nothing was there. Following the direction of the people screaming, we finally came across one of the guards running down the hallway.

"Why are people screaming through the hallways?" asked the King.

"A Dragon is flying outside the castle, your Majesty," said the guard.

"A what?" asked the King.

"A Dragon, your Majesty," replied the guard.

Without hesitation, the three of us headed toward the top of the castle to see what the guard was talking about.

Trying to get to the top of the castle took longer than I thought. People were running back and forth, some carrying weapons and provisions. Some were just ordinary citizens trying to get a look at what was going on. Others were praying in the hallways, which left little room to pass by.

Once we finally reached the top, we looked around but saw nothing flying around the castle. We could see the guards preparing for battle, but there was no sign of this dragon. So the King reconfirmed the excitement.

"What is going on up here?" asked the King.

"Your Highness, you shouldn't be up here," said the guard. "A dragon is flying around the castle."

"Where is this dragon?" asked the King.

"Last we saw, the dragon was headed towards the East, your Highness," replied the guard.

Of course, we looked in that direction without thinking. However, we still hadn't seen any signs of this dragon. I was starting to wonder if there was a dragon at all. Of course, if there was a dragon, what would the chances be that two dragons existed within this time frame?

As soon as I thought that, the dragon flew over our heads. It didn't come from the east but from the west. It must have circled back around, and while we were looking in one direction, it was coming from the other.

We all quickly ducked down, like it was close enough to grab one of us. I still wasn't sure what ducking down would have done, but it was instinct. However, when I looked back up at the dragon, I quickly realized that the dragon that terrified everyone was friendly.

"Your Highness, have your people stand down," I said.

"What? Are you mad? A dragon is flying around the kingdom; we must defend ourselves," replied the King.

"I understand your rationale, but the dragon is on our side," I replied.

"With you? What do you mean with you?" asked the King.

"Well, not with Ethan and I, but with Thalondor," I quickly replied.

"How? A dragon hasn't been seen in centuries based on folk tales," said the King.

Ethan jumped in and proceeded to explain the events that had taken place on Serpent Pass. He explained how he had fallen through an opening, and the team had found the egg. Then further explained how the egg hatched around the warmth of the fire.

I could see the puzzled look on the King's face as he attempted to take all of this in. As the stories continued, surrounding the mystery of Thalondor, I could understand how people would have a hard time believing the tales. I was in the middle of the story and had difficulty accepting it.

"How can you be sure the dragon is with you?" asked the King. "What if there happens to be another dragon in this era?"

"I suppose the possibility exists, but based on the markings and color, I'm certain that it is Scorch," I replied.

I didn't want to go into the details, but based on the last time I had seen the dragon, the dragon that had just passed over was twice the size of Scorch. The color pattern looked the same, but he was much bigger now. I couldn't explain why the dragon was a lot bigger, but I felt confident that the dragon was Scorch.

"If the dragon is with Thalondor, then why is he circling the kingdom?" the King asked.

"If I had to guess, the dragon is not alone," I replied.

"What do you mean, not alone?" asked the King.

"If I had to guess, King Valaric is here too," I said.

"What, that's impossible," replied the King. "It has been two days, and my messengers would have just made it to Thalondor. There is no way he could have made it here in time."

"It is possible," I said as we explained how Glimmering Caverns came into play.

We decided to focus our attention down rather than up in the skies. Out in the distance of the kingdom, we could see a small force heading towards the kingdom. I could barely distinguish the flags being flown, but I was confident it was King Valaric.

Chapter 38 Fear of the Unknown

With a small group of guards, Queen Amelia, two messengers from Thaloria, and I walked towards the big gates of the Kingdom of Thaloria. We weren't planning to fight; we just wanted to figure out what was happening. Even though we didn't mean any harm, I still felt careful because we were in a place we didn't know. I quietly told my loyal pet bird, Scorch, to fly up and watch things from above.

Scorch had two critical jobs during our trip. First, he flew above us, watching things and telling me what he saw using our special connection. Second, he was there to protect us in case anything wrong happened.

Even though I worried a little about Thaloria possibly attacking us because they were keeping Ethan and Roderick confined, I couldn't be sure. It was strange that King Matthias had locked them up, especially since they were supposed to be messengers. It didn't make sense to limit their movements when their job was to communicate.

If Matthias wanted to hurt Ethan and Roderick, he could have punished them badly or locked them in the dungeons. But the messengers said Matthias seemed fair. He was careful when dealing with important stuff, wanting to know all the facts before making significant choices.

Matthias sounded like someone who liked to stick to the facts and not let emotions get in the way. I liked that because it meant we could work well together. If things went smoothly, we could become good friends and make a strong team between our kingdoms.

We didn't stay long in Thalondor because I wouldn't say I liked it when my people couldn't move freely. We ensured the messengers got something to eat when we arrived since they'd been walking all day. Queen Amelia and I went to talk to the elders to learn more about the next place where strange creatures had been seen.

As we walked around Thalondor's big rooms and hallways, I had to keep reminding Amelia to keep moving. She was amazed by all the fancy designs on the walls, but to me, they seemed like regular rooms and hallways compared to the ones in Serendell, which were much fancier.

However, Amelia found everything fascinating. Thalondor was super old, one of the oldest kingdoms around. It had been in ruins for over a thousand years, so few people ever saw it up close. A lot of folks thought it was cursed because of old stories. Long ago, when the King of Thalondor defeated darkness and saved the land, people told stories about how great the kingdom was. But as time passed, those stories changed into cautionary tales about curses on the kingdom.

From what the elders had told me before, Thalondor was older than the other locations in the realm. Hearing about the Kingdom of Thalondor, which used to be grand but was now just ruins, was incredible. It was hard to wrap my head around how much history it had, significantly, since I grew up in simple Aurelia.

One of these days, I would have to look at things within the kingdom. Unfortunately, right now was not one of those times, as we still needed to get to the elders. I wanted to see if they had found more information on the uprising.

Once I could pry Amelia away from the portraits and carvings on the wall, we finally reached the elder's location. We opened the door; they were in a heated debate on items and history. I often wondered how they got anything done when it appeared most of their time was spent arguing back and forth.

"Good evening, elders," I said, breaking up the conversation.

"Good evening, your Majesty," one of them replied.

"This is Queen Amelia. We have dropped in to see if you have more information," I said.

"Evening, Queen Amelia," they answered.

"Have we discovered any more information or trends of how the creatures appear?" I asked.

"Unfortunately, I don't believe the ancient parchments get into that type of detail," the elders said.

"So basically, we are blind as to where the creatures will come from," I said.

"As of right now, yes," the elder said. "We can't even tell you how many will come through."

"Well, if it helps, they are coming through in the Kingdom of Serendell," Amelia said.

"That does help, your Majesty, as we can record that in today's scripts, so we have the information documented," answered the elder.

"There doesn't seem to be any sighting in Eldoria Forest from what we have seen or heard," I replied.

"Interesting," said the elder.

"Why interesting?" I asked.

"They seem to be popping up all over the place, but no one has seen them there," replied the elder. "I wonder if it is because of Eldoria Forest or just the fact that no one has seen anything as of this moment."

"That is a good question," I replied. "We will have to head there after we get back from where Roderick and Ethan are being held."

"Held?" asked the elder. "I thought they went to the east as messengers."

"Yes, they did, but the King there has them confined to quarters until his two messengers return, confirming that Thalondor is no longer in ruins," I replied.

"Oh, I see," said the elder. "Do you think you will have trouble getting them out of there?"

"I don't think so, based on my discussion with the messengers they sent this way," I said. "The intention is to get them there faster than they took to get here."

"Glimmering Caverns, I presume," said the elder.

"Yes," I replied.

After explaining the rest of the details, we told the elders good night. I brought Amelia to her room for the night and then returned to my room to get some much-needed rest.

It felt rather nice to be in my bed for another night. Of course, I had to move Whisperwind out of the middle of the bed. Living in a castle suited him more than living in the woods.

After a night's rest, we headed towards the Kingdom of Thaloria, which brings us back to our current situation. The group of us headed towards the gates of Thaloria as Scorch flew overhead.

I didn't think we would run into trouble, but there was nothing wrong with showing strength by letting a dragon soar through the skies. Plus, Scorch told me telepathically that he had seen Roderick and Ethan on top of the castle. This was a good sign and should be less aggressive than we had thought.

As we continued walking towards the gates, we noticed the drawbridge and gates were open. This was a good sign as they didn't see us as a threat, with only a few guards escorting us to the kingdom.

As we drew closer to the gate, we noticed a group of people comparable to the size of our group come out of the gate. We were still too far away to see if they were friendly or foe, but we assumed this was either the welcoming or fighting party.

To be safe, I asked Scorch to circle above us, just in case. They had already seen the dragon overhead, so this wouldn't be anything out of the ordinary nor show any aggression, especially since Scorch hadn't attacked anything yet.

This turned out to be a good move because Scorch let me know that Roderick and Ethan were among the people who had come out of the gate, which showed good faith that this was more of a welcoming party than a fighting party. This news made me happy, as we already had enough to deal with, that we didn't need to fight amongst each other.

Once closer to the gate, Roderick and Ethan approached us and welcomed us to Thaloria. I was happy to see them, even though it had only been a few days. I was even happier to know that they were unharmed. They filled us in on the findings and issues within the Kingdom of Thaloria.

"King Valaric, let me introduce you to King Matthias," Roderick said.

"Nice to meet you," I replied. "This is Queen Amelia of Serendell."

"Nice to meet the both of you as well," replied King Matthias. "Welcome to the Kingdom of Thaloria."

"Thank you for inviting us in," I said.

"I see you have returned with our messengers a little early. You will have to tell me how you accomplished that task over some drinks," King Matthias stated.

"We can talk over drinks," I said, motioning for the messengers to step forward.

"Let's head to the castle and complete our talks there," said Matthias as he motioned for us to follow him through the gates.

Without hesitation, we followed the entourage towards the castle. I asked Scorch to stay close to the area, just in case. People may look and sound friendly but also have ill intentions. Hopefully, that wasn't the case with this group, but one can never tell exactly.

Walking towards the castle, I looked around at the buildings and ornate designs. The detail was nowhere near what I had seen in Serendell, but it was still lovely to look at while we walked. There wasn't anything special about the buildings. They looked like ordinary buildings that people used to live in, conduct business in, and eat in.

Once we made it to the castle, we headed to a room with a large table surrounded by chairs. This could have been the dining hall that King Matthias used to entertain guests or a meeting chamber. I wasn't sure which one it was at that moment. Maybe the room doubled as both.

Matthias stood at the table's end and motioned for us to sit down. I sat off to Matthias's right while Amelia sat in the chair to his left. Roderick and Lucas sat next to me. The remainder of our guards and people stood against the walls.

"So what brings you this way, King Valaric?" asked Matthias.

"To be honest, I wanted to check up on my people," I said as I gestured towards Roderick and Ethan. "I had expected to see them back in Thalondor but instead found your messengers."

"I can certainly understand your concern, but I hope you can understand mine as well," said Matthias.

"Which was?" I asked.

"Two strangers show up at my gates, stating they are from a kingdom that has been in ruins for hundreds of years while trying to convince me creatures are coming from the ground," Matthias stated. "That story sounds a little unbelievable."

"When you put it that way, the story does seem a little unbelievable," I said with a bit of a chuckle.

"So, as my messengers probably told you, they were sent to the

Kingdom of Thalondor merely to ensure it was no longer in ruins," Matthias said.

"Yes, the messengers did relay that message and stated you had confined Roderick and Lucas to a room within the palace," I said. "Thank you for not leaving them in the dungeon while you were waiting for information."

"I am also thankful that I didn't leave them in the dungeon as well," Matthias stated. "If I had left them in the dungeon, we would probably not speak right now."

"Why's that?" I asked.

"Because if they were in the dungeon, my family and I would have been killed had it not been for these two fine warriors," Matthias stated. "They quickly came to our aid once the creatures started roaming the castle."

I glanced in the direction of Roderick and Ethan, who were giving up and down nods with their head. They had already told me there was a portal in the dungeon, but Matthias's men had already controlled the situation. They hadn't said anything about the creatures roaming the castle, though.

"I assume you have eliminated all the creatures roaming the castle?" I asked.

"We assume so," replied Matthias. "We checked on the soldiers in the dungeon first thing this morning but were quickly pulled away as screams filled the castle because a dragon was flying around the kingdom."

"I suppose you are referring to Scorch," I said, looking innocent. "As you can see, he didn't cause anyone harm or damage; he was relaying the things he could see."

"What do you mean relaying?" asked Matthias.

"I can communicate with him through telepathy," I said. "It is the same as you and I talking, except we don't have to be in the same room."

"Well, isn't that convenient," Matthias remarked. "Now that we cleared the air, how can we work together to clear these beasts from our lands."

"We are going to have to pool our resources to defeat these things," I said. We have already made agreements with the village north of

Thalondor and the Kingdom of Serendell.

Amelia took a moment to shake her head up and down, showing that she agreed with the solution.

"What is our ultimate plan?" asked Matthias.

"Unfortunately, we are still working on that as we speak," I said. "The elders in Thalondor are searching for clues to give us the upper hand in this battle."

"What do we do in the meantime, and how do I stop the creatures from entering the dungeon?" asked Matthias.

"Right now, we need to agree to work together to try and stop what lies ahead," I said. "As for the dungeon, Queen Amelia has the same issue in her dungeon. She controls it, so we left the portal open for now."

"Left the portal open," remarked Matthias. "Why would you leave the portal open?"

"Right now, we have been able to handle what comes through the portals as long as we leave them guarded," I started. My fear is that if we start closing portals, where will more pop up, and at what rate?"

"I can understand your rationale, but I don't want to leave those things coming into the castle and putting my family in danger," Matthias stated.

I looked at Amelia to see if she had anything to offer. In Thalondor and Serendell, things were confined to the dungeon. Here, though, they had made it into the castle and threatened his life. I could understand his desire to close the portal, but I didn't know what happened when we did.

Just as I was about to offer a suggestion, Scorch spoke up. He told me a commotion from the north side was outside the kingdom. I wasted no time in relaying this to everyone in the room we were sitting in.

"Let's head to the top of the castle to see what the commotion is all about," Matthias said.

"Seems like we just did this a little while ago," Roderick said with a laugh.

We all followed Matthias up the stairs. None of us knew what we would see, but once we arrived at the top, nothing could have prepared us for what we could now see.

Chapter 39 The Portal

As we overlooked the castle walls to the north, in the distance, we could see a massive force of creatures heading in this direction. They weren't moving quickly but would arrive at the kingdom before nightfall. I didn't know how many were headed in this direction, but thus far, this was the largest group of creatures we had seen thus far.

Of course, this led me to wonder where exactly they came from. I also thought about how many went through that portal in an hour. Maybe this portal was one of the first ones open, which is why so many creatures were heading in our direction.

"Sound the alarms, set defensive positions," Matthias called out.

"Yes, your Majesty," answered one of the guards.

"We have soldiers outside the walls to the east," said Roderick. "We need to bring them in so they don't get slaughtered."

Matthias grabbed one of the soldiers running past. "Bring this man to the stables at once. Roderick, grab one of the horses and get your people as quickly as possible."

Roderick quickly nodded in Matthias's direction and then gave me a nod. Then he headed down the stairs right behind the soldier. We knew the extra thousand soldiers wouldn't help much, but we couldn't afford to lose a thousand soldiers either.

"Matthias, what do you need us to do?" I asked.

"Is there any chance that Scorch can count and estimate how many are headed this way?" Matthias asked.

"What exactly does he think I am?" Scorch stated. "Some type of dumb animal that only meows or something."

"That's not what he meant," I told Scorch. "Remember that he had never seen a dragon before today, so he has no idea what capabilities you possess."

"Ya, Ya, Ya, the big dumb animal will be over the horde in a moment," Scorch said sarcastically.

"Scorch is headed in their direction now to get a closer look at how many are headed this way," I told Matthias.

"Thanks. Maybe we can get an idea of how many we are dealing with to develop a better plan," Matthias said.

I turned and looked at Amelia, "you doing alright?"

"Yes, there isn't much I can do from here, but see what happens," Amelia said.

Meanwhile, I could hear Scorch in the background, "One hundred twenty, one hundred twenty-one."

"Alright, Scorch. You proved your point; give us an estimate of what you see from up there," I said. "How many do you see?"

"Well, you aren't going to like the answer," Scorch replied. "There has to be at least thirty thousand or more headed your direction."

"That's not good," I said aloud.

"What's not good?" asked Matthias.

"There's at least a group of thirty thousand heading this way," I relayed.

"What? How? Where did they come from?" Matthias asked.

"Right now, I can't answer any of those questions," I answered. "Let me see if I can find more information while you continue to set up defenses."

Matthias and his soldiers continued to prepare the kingdom for battle. I continued to watch as they brought barrels of oil, baskets of arrows, and other weapons atop the castle walls. Of course, most of the defense was on the northern side.

Matthias's soldiers worked together like a cohesive unit as they prepared for what would come. I couldn't tell if this kingdom was often attacked or if they practiced for scenarios like this one. At this moment, I felt confident that we could defend against the upcoming threats.

I glanced over the eastern side to see if our troops were headed this way. Currently, I don't see any movement in that direction. Either

Roderick hasn't made it there yet, which would be a little concerning, or he is getting everything in order.

While I was lost in thought, Scorch spoke up again. He had located what he believed was the source of the horde headed our direction, but there were at least another twenty to thirty thousand creatures in that location as well. Attempting to clear that would be a challenging task.

Of course, that would have to be a battle on a different day. Right now, we had to focus everything on the imposing fight in front of us. This was by far the most significant force of beasts we had ever encountered, and I wasn't exactly sure how the entire battle would go.

Thus far, the visions have only shown open combat in wide open spaces, but could we better defend from a fortified position? Our position was way better behind the walls, but eventually, we would have to face them in open combat if we wanted to eliminate the other twenty to thirty thousand near the portal.

My thoughts of how this day may end forced me to become sidetracked. I almost forgot that Roderick was headed to get our troops. I saw them heading this way with a glance over the side of the walls. That was the good news, having them make it inside the kingdom walls.

There wasn't much more that I could do up here. Matthias's troops had everything in order as they continued to set up the defenses and reinforce the walls. So, I decided to see if my presence was needed elsewhere.

"Matthias, anything else we can do for now?" I asked.

"Yes. Roderick mentioned that you could close the dungeon portal, " Matthias answered. "I don't want to worry about those things coming in from the inside while having to fight them on the outside."

"Yes, my concern is that we don't know what closing the portals does yet," I answered. "What if every time we close a portal, the other portals increase the number of creatures coming through per hour."

"I think we have to worry about what is happening right now and deal with the outcomes tomorrow," said Matthias. "That's hoping there is a tomorrow."

I took a second to look at Amelia, "What do you think?"

"I believe Matthias is correct, Amelia stated. "With that portal open, we increase the risk of losing the battle today."

"Alright," I said. "Let's go to the dungeon."

Matthias led the way, and Amelia and I followed. Ethan stayed on top to continue helping the soldiers prepare for the impending battle. Matthias led Amelia and me down the stairs and numerous hallways before reaching the dungeon stairs.

"Right through this door is the stairwell to the dungeon," Matthias said. "Last we saw, my guards had everything under control just before you arrived."

We walked through the doorway, and the scene looked familiar. The guards had the portal surrounded and seemed to have everything under control. Now we needed to get some more information, so I hopefully didn't get stabbed in the shoulder.

"How are things going down here?" asked Matthias.

"Well, your Highness," answered the soldier.

"How often are the creatures coming through, and when is the next one due to come through?" I asked.

"The creatures seem to be coming through about every thirty minutes," the guard said. "We expect the next one in approximately ten minutes."

I glanced at Amelia, "they were only coming through hourly in your castle."

"Yes. Do you think they are coming through faster now?" Amelia asked.

"I don't know, but when we finish this battle, we will have to go back and see," I replied.

"Agree," Amelia answered.

"Where are these creatures coming from?" Matthias asked.

We took a few minutes to explain the current situation to him. Like most people, he had always heard of tales from the past, but most things a thousand years ago were hard to believe. Sometimes, the line between reality and make-believe was fragile.

While talking, we noticed the portal starting to flicker with light. One of the guards yelled, there's another one coming. So we moved back and let the soldiers handle whatever would come through the portal.

We quickly drew our weapons, just in case. We probably didn't need them, but I would instead be prepared rather than caught off guard. In the background, I could hear a soldier getting the archers ready.

As soon as the creature started coming through the portal, I could hear the soldier yell loose. The arrows flew through the air and impaled the intended target. Before the creature could react, the archers had already released another volley of arrows in its direction.

I was impressed with their techniques. The arrows did most of the work, allowing the soldiers closest to the portal less to deal with. Besides closing the portal, the only thing I may have changed was finding someone who could conjure lightning or fire spells.

The soldiers around the portal engaged the staggering creature. Their techniques eliminated the issue quickly, which was good because fighting these things up close was extremely dangerous.

With the threat eliminated, I was left to close the portal. I reached into my bag to grab my dagger and headed towards it. Once I reached the portal, I approached it slowly, still slightly suspicious, as I rubbed my injured shoulder. I couldn't afford to get stabbed again as I attempted to close the portal.

Not wanting to waste more time, I plunged the dagger into the portal. As the dagger entered, a bright light flashed from the portal, and in seconds, the portal was closed.

We could focus on the enemy outside the walls with the portal closed. Everyone was correct; we didn't want to fight the creatures inside and outside the kingdom. Now, we could finish preparing for what was soon to come.

Chapter 40 The Impending War

Now that the threat of creatures coming in through the dungeon was gone, it was time to focus on the impending danger. We wasted no time returning to the castle's top for a better view. We have yet to face a significant threat, but this could tell how the future would go.

Once we reached the top, I saw that Roderick had returned to the castle.

"You get everyone inside the walls?" I asked.

"Yes, your Highness," Roderick replied. "They had no idea that the horde was headed this way."

"If it hadn't been for Scorch, we wouldn't have known either," I replied.

"Good point," answered Roderick. "Speaking of Scorch, where is he?"

It was almost as if Scorch was sitting there, waiting for someone to ask that question, because he appeared out of nowhere as he flew over the castle.

"Did you miss me?" Scorch asked in my head.

"Well, I was starting to wonder where you were," I replied. "Anything new to report that might be beneficial?"

"Nothing new," Scorch replied. "They are still headed in this direction if that helps."

"Believe it or not, that does help a little," I replied.

"How so?" asked Scorch.

"We don't have to chase them down and face them in an open battlefield," I replied. "This should allow us to reduce the number of our casualties."

At least, this is what I was hoping. Thus far, the engagements have been much smaller. This was going to be a lot more complex than the previous battles.

Thank goodness I had sent Scorch out with ulterior motives. Had he not been flying around, we may not have known the horde was headed in this direction, and we wouldn't have had the opportunity to prepare for the battle. Hopefully, this will tip the odds in our favor.

"Nock," someone said in the distance.

"Draw."

"Loose."

The time for planning was now over. Based on those words, the enemy was now close enough to engage, and I wanted a better view.

I made my way to the fortified wall where our archers stood, ready to unleash their arrows upon the enemy below. The sight that greeted me was awe-inspiring. At least two to three hundred archers lined up along the wall, each poised with their bows drawn and arrows ready to be released. The air was filled with the rhythmic sound of bowstrings being drawn and arrows soaring through the sky, one after another.

I observed the precise coordination among the archers with a sense of wonder. As soon as one set of archers released their arrows, the next set prepared to do the same. It was a seamless loading, drawing, and releasing process, executed with flawless timing and efficiency. The first set of archers loaded their arrows while the second set drew theirs, and as the first set released their arrows, the second set drew back while the third set prepared to release. It was a continuous cycle of action, with each set of archers seamlessly transitioning to the next stage of the firing sequence.

The archers moved with a fluidity and precision that spoke of extensive training and practice. Their movements were perfectly synchronized, a testament to their dedication and skill. They had honed this technique through rigorous practice, ensuring they could defend the wall against any approaching enemy with unwavering efficiency and discipline.

I leaned over the fortified wall, my gaze fixed on the battlefield below, where the arrows from our archers found their marks amidst the enemy ranks. A sense of satisfaction washed over me as I witnessed the effectiveness of our ranged assault, noting with approval the significant hits on critical targets. However, my satisfaction was short-lived as I realized the enemy soldiers were brutal, requiring multiple arrows to bring down just one.

The realization hit me hard – if we didn't devise a new strategy to thin their numbers swiftly, we'd face overwhelming odds in close-quarters combat. Our current forces weren't sufficient to achieve victory without suffering heavy casualties, a risk we couldn't afford to take in these precarious times.

When despair threatened to overwhelm me, a miraculous turn of events unfolded. Out of nowhere, lightning bolts crackled through the air, striking the enemy forces with lethal precision. I scanned the horizon, puzzled at first, until my eyes caught sight of figures atop the towers, wielding powers beyond comprehension. Old King Matthias had a few battle tricks up his sleeve.

I was inspired as I watched the devastating impact of our archers' arrows and the sudden appearance of lightning bolts wreaking havoc upon our enemy. Before I could even voice my thoughts, Scorch, my loyal companion, was already taking decisive action. With a swift flap of his wings, he soared into the air, a streak of fiery determination against the backdrop of battle.

Scorch maneuvered behind the enemy's lines with a precision born of instinct, his keen eyes locked on their vulnerable flank. And then, with a mighty roar that echoed across the battlefield, he unleashed a torrent of searing flames upon our unsuspecting adversaries. The sudden eruption of fire sent shockwaves through the enemy ranks, scattering them in disarray as they scrambled to evade the blistering inferno.

As the battle continued, our plan started to work better and better. The enemy's large group of creatures was getting smaller because of our arrows, lightning, and fire attacks. Everything we did worked together perfectly, making it hard for the creatures to fight back.

The air was full of energy as our arrows hit their targets with deadly accuracy, causing chaos among the enemy. Lightning bolts lit up the sky, hitting the creatures hard and taking them down. And then there was Scorch, breathing out a fire that burned everything in its path, leaving behind destruction.

As our attacks kept hitting the creatures, there started to be fewer of them. Even though they were still tough, they were slowing down. We knew we had to get ready to fight them up close, but we felt more hopeful now. We could see that victory was possible.

Amidst the chaos of battle, memories from the past flashed through my mind. I pictured my ancestors fighting against these same formidable enemies, just like we are now. It felt strange to see history repeating itself right before my eyes.

But as I looked at the battlefield, I noticed something different. Unlike my ancestors, who fought in open fields, we were battling within the safety of our kingdom's walls. I wondered: was our kingdom the reason for our success, or were we just lucky?

I knew we'd have to consider it later. With our people's lives at stake, I had to stay focused on the fight. I couldn't let thoughts of the past distract me.

What made the creatures dangerous was that they threw caution to the wind. Where most enemies would have stayed outside of archer range or used preventative measures, they continued to press forward. This fact made them more dangerous, and they could overcome any fortress if they had hundreds of thousands of them.

That was a thought for another day. Right now, we had to get through today before we started worrying about what may come in the future.

Shaking off my deep thoughts, I took a moment to look around. I realized I hadn't noticed that our archers had stopped firing arrows. The enemy had gotten too close to our kingdom's walls, so the arrows wouldn't be as effective now. It was time for the real battle to begin.

From where I stood, I could see everything. The King took charge, leading our ground troops with confidence. He led the charge with our strong cavalry unit. I couldn't count exactly how many soldiers there were, but a lot—maybe ten to fifteen thousand—were charging ahead on horseback, their hooves pounding the ground loudly.

After the cavalry charge, foot soldiers armed with spears and swords followed closely behind. They marched forward determinedly, ready to face the enemy in close combat. Their movements were precise and coordinated as they closed in on the enemy.

With our army significantly outnumbering the enemy, we held a clear advantage, nearly three to one. The cavalry led the charge, crashing into the enemy with fierce momentum, breaking through their defenses like a sharp blade through the grass.

As the cavalry charged ahead, their riders attacked with swift and deadly strikes. Swords and spears gleamed in the sunlight as they slashed through the enemy ranks with precise skill. The horses, spurred on by the urgency of battle, trampled over the creatures with mighty force, crushing bones and ligaments in their path.

In the aftermath of the cavalry's assault, the once-green fields were devastated. The ground was soaked with the blood of our enemies, painting a grim picture of the fierce battle that had unfolded. Rivers of red flowed across the earth, a stark reminder of the brutal reality of war.

Although the number of creatures had significantly decreased, the battle continued. The front line of our foot soldiers had now joined the fight, determined to defeat the remaining enemies and end the day of battle.

The soldiers at the front carried strong shields, shielding those behind them. Behind them, the second line of soldiers held their spears up, ready to attack any approaching creatures. They moved forward carefully, staying close together to keep their defense strong.

The creatures launched a wild attack on our foot soldiers' shields, driven by their basic instincts to break through the barrier between them and their enemies. They relentlessly slammed into the strong defenses, trying anything to get past the soldiers' shield wall. But despite their efforts, the soldiers' organized formation held strong, stopping the creatures at every attempt.

Despite the fierce assault, our foot soldiers stood firm, their shields steady against the constant attacks. With each strike, they remained determined to defend their fellow soldiers and protect their kingdom from the advancing threat.

Soldiers wielded their spears precisely at the front of the line, jabbing at the creatures carefully. Each strike weakened the enemy's numbers, thinning their ranks as the soldiers pressed forward.

As the battle raged on, our foot soldiers continued to fight with unwavering determination. With every step, they moved closer to the next group of enemies, their resolve unbroken despite the chaos around them. This battle ended as their numbers significantly decreased, and we could see an imminent victory in our future.

We thought we were in control, but that didn't last long. Without warning, a second wave of creatures surged from the forest, catching us off guard. There were so many of them, and they were determined to attack. Our soldiers on the ground were suddenly in danger.

Earlier, Scorch had told me twenty to thirty thousand more creatures were near the portal. We only had fifteen thousand troops with us. The odds were not in our favor, and things could go badly if we didn't act fast. Our survival was on the line.

"Archers, start firing at the new line of creatures coming in," I said with panic.

"Your Highness, our King and soldiers are down there," replied one of the archers.

"If you don't start firing arrows now, the King and the remaining soldiers don't stand a chance," I replied. "So either get to firing and hitting creatures or them, and all of us are surely doomed."

With a hesitant reluctance, the archers reluctantly started shooting arrows at the approaching enemies. The creatures were still far away, so the arrows flew over our soldiers' heads. However, some arrows might accidentally hit our troops. But we had no other option at the moment. We had to try to thin out the creatures' numbers from a distance, even if it meant risking harm to our people. It was a difficult choice, but losing everything was not an option.

"Scorch, can you rain down fire upon them as they exit the forest?" I asked.

"Let me see what I can do, but there seems to be a great deal of them spread across the terrain," Scorch replied telepathically.

"Do what you can 'cause the result isn't looking too great at the moment," I said.

Scorch flew high and dove down, breathing fire onto the creatures below. His fiery attack, combined with the arrows from our archers, was impacting the enemy. Yet, despite our efforts, I worried it might not be enough.

Meanwhile, our cavalry and soldiers on the ground were still battling the first wave of creatures. They didn't realize the danger coming from their flank. They needed to focus on defeating the first wave, or they'd be caught between two enemies. If that happened, our forces would be in serious trouble, and defeat would be inevitable.

As the archers continued firing arrows into the sky, the enemy drew nearer, endangering our soldiers with the risk of being hit by our arrows. We knew we had to change our strategy quickly before we ran out of choices.

Before I could devise a plan, Scorch sprang into action. Incredibly fast, he created a barrier of flames between the oncoming creatures and our troops. While it wouldn't stop the enemy completely, it would hurt them badly and signal to our ground forces that danger was approaching.

As time passed, the tension on the battlefield grew as our forces clashed with the advancing enemy. Despite using fire and arrows to weaken their numbers, the enemy kept coming, and their sheer size made them a formidable opponent.

From where I stood, I watched with worry and determination. Our tactics had worked somewhat, but more was needed to ensure victory. We needed to act fast if we wanted to win this fight.

Looking at the battlefield, I guessed we'd taken out about half, maybe more, of the enemy. It was a significant achievement, but we still had a tough fight. The enemy kept coming at us, and we were losing more of our soldiers as time went on.

Our ground troops quickly changed their formation, moving closer to the safety of our kingdom's walls to avoid being surrounded by the enemy. Meanwhile, the cavalry moved back behind the infantry, preparing to devise a new plan for the battle ahead. It was a crucial moment, and the future of our kingdom depended on how we faced the enemy's next attack.

The ground troops at the forefront of our defense wielded their sturdy shields, forming an impenetrable barrier against the oncoming enemy. Behind them, the second line of soldiers held their pikes at the ready, extending past the shields to impale any creatures foolish enough to charge forward. It was a well-thought-out strategy designed to maximize our defensive capabilities against the overwhelming force of the enemy.

However, despite our formation's advantages, the sheer number of enemy forces posed a significant challenge. We were facing an onslaught that tested the limits of our defenses, and it was clear that we needed to find a more effective solution to ensure our survival.

As the creatures emerged from the firewall, they relentlessly charged toward our front lines. Despite being engulfed in flames, they pressed forward with a ferocity that bordered on madness. Our defenses repelled the initial attacks, but it was evident that the line couldn't hold indefinitely against the tide of enemies. With each passing moment, more advanced, threatening to overwhelm us through sheer force of numbers.

In the face of this relentless assault, it became increasingly clear that our survival would depend not only on our skill and determination but also on our ability to outmaneuver and outwit the enemy. It was a battle that would test the very limits of our courage and resilience as we fought tooth and nail to hold the line against overwhelming odds.

As the creatures multiplied, our front-line soldiers began to bear the brunt of their attacks. We were losing soldiers faster as the enemy pushed through our defenses. Scorch intervened again, unleashing another wall of fire to target the rear of their formation. Yet, despite our efforts, many creatures remained between the flames and our troops.

The cavalry, having regrouped, swung back around to drive the enemy towards the wall. Despite our coordinated efforts, we were sustaining heavy losses. What had seemed like a sure victory moments ago now descended into chaos.

As we pressed forward, we found ourselves in a decisive moment, with the creatures hemmed in by our swords, the castle walls, and the encroaching flames. Though they fought fiercely, their resistance began to wane as the battle neared its conclusion. This day would undoubtedly be remembered as one of the most epic clashes of our time, a testament to the courage and resilience of our troops.

Despite our challenges, our soldiers continued to whittle down the enemy's ranks, ensuring that we would live to fight another day. While we mourned the loss of nearly half our forces, we took solace in knowing that our kingdom would endure. The lessons we learned on this battlefield were invaluable, offering insights into our enemy's tactics and revealing opportunities for unity in our struggle against them.

Today's victory came at a steep price, but it served as a reminder of the sacrifices required to safeguard our lands. We knew that many more battles lay ahead if we hoped to rid our kingdom of this relentless foe and restore peace to our people. But with each triumph, we grew more robust, resilient, and determined to reclaim our way of life from the shadow of war.

The End

www.ingramcontent.com/pod-product-compliance
Lightning Source LLC
Chambersburg PA
CBHW060440310726
48977CB00001B/274